MRS. FANNERY'S FLOWERS

Bethanne Kim

Cover designed by Laura Givens

Learn more about the author at https://bethannekim.com/

Printed in the United States of America

First Printing: Aug 2021
1632, Inc.

eBook ISBN-13 978-1-956015-07-2
Trade Paperback ISBN-13 978-1-956015-08-9

CONTENTS

Dedication
For my dad, who introduced me to this series and with whom I have continued reading it, and my mom, the real Julie Marie in my life.

Bethanne Kim

PROLOGUE

April 2000

Krystal Reed drove over to her Aunt Bethel and Uncle Raymond Little's house after finishing her shift at the drug store. Her parents were bringing Nana over from Bluemont for the afternoon and if she timed things right, her mom would take over and finish the overstuffed laundry bags she had brought from her dorm. The machines there always seemed to be broken or steal your quarters and promptly malfunction, so she tried to do her laundry when she visited family. Besides, this way, she could send her winter clothing home with her parents. With luck, she just might have a small space to see out the back window on her drive home.

Bethanne Kim

PART 1
1631

Bethanne Kim

CHAPTER 1

May 1631

Krystal was lost in the simple pleasure of an ice-cold soda and porch swing a warm spring day when the sky lit up with fire. Confused, she slammed her feet down while she worked out what was wrong. The neighborhood was abruptly quiet. No music playing. No bathroom fan growling, porch fan swirling, or window fan buzzing. And no machines washing and drying her clothing. Everything was silent. The only sounds left were nature and cars in the distance.

She was still on the porch, talking about what might have caused the power outage and flare of light with her Little cousins and the neighbors when their mutual cousin Sam Reed (Donovan's son who lived with his mom down in Beckley) drove up. Sam's face was paler than usual, downright pasty, and serious as he walked toward them. "Someone shot Chief Frost! I drove around a bit after I finished mowing Mrs. Flannery's lawn for Donny, then I stopped at the high school because a ton of people were there for the wedding. I thought maybe they would know what was happening. Mr. Hobbs brought Chief Frost in and he looked pretty bad. At least everyone said it was Chief Frost. I'm not here often enough to be sure. People were almost carrying him. His shoulder was messed up. I've never seen anything like it."

Sam had to repeat the story about Chief Frost after more neighbors walked over, then everyone started talking and asking questions. He just shrugged a lot in reply, looking as uncertain as everyone else. "I'm just saying what I saw, that's all. But, uh, carrying a weapon is probably a good choice right now. They said other people were shot at, and they had to kill some really bad guys outside of town. If, uh, you're old enough to be allowed. Even the Principal sounded awful nervous." That quieted them down. No one would call Ed Piazza a Nervous Nellie.

"Boy, this is West Virginia. If you're old enough to shoot straight, you're old enough to carry. Everyone knows your daddy is a useless, lazy, good-for-nothing so-and-so but your great-Grandpa Eli certainly taught you that much. Might not be old enough to let the law *know* you're carrying, but you're old enough to do it." No one disagreed, but the whole situation left them with a lot to think on.

Sam kept answering questions, like where else the power was out (everywhere) and whether the phones lines were working (they weren't, including cell phones). Finally, everyone seemed to accept that he didn't know anything more.

Bethel the Younger (daughter of Bethel Reed Little and Raymond Little) looked worried. "Aunt Sonia and Uncle Donnie Joe were supposed to come here this afternoon and we haven't seen them yet. Krystal, have you heard from them? Will you be able to get home okay?"

Krystal hadn't thought through the situation that far. "Uh, can I stay here? I'll sleep on the sofa. Some of my laundry was mid-cycle and it's soaking wet. Unless the electricity comes back on soon, there's no way it'll be dry tonight, even if I hang it outside to dry. And no, I haven't heard from my parents."

Everyone in the family knew Krystal had been born a world-class worrier, just like her mom, so Bethel and Sam tried to distract her. "We all know the no-power drill: no needlessly opening the refrigerator and freezer and close them fast. Eat or cook fridge food within a day. Don't flush if you can avoid it; keep a can of water handy to refill the toilet tank until we get power to the water pump again."

Sam picked up where Bethel left off, in a perfect imitation of their great-grandmother Grannie B. "Use food in the freezer within two days. Empty the pipes to the tub and sinks into pitchers for drinking water. Check the flashlight batteries and keep one with you. Cook outside on the grill. Not inside—*outside!* Heathens." Grannie B always muttered the last comment under her breath, after someone threatened to start a cooking fire in the kitchen. "Check the dryer. Move anything in there onto the clothesline. And hope you don't have laundry in mid-rinse." The neighbors laughed at his spot-on imitation, but it reminded them of chores they needed to do, so everyone headed home, and Krystal started hanging up her clothing from the dryer on the drying rack in the back yard, ignoring everything in the washer for now.

Just as the family was finishing dinner on the front porch, a pair of horses pulling a not-quite-wagon turned onto their street, headed toward the high school. After the initial shock, Krystal grabbed her newish birthday camera out of her not-so-new car. Her parents would never believe it if she told them a horse and wagon randomly went down the street in Grantville.

"Barbara Reed," barked Irene Flannery as she charged into Barbara and Eli's room at the Bowers Assisted Living Residence the next day. "Control your great-grandchildren." Barbara waited calmly for the other half of Irene's complaint-of-the-moment. "Donny Higgins was supposed to mow my grass and that lazy Tom Sawyer wannabe got his cousin Sam to do it. And that boy cut it too high. He probably didn't think I'd notice before he went back home to his momma in Beckley, but I noticed all right."

"Irene, you may be old, but you aren't half as deaf as you pretend, and you certainly aren't blind. The whole town lost power yesterday and something happened to the phones, and no one is going anywhere right now, including Beckley. With the Chief of Police being shot and armed strangers wandering around town, your lawn is nobody's biggest problem. Not even yours. Don't start in on your rose bushes, either. Donny never did anything to them on purpose."

Irene sniffed. "Any foolishness Danny Frost has gotten into is none of my concern. Unlike my yard. You tell that Sam Reed to fix my grass if he expects to get paid, and not to get lazy when he mulches my roses like Donny does. Kids these days just don't take good care of other people's things."

"Why are you yelling at me instead of their parents, Irene?"

"You know there is no point in talking to Donovan Reed as well as anybody does. I told you letting him marry that woman from out of town was trouble."

"Huntington is hardly a far-off crazy-town like Hollywood, a place I recall you wanting to live once upon a time, and Michelle is a better woman than anyone expected him to end up with, even for a few years. Lord knows Sam was better off living with her in Beckley than he would've been living with Donovan here. Besides, you are from out of town yourself."

"As you like to remind me, you were there when I came to Grantville from my grandparents' home. I was an innocent wee bairn barely a week old and you hit me over the head with your doll. It's no wonder those children are uncontrollable, Barbara Ann."

"You pulled my hair and even your own mother never denied it. My only regret is that I didn't have a china doll to hit you with instead of a rag doll. Maybe you would've learned something that way!"

Now Irene looked smug. "*I* went to college, unlike you, so I know plenty. Like that the people who rented your old place are not there and the house is empty, with all these criminals running around. Krystal and Sam are both in town and staying with Bethel and Raymond Little, as if their house is big enough for all those people. But I am happy to take you and Eli over to see for yourself that I am right."

Eli slowed his walk as soon as he saw Irene Flannery heading toward their room, arriving just in time to hear her offer to take them over. "Ladies, I would purely enjoy seeing my great-grandchildren, so I, for one, will take up Miss Irene on her kindly offer. Barbara, will you join us?" After a gentlemanly bow, Eli Reed offered one elbow to his wife and the other to Irene Flannery, who was now obliged to drive them to visit their old home. "Miss Irene, you are *still* lovely enough to be in pictures."

Hearing that bit of flattery, Irene perked up, a bit of her youthful flirtiness shining through for a moment. "You know, a motion picture talent scout offered me a contract back in the Great Depression, but I didn't really want to move the whole way to Hollywood." Grannie B rolled her eyes, safely out of Irene's sight. "I'm not sorry I stayed here. I never would've married my Patrick if I had gone swanning off to star in the motion pictures. But then again, I wouldn't be acting as a taxi service for you." Irene just didn't have it in her to end anything on a happy note.

"Grannie B and Grandpa Eli!" Krystal was relieved when they arrived at the Little's house. "My parents never got here with Nana yesterday. They were bringing her over for the afternoon. Everyone is saying there's some kind of ring around the town and we can't get out to go home. All I have is the stuff that was in my car. Sam has a little bit he left here when he stayed before, but that's just some odds and ends like toothpaste and a few pairs of underwear that he didn't notice under the bed when he packed up and went back to his mom."

Hearing Krystal greet their great-grandparents', Sam came in from the kitchen with a big Dagwood sandwich he'd made himself. Seeing Mrs. Flannery, he stiffened up and almost left the room. He didn't live in Grantville, but she had yelled at him a lot over the years when he visited. Cautiously, "Hello, Mrs. Flannery." With much more enthusiasm and hugs, "Grannie B and Grandpa Eli! Why are you all here? Did you hear that Aunt Sonia and Uncle Donnie Joe haven't come back and the roads don't seem to go anywhere anymore?"

"Mrs. Flannery told us you and Krystal were staying here with your Aunt Bethel and Uncle Raymond. We wanted to see if it was true. Folks at our place are saying no one has seen anyone who was out of town when that big flash of light happened yesterday, but folks at our place don't exactly have reliable memories, or hearing, so we wanted to check on you ourselves. Mrs. Flannery was kind enough to volunteer to drive us here." Seeing their skepticism, Grandpa Eli laughed. "There *is* something in it for her. Sam, Mrs. Flannery wants you to go cut her lawn again. She says you cut it too high."

Sam looked angry but it didn't stop Grandpa Eli. "Just cut it again, Sam, it's not like you have to do it every week. You'll probably be home before it needs cut again. As for you, Irene, next time you can check the mower height or live with it. Be glad Sam didn't butcher your precious rose bushes like you always complain about. He helps his mom with her garden in Beckley and he's in the 4-H, so he knows how to take good care of them. He's even won prizes for his own roses, but he doesn't like to talk about it."

Unsatisfied but knowing it was the best she would get, Mrs. Flannery gave an abrupt nod and headed for her car, letting the screen door slam behind her as she stomped down the steps.

"Have you checked on your dad, Sam?" asked Grannie B.

"Yeah, I checked. Bad news, there. Donovan Reed is still in town, and still the miserable SOB he always has been. Don't give me that look. That's the nicest description I've ever heard of him, including from you. I guess Mom's still at home in Beckley, so I'm pretty much an orphan if things don't get fixed." Sam's eyes widened and he started to panic. If he really was an orphan, someone might force him to move and live with his father, and he did *not* want that. "If I'm stuck here without Mom, don't make me go live with him again! Aunt Bethel and Uncle Raymond can be my guardians. Or Bethel or Krystal—they're my cousins and both are over eighteen and I think that's old enough. Donovan Reed doesn't want me. You know he doesn't!"

Grandpa Eli pulled Sam in for a comforting hug to stop the building panic. "Son, we won't let that happen to you. Everyone around here knows enough about Donovan that they wouldn't saddle any kid with him. If that happens, we'll find someone you can live with. In fact, Mrs. Flannery told us that our tenants are out of town. You and Krystal can go ahead and stay in our house for now because you're right, it's no secret that Donovan doesn't want any kids living with him. If things don't get fixed soon, we'll figure out the guardian thing so you don't have to worry about Donovan at all." Sam looked very relieved at that. "But right now, you need to go cut Mrs. Flannery's grass because if you don't, even if you leave tomorrow, Grannie B and I will have to hear about it until either we die, or Mrs. Flannery does." With that, Grandpa Eli shooed Sam out the door.

Two days later, everyone in town went to the big meeting in the high school gym, hoping for answers. Everyone had someone they hadn't heard from since the flash of light on top of not having power or phone service. Krystal still hadn't heard from her parents, and she was scared sick about what had happened to them. A born worrier, she had barely eaten since dinner the first day. Grannie B, Grandpa Eli, and Sam were worried that Krystal's parents might have been in an accident but didn't want to mention it to her. Maybe the meeting would tell them something that made sense, like a rockslide had taken out the phone lines and blocked the passes so no one could get back home, something like that.

Krystal's mind wandered when people got long-winded, but she tuned in again to hear, "You heard what Ed Piazza and his teachers told us. Somehow—nobody knows how—we've been planted somewhere in Germany almost four hundred years ago. With no way to get back." Her face set in a hard line at that, but she stayed silent and kept listening. She wasn't giving up on getting her parents, her Nana, and her *life* back that easily, no matter what anyone said.

She and her cousin Bethel had both gone away to college for a reason: they had no intention of spending their lives in a backwater, hillbilly town in Appalachia. Krystal's life, her future, was still out there, and she would find it. No one knew what had happened or why, but that meant that they couldn't be sure it wouldn't happen again. She was going to hang on to her hope that life would return to normal for as long as it took to get there, no matter what anyone told her.

Mayor Dreeson finally ended all the speechifying with a call to vote for Chairman of the Emergency Committee. "Under the circumstances— running unopposed and all—I think we can handle this with a voice vote. All in favor?" Of course Mike Stearns won, running unopposed and with the only one speaking out against him being a big-money, big-city CEO. Krystal thought the pictures she took for her parents captured the moment nicely.

He didn't live in town, but Sam had spent more than a few weeks of vacation there, and every day of his vacay for years had focused on not being with his paternal unit, so he was friends with quite a few guys around his age, and their parents knew him too, from sleepovers. Since it didn't look like he was going home soon, his great-grandparent's house wasn't his home, and Krystal was a moody stick-in-the-mud, he started arranging sleepovers with any friendly families he saw in the gym or around town. Krystal waved off the few friends she had in town when they tried to talk to her, completely uninterested in socializing until she could see her parents again. This nightmare had to have a reasonable scientific explanation.

When they caught up to her, Grannie B and Irene Flannery were having a 'discussion' while Grandpa Eli looked on serenely, hearing aids turned off. He was fond of that old joke, "Why do men go deaf before women...Because they want to." It got him a swat every time he told it, but according to Grannie B, some husbands are just hard to train.

Mrs. Flannery was on a rant. "Barbara Ann, you know I have never liked Mike Stearns. That boy's mama coddled him. I don't care what she says, being three is not an excuse for peeing on another person's prize rose bushes. And Mikey Stearns is a Presbyterian, whenever he bothers to go to church at all." Sniff, sniff. "Mr. Simpson looks like the kind of person who never peed on a rose bush in his life, and an Episcopalian like him is closer to being a good Catholic than the Stearns boy is. Why would a good Catholic like you vote for someone like Mikey Stearns?"

Grannie B gave as good as she got. "Irene, first, you know good and well that my Eli and half my own children are Methodist, so I won't hold that against anyone. Second, Mike Stearns is no boy, and you know it. He's been a UMWA organizer for decades. He could even outmaneuver that bastard Quentin Underwood, and I know you don't like Underwood. This Mr. Simpson is trouble. You've seen it enough in your life to know it's nothing but trouble when big city types come through here trying to throw their weight around. Next thing you know, he'll be trying to get us to do some fool thing like building a navy up in our hills and hollers. Mike Stearns was with the group who helped rescue that poor farmer while Mr. Pittsburgh, over there, stayed safe in town. It's what the fat cats always do:

have the little people take the risks and do the work while they watch somewhere safe."

Irene sniffed again and turned to leave. "At least Mr. Simpson and his wife *look* respectable and *sound* respectable, which is more than Mikey Stearns can say."

✱ ✱ ✱

Krystal almost slipped as she raced down the steps, through the living room, and around the corner into the kitchen the next morning. "Sam! Where are the car keys? I have to get to work. Sam!"

"I hid them."

"What?"

"I hid them. It was too depressing to look at them, so I put my car and your car around back and hid the keys for all our vehicles. Even the mower."

"WHAT?"

"We can't drive anymore. They said 'only for emergencies' because there isn't any more gas 'cause we're in medieval times now. So, I put the keys where we can't see 'em. I just got my license last month and now I can't drive! I don't want to see the keys, or my car, and I put them in there." He gestured toward the kitchen junk drawer. "I pumped up the tires on an old bike for myself and left the pump out so you can do one for yourself."

"WHAT?"

"I told you, no driving. It's not that complicated, Miss Krystal Marie Reed, high and mighty college nursing student. After the meeting yesterday, that's one of the things the new committee decided. Mrs. Flannery came over this morning, special, and told me, 'Just because that committee says we can't use anything with a gasoline engine except for

14

genuine emergencies doesn't mean you can stop cutting my grass, young man. I still have my Patrick's old push mower, and I still have standards, even if no one else in this town does.' I tried to get out of it. I mean, it was Donny's job, not mine! But she just kept talking. 'You'll have to clean it up some and sharpen the blade, but I expect my lawn cut and my roses taken care of every week. Donny used to do it but since you know how to take care of roses and he never did, it's your job now.' Figures that stupid lawn would be her first thought, that, and her rose bushes. Again. Why does she care so much? Anyhow, no more cars, or trucks, or…" He trailed off, overcome by grief as only a sixteen-year-old boy with a new driver's license can be at not being able to drive anymore.

"Sam, I don't care what that cranky old biddy says. I'm driving my car to work today. I'll be late for my shift if I try to bike. Maybe she exaggerated. She loves making everyone around her miserable."

Krystal was in an extra big hurry because she needed to pick up some things for herself and Sam before she started her shift as a clerk at the drug store. Uncle Raymond said they could have some basic toiletries on the house since Krystal didn't have any toiletries with her and Sam only had enough for a weekend trip, but there were some other things she wanted, like some make-up. When she got inside, she saw a new sign on the community bulletin board near the front door.

The Emergency Committee chaired by Mike Stearns has declared the remaining motor vehicle fuel to be a vital military resource. That means that the fuel in your tanks is all the fuel you've got, unless you donate that too. A bus service is being organized and there will be help for the elderly and disabled to get where they need to go, including shops as they reopen. Please contact the hospital operator, police office, or assisted living home operator if you need assistance with transportation.

That answered that. Bicycles, scooters, skates, etc. were about to become all the rage. Krystal spent most of her shift ringing up other practical people who were stocking up on basic toiletries and over the counter medications. Then there was Mrs. Flannery. Never one to let practicalities intrude overly much, she bought several bottles of her favorite bluing hair rinse, hair pins, hair spray, cold cream, baby powder, and bunion pads.

June 1631

"Krystal, your Uncle Raymond, Sam, and I are all worried about you. What have you done other than your shifts at the pharmacy and sleeping since the big meeting at the high school? Anything?" Bethel was the kind of person who brought stray birds into the house to heal. Seeing her niece in such clear pain hurt her to the core. If Krystal hadn't stopped in to do laundry after her shift at the pharmacy, she would be up-time with her parents right now. But she had, so she lost her university, her (new and seemingly not serious) boyfriend, her parents, her best friend, Julie Marie, her home… In short, everything except her car, a few bags of laundry, and her Grantville relatives. At least she had a few CDs in her car, so she had a little bit of her own favorite music.

"Nothing. What should I do? No one knows why we are here or for how long. I'm just waiting to go home. I hate living in someone else's house, and this is definitely someone else's house. When I go to the fridge, they have Pepsi instead of Dr. Pepper. Pepsi! What kind of person drinks Pepsi when they could have Coke?" Krystal's strong anti-Pepsi feelings (and rants) had amused her extended family for years, but her current distress was no cause for amusement, so Bethel bit back the smile that came unbidden. "The family pictures, the books, the magazines, everything is wrong." She looked ready to either cry or hit something.

Bethel hugged her close and let her simply be young and hurting. "Krys, I know you don't want to hear this, but we may not go back. This may be permanent. If it is, you know Grannie B and Grandpa Eli will let you keep living here, in their home."

"I won't accept that! We are going to go home. I *will* see my parents again, and Julie Marie, and my college, and my whole life! Medieval Germany is not my future!"

Bethel considered the situation while Krystal sulked. "How about this, Krys. If we are still here in July, we will pack up some of the Clevenger family' things. They will have rented a new house by then. When they moved to assisted living, Grannie B and Grandpa Eli packed their things into the attic. You can pick through their stuff and put what you like best back out in the house, including family pictures. I have the family Christmas card your mom sent out last year. Frame that. Try trading books with other families for things of more interest to you. If things return to normal, you can always trade back." Krystal still looked unconvinced, but she agreed, certain things would be back to normal by next month.

CHAPTER 2

July 1631

"**M**rs. Reed, the Refugee Center asked me to talk to you. They never expected this many families, or orphans, when it started. Almost everyone except Jimmy Dick and Mrs. Flannery has agreed to have people live with them. Do you think you could talk to Mrs. Flannery and get her to agree to have a family live with her? In her garage, if nowhere else? Everyone says no-one but you could convince her to wear a raincoat in a hurricane but that she listens to you sometimes. They would really appreciate it."

Grannie B laughed. "No one else was willing to beard the lioness in her den, eh? Fair enough. I'll take her on, but you have to drive us there and back. I'm not going into town without my Eli."

The next morning, the Reeds were dropped off at St. Vincent's where Irene would be cleaning, just as she had for decades. "Irene McClanahan Flannery, what is this I hear about you not letting any of these poor refugees live in your house?" Grannie B cornered her in the choir loft.

"It's my house, Barbara Ann Reed, and I don't have to let anyone live in it. This is still America and I have my rights."

"Is it, really, Irene? *Your* house, just Irene's house? And all these years you've said it's yours—*and Patrick's.*" Hearing Grannie B's subtle emphasis on her dead husband's name, Irene Flannery stiffened, sensing she wouldn't like what was coming next. "What would Patrick think about you making women and children live in tents while you have those empty rooms in your house?" Barbara and Irene knew exactly what buttons to push on each other.

"Don't you talk about my Patrick like that," Mrs. Flannery hissed, furious because it was true. Her Patrick would have been one of the first to open their home to refugees, especially orphans. "I'll have you know I was going to go over this afternoon to see if they have any good Catholic widows or children who need a room. None of those whore camp-followers are welcome in my home, but my Patrick would've agreed with helping good Catholics and that's what I'm going to do." With that, she turned her back on Grannie B and went back to cleaning.

"Glad to know I heard wrong, Irene. If I can help you with the new family, just let me know." Satisfied she had done her good deed for the week, Grannie B left for a stroll with Grandpa Eli.

"I've never seen the streets this quiet. Do you remember when you were courting me? There were hardly any cars back then but there were plenty of horse-drawn vehicles and just plain horses. This quiet is nice. It feels safe." They spent a few minutes lost in thought as their feet carried them toward their old home and up onto the porch. Since Grannie B and Grandpa Eli lived in assisted living, Krystal and Sam's Uncle Raymond and Aunt Bethel were helping around the house, including getting the new refugee family settled in. As a result, Grannie B and Grandpa Eli hadn't met the new family living in their old house yet, so they sat down on the swing and had a nice, if slightly uncomfortable, nap, while they waited. It wasn't much, but the income from the refugees living there helped make up for their tenants being left behind, especially with Krystal and Sam there to keep an eye on things. Assisted living isn't cheap in any century.

As they started waking up, Krystal turned into the driveway on her bicycle. "You were supposed to call for a ride home! They were so worried about you that someone called me at work and asked me to come see if you were here. Now I'm supposed to take you back unless you want to spend the night here? I'll call them if you do."

"Where would we sleep? We aren't going to put anyone out of their bed."

Krystal was torn up inside. She missed her parents but didn't want to be a big baby. Other people had lost more. But Grantville wasn't her home, and this house wasn't her home. Even Mr. Bigshot from Pittsburgh still had his wife and son with him. "You can sleep in your old bedroom. I don't want other people sleeping there when my parents show up and need a room. You'll only be here for one night, so that's okay."

Grannie B and Grandpa Eli both gave her small, sad looks, then conferred in hushed tones. "We will spend a night here so we can get to know this fine family you have living with you, but we have to go back first thing in the morning so we can get our medicine. They still have a few things we need to take, you know."

After everyone else was in bed, Grannie B went into Krystal's room and sat down on her bed for a chat. "Little one, we need to talk. It's not good, you insisting that the people we lost will come back or that we'll return to them. We all want to believe we will get everyone back; we all miss the people we lost, but we have to live the life in front of us, not the one behind us."

Krystal looked mulish. "It's only been two months. We don't know what happened or why. We don't know if it will happen again. It could. Before the Ring of Fire, no one would have believed that could happen. Now everyone says it can't happen a second time and it can't be reversed, but I don't believe them. It could happen again, and I just know we'll see them before school starts again. I'm not giving up on seeing my parents again, or on going back to college. I can't give up on Mom and Dad!" Grannie B hugged her close, letting the tears soak into her nightie as the sobs gradually turned into hiccoughing and Krystal finally released her. "I know you don't agree, Grannie B–it seems like no one does and I don't understand why–but I'm not giving up on them."

Grannie B brushed Krystal's hair back, looking into her eyes as she held her chin. "I see that. You miss them too much to even start to let go yet. I guess you lost too much. I will let you be on what you believe. For now, as long as you enroll at the vo-tech to continue your nursing studies there, just in case. But if they do not come back, you will have to let go someday, just like we have to let go when people die. We all hurt for the ones we lost, not just you, but we still have to live our lives. Since we still own this house, Grandpa Eli and I want you to make sure *all* the rooms are being used, including our old bedroom." Grannie B gave Krystal a long hug and a quick kiss on the top of her head before going back to her old bedroom for the night.

✳ ✳ ✳

"Are you sure Krystal won't get mad, Aunt Bethel? She's awful insistent everything will just snap back." Nearly two months of living with his cousin had convinced Sam that she wouldn't see reason on the subject of life returning to normal. She had never wanted to live in West Virginia, much less Grantville, and the reality of being stuck in a century that, in her opinion, made the most backwoods area of the USA in 2000 look like something from a sci-fi movie had hit her harder than most.

Bethel snapped at him, out of patience with Krystal. "She agreed last month. She probably thought we would be back in 2000 by now, but she did agree, and she can live with it. We are only boxing some of this stuff and storing it in the back of the bathroom, not getting rid of anything. If things ever go back to how they were before, everything is still here for the old tenants to claim. If not, it's still here for you two to use. Right now, that girl could use some familiar things to help her. And part of that is packing up Linda Abernathy's ivy-covered Corelle dishes and putting out your great-grandparents' Fiestaware dishes and kitchenware. So will packing up all their toiletries. No one needs to be looking at another person's toothbrush every morning!"

"What about the family pictures? They have a ton of them lining the steps upstairs. Having strangers staring at me walking around in my robe is kind of creepy."

"Let's leave those for another day. Krystal will be home soon and we'll enlist her help. I'd rather keep to small steps for now, like the dishes and toiletries they will clearly take with them to their new home. We may swap out the photos in the picture frames in the stairwell. If we change them slowly, she may not notice. They have a bunch of photo albums. If we can't find scenic pics there, we can cut them out from magazines. If she asks, Linda and her kids can take the frames as is, but their family won't be staring you down anymore."

"Do you have any family recipes? She keeps complaining that the Clevengers' cookbooks suck. Whatever kind of cookbook she is looking for definitely isn't here."

Bethel gave the Clevengers' cookbook collection a quick once-over. "Hmmm. I'll look, Grannie B gave most of her cookbooks to different family members when she moved into assisted living, but I think she still has a few. Pack these away and we'll find cookbooks with more biscuits and gravy, less *Zone Diet* and food fads. I have an old *Good Housekeeping* cookbook, and a new one. I'll choose one and bring the other over here. That's a safe one to start with."

CHAPTER 3

August 1631

Krystal was out of sorts. Nothing had gone back to normal yet and everyone else seemed convinced things never would. Instead of heading back to her friends, her boyfriend, and her college life, she was stuck in Grantville going to their so-called nursing program, which really just trained LPNs and nurse's aides, not RNs. Grantville didn't have a hospital before the Ring of Fire, even if they were building one now, and it certainly didn't have a nursing school, so the whole thing struck her as pointless.

It isn't fair! Uncle Raymond made me register for this stupid, so-called nursing school in Grantville, as if I'll learn anything there. When I am back in real college, I'll be so far behind! Krystal's bad case of self-pity was getting on everyone's nerves. Everyone had lost loved ones, and most had lost children, spouses, parents, and other close family, plus jobs, saving accounts, and retirement income. *I want to leave West Virginia, not spend more years here, making up for the time wasted in this LPN program at the vo-tech instead of a real nursing school, even if Grantville is technically Germany now.*

"Are you ready to start classes in a few weeks, Krys?" She had no idea how Uncle Raymond could be so upbeat when everyone knew the pharmacy had run out of life-saving medications for a lot of people, including asthma inhalers for people like Grannie B. Seeing her grumpy nod annoyed him. "You are lucky, Krystal. Nursing down-time is different than nursing up-time, but at least you can still study and have the career you wanted. A lot of people can't. Look at Bitty Matowski! Ballet is completely gone. You studied ballet with her. Do you remember how much she loves it? Well, ballet was her life's passion, and now it's gone. And you're going to be handling more gunshots and trauma care than an inner-city ER. If you are right and things do somehow go back, you will be *way* ahead of everyone else in basic trauma care and triage.

"You'll also learn a lot about old-school ways to do things, which can be helpful sometimes, especially when the power goes out or in an emergency. I'm starting to learn a lot about herbal remedies, which I'm sure you will too, if we stay here for a while." As a pharmacist, Raymond deeply missed regular shipments of manufactured drugs, but he had never opposed herbal remedies. His issue was the difficulty regulating their potency to ensure patients took consistent dosages, not effectiveness.

"The school might give me some kind of eco-award for washing and reusing my disposable gloves and masks." A weak attempt at a joke, that was still the best Krystal had done in months. "I didn't stay in dance long, so I don't remember much about it. I am sick of hearing about people who are worse off than I am, who lost more, who were left with less, whatever way you want to spin it. This sucks! I hate it. And I hate what freaking Pollyannas everyone is being about the whole thing!" She stomped out of the pharmacy and went for a walk to calm down before saying something she couldn't take back.

When she got back, Uncle Raymond handed her a book. "This isn't the first time you have accused me of being a Pollyanna, as if I'm in some kind of denial about what is happening around us and, frankly, you are getting on my last nerve about it. *Pollyanna* was one of Grannie B's favorite books as a girl, which means all her children, and grandchildren, were read the story. When I asked her, she still had her copy, the one I just gave you. Read it. Once you are done, I don't ever want to hear you use 'Pollyanna' as a pejorative again. Clear?" Krystal nodded. "Good. It shouldn't take long for you to finish that. Bring it back to me when you are done so I can return it to Grannie B. She loves that silly book."

September 1631

This was far from the first "first day of school" for Sam or Krystal, but none of the others had been anything like this. For starters, the high school now required German, and Latin was *highly* recommended. The vo-tech wasn't requiring either yet, but that was only because of the teacher shortage. Most importantly, their moms weren't here to see them off. Sam even missed the teary hug that had gotten embarrassing the last few years. At college, Krystal had seen herself off to her first day of classes, and her mom had been working and unable to see her off the last few years, so that part was easier for her, but she still had a first day of school picture at some point in the day and she missed her parents.

While their down-time classmates were amazed by the books, desks, and all that went with an up-time school, Sam and the other up-time students missed a backpack filled with new pencils, notebooks, erasers, and other school supplies. And, of course, a new back-to-school wardrobe. Even if part (or most) of it was hand-me-down, at least a few items would have been brand new. Socks and underwear, if nothing else. This year, everyone had leftovers from previous years, things from around the house, and nothing but hand-me-downs.

Krystal snapped a quick first-day-of-school pic of Sam, then shrugged into her backpack, looking at him a bit enviously. "Thanks for making breakfast. Have a good first day at school. I'm glad one of the bikes fits me since I, unlike some pampered youngsters, don't have a bus to drive me to school."

"Why not? Your classes are in the vo-tech space near the high school. Just catch the bus with me if you don't want to ride the bike."

Krystal had told him several times that here classes were half-days with half-days working with patients, so she rolled her eyes in reply, then pedaled as hard and fast as she could, taking a few short cuts across grassy areas, hoping to be first to class so she could be settled and reading when the others arrived. Once things went back to the way they were before, she expected all the down-timers to be gone. Since either they would be gone, left down-time, or she would be gone, back to her real life soon, making friends would be a waste of time. Uncle Raymond's argument that learning some herbal remedies and old-school techniques could be useful was the only reason she was here at all. Well, that and boredom. It was definitely a chance to treat injuries and illnesses that those left behind would never see.

As she locked her bike and looked up at the vo-tech center where the LPN, EMT, nurse's aide, and combat medic classes were being held, the term "gird your loins" randomly popped into her head. After a deep breath, she took her first step through the door and into her future. Then she turned around, ran outside, and threw up in the bushes. When the teacher arrived ten minutes later, Krystal was still sitting on the steps while a small gaggle of other students stood around, quietly watching her and talking behind their hands.

"Why are we outside..." Krystal dry heaved at just this moment. "Well, I guess that explains it. You look to be one of my students. LPN students, please help your classmate into the room. Later, you will be explaining any efforts you made to help and why you were standing there, not helping, when I arrived. For now, one of you must carry her things. Instead of our planned lesson, we have our very first patient to diagnose and help!"

As they all settled into their seats, Alice Sims started talking. "Mikki, welcome and please find a seat, we are just starting. I am Nurse Sims. My husband, Doctor Sims, and I retired from nursing six years before the Ring of Fire. He is a medical doctor and not a dental doctor like our esteemed son. We run a well-baby clinic at the Refugee Center two afternoons a week. You will all work there, learning about infant and post-natal care, which is the only time most of you will see us. Even by up-time standards, we are *old*!" Alice said this last with a grin and a wink. "The requirement for fluent written and spoken English means we have no Germans in our course this year, but the medical staff hopes apothecaries, barber-surgeons, and herbalists will join within the next year or two."

"As you should know, our shortage of teaching staff means many of you will be teaching lessons based on your personal skillsets. Someone will take notes and videotape your lessons to create lesson plans for next year."

"Now, let's see what you know! Who would like to lead the examination of Miss Reed?" Alice's palpable enthusiasm infected her students. The final diagnosis was that Krystal ate some greasy, slightly "off" sausage for breakfast. Add in a bumpy, fast bike ride to dumping the grease on an otherwise empty stomach and too much general stress and anxiety, tummy troubles were inevitable. The recommended treatments were mostly up-time medications that were either gone entirely or being kept for more serious health problems. Krystal refused to eat or drink anything with ginger since it had become rare and expensive, totally unrelated to her intense dislike of its taste. A down-timer woman assisting Nurse Sims for the first day of class suggested lavender tea, which worked quite nicely.

"I hope that is a good lesson for you class. You can, and should, learn from everyone, not just doctors and nurses. There are a lot of good home remedies. Chicken soup really is good for colds. Honey is a good antibacterial. Lavender tea helps with upset tummies. Don't dismiss something just because it didn't come from a textbook!"

Englishman, tool, and the only down-timer in the class, Justin Marbury interrupted. "Clearly, up-timers are not the only ones with medical knowledge. You depend too much on things others made. You can't even treat a simply upset stomach without medicines that are gone now!"

Alice glared at him before continuing as if he had never spoken. "But do test down-time and home remedies first. Lots of home remedies are so much bupkis. Use your common sense. Much like blood-letting, filling a cavity with crow dung will not make anything better!" Justin turned red and his eyes narrowed at the mention of bloodletting.

"Seriously? People put poop in their mouth *on purpose?*" Mikki asked.

"Yes, that is something some people, dentists, technically, actually do here and now. Doctor Sims and I have been collecting some of the more…questionable medical practices. We plan to add explanations of why they aren't the best course of treatment and give alternatives, then have copies printed to send anywhere and everywhere we can."

✳ ✳ ✳

Alice Sims looked tired as she smiled at the nursing students. "You young people have been doing a fabulous job in the well-baby clinic. The first down-timers who came were nervous but it's a hit! However, the refugees feel overwhelmed by all our staff. Director Szymanski agreed that starting this week, you will be split into two groups. You will alternate weeks at the Refugee Center, helping with triage and other basic care in addition to the well-baby clinic, and the Bowers Assisted Living Center, where you will treat some long-term illnesses and help with rehab exercise."

Krystal spoke up. "At the Bowers, will any of the residents be teaching us?"

Justin sneered. "What can a bunch of old people teach us? Most of them can't even feed themselves anymore."

Krystal and Alice glared in unison, but Krystal answered, voice as cold and clear as ice. "My Grandpa Eli was in WWII. Many of the men out there were, and some of their wives served, too. They saw things. Many can't remember what they said thirty seconds ago, but most can remember fifty or seventy years ago like yesterday. Grandpa remembers holding pressure on a leg wound so a soldier he never saw before, or since, didn't bleed out. He remembers when and how they put a tourniquet on it. He can tell you exactly what the stretcher looked like. Ask him. He'll tell you about the tan canvas and the straps used to hold people in. Without straps, some patients fell out, especially in ambulances. Others didn't believe they were really hurt and got up when they shouldn't, if they weren't strapped in. There was a metal rod underneath. It locked in place across the width of the stretcher when it was open and folded for storage. But Grandpa's shirt got caught when one locked open, so he had to stay with the stretcher until they got to hospital and the patient was removed. Another old guy mentioned some kind of wheeled 'litter carrier' to help remove wounded from the battlefield or move them around at the hospital with only one orderly carrying the stretcher." Krystal finished with a withering look. "They remember plenty, Justin, even if they won't remember you a minute after they meet you."

After a pointed pause, she continued more warmly. "So, *Frau* Sims, will the old folks be teaching us anything?"

Alice took a moment to compose her answer. "We honestly hadn't thought of that. All we were thinking about was how to help the staff, stretched thin as they are. Some of what they know or remember is probably dangerously out of date. In 2000, tourniquets were out of favor,

31

for example, although military medics here brought them back this summer for battlefield injuries, especially amputations. That's not as bad as trying to bring back bloodletting, but we'll still need to be careful. I'll talk to Beulah, Director MacDonald, that is, Doctor Adams, and the other hospital staff to see what they think. In the meantime, your next instructor has arrived, so I will take your leave."

"*Guten morgen,* class. I am *Frau* Zimmerman. The doctors of Leahy asked me to teach you about herbal remedies. This I cannot do, not entirely. To learn herbal remedies takes many years. You will start by learning some of the simplest remedies, such as for heartburn, fevers, and aching heads, and I see you have already learned one for upset stomach. The doctors at Leahy will be telling me what important up-time medicines they no longer have. Together, we will find the best herbal cures, and I will teach these to you. Some herbal remedies do not work and may even be dangerous. I have done this for many years, and my mother and grandmother before me. Problems happen when inexperienced herbalists, or those with no training at all, try to make remedies, or with new patients, when unexpected reactions can occur. You will learn about some remedies that do not work as well, so you know what to look for.

"We will start with tincture to reduce fever. Before you finish the course, you will learn how to make a potion with sage, dandelion roots, and a flower you call lily of the valley. This can help problems of the heart, but can also kill, if the dosage is wrong or the heart muscle is not the problem. Normally, I would not teach it to anyone who has been studying herbalism for such a short time, but the doctors at Leahy are most adamant this medicine is needed very much.

"What questions do you have for me?"

"What can a *person* like you possibly teach me that is worth my time? When I return to England, I will study under a real medical doctor. Someone who has forgotten more than you ever will know." Justin's sneer was epic. He was almost thrown out of the program that day, but the need for trained people saved him.

"Such as bloodletting? And the humors? Will this 'real medical doctor' teach you how much weaker women are, and that they can't handle anything? Pah! Up-timers have shown how foolish these things are. Some herbal remedies, like willow bark tea, were still used in 2000, in a different form. If you aren't too stupid to listen, you will learn more cures from me than that 'doctor' is ever likely to teach." *Frau* Zimmerman had heard this line of attack many times before.

"Aren't you afraid to teach us this? What if we get it wrong?" Krystal asked, but other arms went down, their owners nodding in agreement.

"No. I am working with an up-timer on 'curriculum development'. You will have the needed skills before you make anything. It will build on other things you learn during the year. Making it will be your final test for herbalism, at the end of the year. The up-timers will make sure you have the knowledge of when to use it. We will both discuss dosing. If it ends up being too much, we will not do this. So, no, I am not afraid. A little worried with so little time, yes. Afraid, no." Her smile set most of the class at ease.

Two weeks later, Krystal's stress level hadn't improved and *Frau* Zimmerman announced they were going to start studying uses of Belladonna.

"*Frau* Zimmerman, are we seriously studying deadly nightshade?" Krystal's stomach was constantly knotted up and she felt sick to her stomach more often than not. Being told they would make potentially deadly herbal remedies was the last straw.

"Please do not use that name again. It is Belladonna and this plant has many good uses in medicine. You must to know them. If it makes your stomach better, you will not prepare any remedies using Belladonna. It is too dangerous with so little knowledge." *Frau* Zimmerman didn't look pleased.

"Why bother studying it at all then? It seems pointless."

"Because when you know what it can do, you can find a good herbalist to make what your patient needs, if it's complicated, or make it yourself, if it isn't. Did you ever make the medicine yourself up-time, or did you always buy it from someone else? As much as you fuss about medicines you no longer have, it seems that you must not have made any medicines at all yourself." The tart answer didn't make Krystal feel any better. The idea of making medicines herself, even uncomplicated ones, made the knots in her stomach curl a titch tighter.

"May I be excused? I am not feeling well." Krystal went directly from the classroom to find Garnet.

"Director Szymanski, I need a few minutes of your time, please."

"Wait outside my office. When I finish here, I'll come find you."

By the time Garnet was finished and came back, Krystal felt calmer. "Please come in. Something must be quite wrong for you to be here before class is over for the day. What is it?"

Krystal saw no point in prolonging the pain. "I need to quit. I'm too stressed. I feel sick every day. I don't sleep well and I'm not retaining enough. I wish I could stay, but I just can't. I'm sorry. I know I'm disappointing everyone."

"Krystal, no! You just lost both your parents, all your grandparents, your friends, and so much more. You need some time. That's okay. Do you think you will want to come back? Or perhaps do the nurse's aide program first?"

"Not the nurse's aide, no. I hope to come back next year, but we'll have to see. I'm going to ask my Uncle Raymond for more hours at the pharmacy and maybe I can work at the Bowers a few hours a week. I already volunteer there."

"Would you like to stay on staff for the well-baby clinic? Nurse Sims and Doc Sims have both said you are a natural. It won't pay much, but you will keep getting experience."

Krystal lit up, just a little. "Yes! I really enjoy that. Helping mothers and babies is so much better than helping the old people out at the Bowers, or even the families at the Refugee Center. Some things like weighing them and actually delivering the babies is almost exactly the same down-time as up-time."

"Consider yourself on staff for the clinic, then. I'll let the Sims know and you can start next week, both days every week. If you want to do any work for the Sanitation Commission, they can use help too. Just let me know and I'll put a word in for you. For now, I'll make sure your teachers know you won't be coming back for the rest of this year, and we will double your pay at the clinic. Fingers crossed for next year!"

"Wait a minute! I'm a volunteer! You said I would be paid for the clinic work?"

"You caught me! Yes, we will pay you, but it won't be a whole lot more than double your rate of 'free', so don't expect much." Garnet grinned, happy to see a small smile on Krystal's face at her corny old joke.

CHAPTER 4

Krystal paused filling out the Refugee Center form and looked thoughtfully at the woman in front of her. "Ursula, you say you are an herbalist. I know someone who might want to hire an herbalist but, more importantly, I know someone who needs an herbal remedy. My Aunt Bethel has been getting hot flashes and night sweats. They started right before the Ring of Fire and her doctor said, 'you're too young' and did nothing to help her. We all know because she keeps complaining about how he wouldn't listen to her. Do you have any suggestions?"

Once Ursula Durer understood what Krystal was talking about, her brow smoothed, and she smiled big and wide. "Easy as can be! Do you know the herb called sage? She must drink sage tea three times a day. Then her symptoms will be better."

"Are you busy right now? I have someone you should meet when my shift is over."

Two hours later, Krystal had introduced Ursula to her Uncle Raymond and explained that she was an herbalist who might be able to help Aunt Bethel. Upon hearing that, she had Raymond's undivided attention. "Do you have a remedy? I'll try anything to help her. Women up-time took something called HRT that we can't replicate easily here and now."

Ursula gave him a slightly pitying look. "You make life too complicated with all your medicines, like this 'artee' you say women took. Do you know the herb sage?" A nod. "Just have her drink sage tea three times a day, at least three days a week. Then it will not be so bad."

Raymond looked skeptical. "It's that simple?" Ursula nodded. "Hmmm. I could use herbal cures for other common complaints, like headaches and fevers. What can you recommend for those?"

Two hours later, Raymond had a list of herbs to grow and buy, and Ursula had a new job making herbal remedies at the pharmacy.

November 1631

"Krystal and Sam, I have to talk to you about Christmas presents." Grannie B now had their full attention. "Krystal, you know your mom always shopped the clearance sales, and you never figured out where she hid your presents. Well, she hid them here, in our house. By the time we moved out, you were bigger and the gifts were smaller, so she started storing them with your Aunt Bethel. She was particularly proud of the year she had all her Christmas shopping done by New Year's Eve–fifty-one weeks before Christmas! Sam, what we hope you didn't know was that your Aunt Sophia bought most of the gifts from 'your dad'. The year we left was no different. She already had some presents with Aunt Bethel and Uncle Raymond before the Ring. You need to decide if you want those presents on Christmas Day or some other time. Think about it and tell me when you decide."

Krystal replied a bit too quickly. "I don't have to think about it. We'll see them again before Christmas and Mom can take care of it like she always does."

Sam was getting fed up with her attitude. "I didn't know who bought them, but I figured out it wasn't Dad years ago. The dead give-away was that they were thing I wanted and liked. I don't have to think about it either. Please choose something to give me at Christmas. Save something for my birthday. Save any stuff that won't be outgrown or useless in a year, so I can keep getting presents from her even though she is *gone*."

Krystal was clearly furious, her eyes flashing anger. "My parents aren't gone, Sam! They'll come back. It may seem like a really long time to a high school kid like you, but it hasn't even been six months yet. Soon, but not yet. They can still come back."

Sam started to talk, but Grannie B motioned him to silence. "Honey, we all want to believe that, but what Sam said makes good sense. If your parents do come back, they can give all the gifts to you themselves. If they don't, then you still have a little bit of them to look forward to." Krystal glared at them both before wordlessly stomping off.

Grannie B broke the tension in the room when she said, "Well, that could've gone worse. She didn't throw a thing."

✳ ✳ ✳

Raymond saw Ursula at the Gardens. "Your beer is on me. Curt, yours too. Ursula, you are a huge help at the pharmacy. I know I've said it before, but Bethel feels so much better since she started drinking your sage tea. I think she's telling all the other women, including the ones she doesn't like. You've done a real service for the community, my friend. Hang on a minute. I'm going to go tell the manager to give you a tab for your beer for the month because it's on me. And cheap at the price!"

Once Raymond explained the situation, the manager refused to start a tab. The wife of Ernie Dobbs, one of the owners of Gardens, took HRT for menopause before the Ring and her symptoms roared back with a vengeance after she stopped having medicine. Until she started drinking the sage tea.

"Now that was unexpected." Raymond plopped onto the bench, prompting Curt to ask for an explanation. "It would seem that your wife's sage tea helped the wife of Ernie Dobbs, one of the Gardens' owners. He was quoted as saying 'that there is a miracle, in my book. I'd saint 'em if I could. Since I'm not the pope, or Catholic, I'll settle for buying 'em drinks for life at the Gardens, if I ever find out who brought back my happy Mo to me.' You and Ursula will drink for free here for the rest of your lives, in thanks."

As Ursula returned from the restroom, she saw Raymond talking as a shocked expression blossomed on her Curt's face. Reaching the table, she looked back and forth at them. "What is it that you have said to my man to make him look so?"

"It's actually your doing." Ursula looked skeptical at Raymond's words. "No, it's true. Your sage tea helped the wife of Ernie Dobbs, one of the owners of the Gardens. He's so happy that you both drink free for life here!"

Now Ursula looked shocked. "That is not a nice joke! You must take it back. My Curt, he believes this is true." Shaking her head. "I thought you were a nice man, *Herr* Reed."

After a few minutes, Ernie came over and confirmed the free beer (but not food) for life. Then he started talking about commissioning a statue of them in the center of town because they were actual, honest-to-God HEROES the way they were helping folks with that tea. That convinced both Ursula and Curt that the whole thing was a mean joke. No one made statues of people like them, ever, for any reason.

"What will it take to convince you? Will a signed note be enough? No? If it's witnessed? If it's witnessed by the mayor?" They finally started to thaw at that suggestion. "How about a note signed by me and witnessed by Mayor Dreeson and Mike Stearns? Will *that* convince you it's a real offer?" Ernie had never, in his life, had so much trouble literally giving something away for nothing.

A stunned Ursula and Curt went home that night with a note, signed by Ernie and witnessed by Mike Stearns and Mayor Dreeson, at the Gardens for dinner, clearly stating Ursula Durer and Curt Bauer were entitled to free drinks for life at the Thuringian Gardens.

Ursula spoke first. "Such important men would not lie when they would be caught so easily, Curt."

"It is true. They lie so they cannot be caught, or so others will be caught in their place. What they signed must be true. I really think it must. I hope." Curt stopped, took his wife's hand, then gave a tolerable imitation of a courtly bow and kiss on her hand. "Thank you for causing this confusing blessing to fall upon us, my beloved." Her laughter tinkled in his ears as they sauntered home, enjoying a perfect crisp fall evening.

"Husband."

"Yes?"

"There is something else to make this perfect evening even more perfect."

"Yes?"

"Next year, we shall be three in our family. The up-timers have confirmed that I am with child." Ursula serenely continued walking while Curt stood frozen in shock before letting out a whoop of delight, then running up, twirling her in a circle, and practically dancing in the street.

"Now this is truly a night to remember!"

❋ ❋ ❋

Beulah looked with pride at the students and volunteers working together at the Refugee Center. A year ago, they were living in different worlds, hundreds of years apart. Now, they were working together to help refugees arriving in Grantville be healthy. Every family had to fill out multiple questionnaires, starting with one when they arrived and were still soaking wet from the showers that asked where they came from, job skills, and how many in their group, and ending with one when they departed asking where they were moving to and where they would be working. Volunteers helped them.

"Where are you going to stay, now that you are leaving the Refugee Center, *Frau* Heydman?" Krystal enjoyed meeting new people this way, no strings or expectations attached.

"We found a place that is cheap. We rent from a person named Fuzzy, like a sheep. There is water and a toilet, which will be good when the baby is born." Anna had given up trying to explain to up-timers that her last name was Banz, not Heydman. Her husband Mathias' last name was Heydman, not hers. "Being in a house before the baby comes, this will be a blessing."

Krystal's brow crinkled. "You mean Wooly?" Anna Heydman nodded. "I heard about that. I haven't seen it, but I heard the place isn't safe. The 'houses' are poorly made and too close together. You might want to reconsider and live somewhere else."

"Do you know a place for us, one that is cheap with water and a toilet?" Krystal shook her head no, brow crinkling harder. "Then we shall live with this wooly-man until we find better." Anna would not be dissuaded.

Thanksgiving Day

"Happy Thanksgiving, Grannie B and Grandpa Eli!" Sam gave them big hugs when he surprised them in their room at the Assisted Living Center. "Krystal couldn't come because she volunteered to work an extra shift at the clinic today. She said it's good practice for when she's 'a real nurse' in a few years, but I'm worried about her. She's always working or studying. It's like she's trying to cut herself off from what's happening around her. Then again, maybe she just didn't want to come all the way out here. The winter weather here is brutal! It never got this cold back home."

"She's still fretting about when she will see her parents again, isn't she?" Sam's nod confirmed Grannie B's suspicion. "It isn't healthy. She's not the only one who wants to believe the people we lost will come back, but most of us are still living our lives. Krystal Marie is putting too much on hold. Is she doing anything but nursing classes and work? Is she going out with friends or dating anyone?"

Sam shook his head no. It wasn't worth reminding Grannie B, again, that Krystal had dropped out of the LPN training program. "Some kids asked her to go out at first, but they are getting busy with the army and whatever else is in their lives now, so they don't come by or call much anymore. She always says no anyway. She still eats lunch with some of the nursing students at the vo-tech, but that's it."

Grannie B's eyes lit up. At eighty-six, she had a new purpose in life. Her great-grand-daughter was going to start living in their new world, not just existing. She pulled the German refugee family living in her old home, the Schultes, into her plans. They could help her with the first step: getting Krystal to do something—anything!—other than work. They all agreed that attending mass was just the thing, even though she hadn't attended regularly before the Ring of Fire. Or maybe because she hadn't gone regularly. Mass at St. Mary's didn't trigger any memories for her, happy or sad. There were no ghosts of 'before the Ring' to feed her dream of going back, and, as much as she hated to admit it, even to herself, she was starting to see that perhaps it was only a dream.

Sam and Grandpa Eli were both Methodist but agreed that if it would get Krystal doing something, and make Grannie B happy, they'd go to mass too, at least through Christmas. Next, Grannie B and Anna Maria brought

Krystal's boss, Uncle Raymond, and some of her co-workers in on the plan. Krystal wouldn't be working on Sunday for at least three months, even if she wanted to, so she had no excuse for skipping mass. Knowing from her family that she had never been a regular at mass anywhere, Father Larry was surprised and pleased to start seeing Krystal regularly join the congregation at St. Mary's.

"Beulah, do you have a minute?" Mikki Barnes was formal in class and on rounds, but this wasn't class, and she wasn't a twenty-year-old kid.

"If you bring a cup of fresh coffee to my office, you can have five minutes."

Ten minutes later, Beulah wrapped her arthritic hands around a mug of hot java, eyes closed while she soaked in the warmth. She let out a deep breath and opened her eyes. "Now, what is it you need, Mikki? Are the youngsters driving you nuts yet?"

"No, nothing like that. They remind me a bit of Ethan and his friends, which is nice since we don't see him much now. It's not even about me. I try to visit the old folks out at the Bowers who have no family in Grantville. You remember that Krystal Reed was in my class until she dropped. Among other things, when I visit the Bowers, I see her helping the therapists and nurses with their tasks. There are two young men who help with PT a lot. Their English is still a work in progress, but they seem like good candidates to become certified physical therapists, possibly even RNs. The taller one, in particular, has a knack for working with the old folks. Good bedside manner on top of the physical skills. I've also seen them using some different equipment that is clearly down-time made. You might want to look into what it is and where they found it."

"Hmmm. I'll make a note and we'll look into it. Sounds like a good catch. Thanks. Did you have a suggestion or concern about Krystal?"

"Oh, right. We all know she has had a harder time than most with losing her family and up-time life. Nurse Sims and old Doc Sims have done a great job keeping her helping with the well-baby clinics and at the refugee center, in addition to helping when she visits the Bowers and working at the pharmacy. You or Garnet or someone should talk her into restarting the program next year. She has the talent and interest, and she will have enough experience that the first semester should be a cakewalk for her. I talked to Nurse Sims a bit and she is friendly with a few former patients as well as two girls in her original LPN class, which is all to the good for her mental health. She is friendly enough with a few former classmates to still have lunch together sometimes. Having friends here should help her deal with the stress better than last year."

Beulah turned to a new page in her notebook, then flipped to a calendar page several months in the future and added a note there. "Done and done. Thank you so much for bringing this all to my attention, Mikki. If you keep this up, you might just end up a supervisor not long after you graduate!" Her grin took the sting out of her 'threat'.

"Before you leave, I think Garnet may have a preview of some new books for your class, if you want a sneak peek." Mikki plopped right back down into her chair, looking expectantly at Garnet as she walked in.

Garnet Szymanski was proud of how the LPN and other programs were shaping up. It wasn't easy, but they were filling in the gaps where teachers and materials were left up-time, resources simply weren't available (or replaceable) down-time, and things needed to be created to bridge the cultural differences. Most of the students from the first class would stay right here at Leahy, but some would start traveling and spreading knowledge. Even Justin, as resistant as he was, would take some knowledge back to England with him.

Garnet raised an eyebrow. "I take it Beulah told you I have some new books here?" Mikki nodded. "Did she tell you what they are?" She shook her head no. "The first one has anatomy prints, basic procedures, and a very abbreviated list of ailments and how to treat them. The second one, hot off the presses, lists the medical terms you absolutely need to know immediately–'stay still!'–and the ones you need to know soon–'nausea'. In January, we expect a second, larger, booklet with the words in Italian, Dutch, French, Swedish, and possibly one or two other languages." For patients speaking anything other than German and English, Leahy was working to find translators, but it was a big job and the mini dictionaries would help.

CHAPTER 5

December 1631

Next step: getting Krystal in the holiday spirit, and that started with decorating. Sam, Grannie B, and Grandpa Eli worked with the whole Schulte family (Heinrich, Anna Maria, Gisela, Agatha, and little Dietrich) to get all the Christmas decorations from the basement/root cellar and attic. Grandpa Eli and Grannie B had left the attic chock-full and locked their tenants out of it, until Krystal and Sam moved in. Krystal arrived home from working at the clinic to find the place bustling.

"How do you fit all of these decorations in your house? Do you put some on the porch and the roof and in the yard? That seems silly. Or are some of these decorations meant to be outside? It is too much." Anna Maria and her daughters were completely overwhelmed by all the boxes of Christmas decorations. The two boxes filled with tiny lights made no sense at all. They were not large enough to light up a book or anything useful and it would take much time to untangle them. Americans could be very crazy people.

The up-timers all laughed. Krystal was getting into the spirit and answered. "Of course some are for outside! The garland, the big Santa Claus, the wreaths, the giant reindeer. The little wreaths go over the front windows on the outside. The rest is for inside, like the little electric candles for the windows."

"Krystal, let's skip the window candles. We have enough work putting up the other stuff, and then we'll have to take it all down later." Sam didn't want to say the real reason Grandpa Eli had suggested not using the electric candles: light bulbs were rare and getting rarer by the day. Saving them for a time when they might not have any other bulbs seemed prudent, but Krystal never reacted well to so much as a hint that they might not go back to their old, up-time lives.

The Germans were more flummoxed by the notion of keeping wreaths from year to year instead of making new ones than by the notion of having fake, electric candles instead of just using real candles. Wouldn't the pine needles dry up and fall out of the wreathes before the next Advent? And, obviously, pine resin makes a sticky mess if you leave pine branches sitting around too long.

Krystal grabbed the biggest wreath and handed it to Anna Maria. "Take this one and put it on the front door. You'll see, it's just fine to pack away year after year. No sticky stuff, no needles sticking you, either. It's called a ribbon wreath."

As a tailor's daughter, Anna Maria Schneider knew a thing or two about sewing, and a lot more about how tailors made money and the things they ended up not being able to use. After examining the ribbon wreath, she decided that sewing scraps would be perfect for making these 'ribbon wreaths'. Not quite as pretty as the ribbons, but much cheaper (free material, almost) to make *and* they could be sold as "genuine American-style wreaths" in a *Christkindlmarkt*.

When Anna Maria and Agatha found an old wooden Advent calendar buried in a box, they got excited and set it aside to fill later, clearly having found a Christmas tradition they understood. Then they found a box with not one but *three* nativity scenes. Grannie B gently removed a set of very carefully wrapped figures of the Holy Family. "My mother brought this set with her from the old country. She called the whole thing our 'o'presebbio' and these are our presepi. Her family lived near Naples and made nativity sets. They sent this one with her when she and my father came to America with my sisters for a better life. She always told me, 'Naples is the only place for a *good* nativity.' To hear her tell it, that was how it had been for centuries." She lovingly put the figures back into the wooden box on a bed of straw. "I wish Grandpa Eli and I could've gone to visit Naples. If wishes were fishes. Sam, I want you to take this when you have your own home."

"Grannie B! That's Dad's! You gave it to him three years ago for Christmas. You can't give it away again."

"Bless your heart. Child, that was mine before it was your dad's, so I most certainly can give it away. If—IF—your father comes back and wants it back, I'm sure Sam will let him have it back—IF my Donnie Joe comes back." Grannie B rarely used that tone with her family but when she did, they listened. It was also a reminder that while Krystal had lost a father, Grannie B and Grandpa Eli had lost more than one grandchild and more than one child to the Ring of Fire. "And if I want to give away any of my other things, or Grandpa Eli wants to give away any of his, we will. Understood?"

"Yes, ma'am."

"Good. Now, where shall we put these other two nativities? And where is the tree stand? We should have that ready when Sam and *Herr* Schulte come back with the tree. Sam and *Herr* Schulte—it is time for you to go cut down a Christmas tree for us!"

As box after box was opened and emptied, the house gradually filled with festive decorations, including a practically perfect Christmas tree Sam and *Herr* Schulte found. There were German lace Christmas ornaments for the windows that Grandpa Eli brought back from WWII. There were small lap quilts from QVC. There were stockings, and pillows, and décor galore!

Everywhere the Schultes looked, they were amazed to find more! It was positively exhausting.

Everyone was admiring the newly decorated tree as Krystal finished the final adjustments to it. "Mom finished the tree skirt for the last Christmas Grandpa Eli and Grannie B lived here. It matches the new sequined stockings she made us all. We would hang them from the mantel, but the stockings are with Mom and Dad, wherever they are. It's good the old ones are still here." Krystal tried to shake off her funk so she didn't ruin it for everyone else. "Has anyone seen the tinsel? It's the last thing we need to add, and Grandpa Eli gets to do that."

Grandpa Eli took the bag of tinsel, paused for a moment and handed the bag to Sam. "Grannie B and I talked about it, and we think it's time for a new tradition. Sam can put the tinsel on now that he's tall enough." *And, he thought to himself, that'll make it easier when I'm gone, Donnie Joe isn't here, and Donovan is still…Donovan.*

After Sunday mass, Irene Flannery walked over to Krystal and looked her up and down, sniffing in disdain. "I thought your mother at least taught you how to dress appropriately for mass, young lady."

Caught off guard, Krystal had to bite back an angry reply. "Mrs. Flannery, you know I didn't live in Grantville and most of my things were left behind, including my mother, my father, and my home. Unlike you, until things go back to normal, all I have of my own things are a few bags of laundry, which did not include my Sunday best, and my car. I am far too busy helping people, working, and studying to worry about finding a church dress."

It was one of the few times in anyone's memory that Irene Flannery looked embarrassed. Krystal was angry, but Grannie B seemed to like the old biddy for some unknowable reason, so she didn't turn on her heel and leave without saying another word, as she deeply wanted to. "I'll try to find something better for next week, so Grannie B isn't embarrassed."

Two days later, as Sam shoveled the sidewalk and took care of Mrs. Flannery's roses, a police officer arrived in response to a complaint she called in that morning. Irene Flannery was the police station's most frequent caller and they expected yet another complaint about some kid going into her yard to retrieve a ball or a person talking too loudly. She actually called the police when someone stopped to *smell* her precious roses.

At the station, they referred to calls over nothing "f-calls", a station code phrase for "Flannery-calls". When Mike Stearns overheard them talking about an "f-call", they all managed to keep straight faces while explaining it was short for "flower-calls" because of people calling about strangers bothering their flowerbeds, which was kind of true since Mrs. Flannery often called for that reason. It was more than a little mean-spirited, but Mrs. Flannery wasted more than a little bit of their time and created more than a little bit of paperwork, and she was more than a little bit mean-spirited herself. Not one of them felt even a tiny bit bad. Having been on the receiving end of Mrs. Flannery's mean-spiritedness his whole life, Mike would have approved the real meaning as well as the "official" one.

In point of fact, the "police" weren't responding to Mrs. Flannery's call today. Jürgen Neubert had been hanging around the station, trying to convince them he had the right stuff to be a police officer. As they got busier, Chief Frost started to think recruiting a bunch of young down-timers (compared to himself) might be a splendid idea. As a result, they hired Jürgen Neubert as an unofficial "auxiliary" helping the police department until the new training program got off the ground. Officially, he was the new office go-fer. As their workload continued to increase, the police staff decided he should help more by answering some of the obvious f-calls, specifically including any actually from Mrs. Flannery.

"I came home and found the door forced open. They only knocked over my Christmas tree! Then the blockheads stole my tinsel, of all the worthless things. How stupid are you people?" This wasn't racism or up-timer arrogance on Mrs. Flannery's part. In her opinion, everyone except her immediate family (who had all been dead for decades) was a stupid, uncultured blockhead.

Jürgen had heard about, but never met, Mrs. Flannery, Men twice his age feared her razor-sharp tongue. As a go-fer and unofficial auxiliary, he was beyond nervous when he realized that this was an actual crime, not yet another call about her flowers. As soon as he realized what had been stolen, a surprised and nervous Jürgen was all business, standing on the front step of her house. "They stole your tinsel? How much do you think they stole? Do you know the weight of what is missing? We will try to find the thieves, but I must be honest, they will melt the tinsel to sell. You should not expect to get it back." As he pulled out a pen and paper and started taking notes, the first note was that she seemed irate but oddly unconcerned about the theft of such a valuable item.

Sam was so utterly confused by this that he broke into the conversation. "Tinsel? I know you can burn it but then you're left with nothing. Why would someone steal something from up-time then destroy it instead of selling it?" Jürgen's English was good for a down-timer, but he couldn't understand everything. He wrote down the confusing statement to ask the other officers later. Even young up-timers like this Sam Reed had to know that silver doesn't "burn." It melts.

So, Jürgen ignored the statement that tinsel burned, an obvious misunderstanding on his own part, and continued doing his job. "Up-time things are most valuable when we do not have things like them already. We have silver tinsel strips, so these are just valuable for the silver. Only rich people decorate their trees with these silver strips, so I think the thieves won't find anyone to buy it. They will melt the tinsel and sell the silver."

As he talked, the reason someone would break in and steal her tinsel dawned on Mrs. Flannery. "Is down-time tinsel made of silver, like the metal in jewelry? Real silver?"

"Yes." Now Jürgen was puzzled. "How would silver not be metal?"

Seeing his clear confusion, Sam reached inside the door and picked up a blob of tinsel from the floor and handed it to him. "Tinsel isn't metal. It's a cheap, shiny, fun holiday decoration colored silver. If you try to melt it, it will burn until there is nothing left."

Jürgen examined the tinsel. "Ah. I see now, but you should perhaps not use so much of it. Others will also think it is real silver like real tinsel and try to steal it." After an intense, but brief, conversation with Jürgen, Mrs. Flannery decided to remove any remaining tinsel on the side facing the windows and put it on the parts she could see from inside the house. Sam volunteered to remove the rest of the tinsel. Since Mrs. Flannery never left anyone inside except for emergency house repairs, he felt safe making the offer, confident she would decline.

"Thank you, Sam. That would be helpful. Please place any remaining tinsel on the other side of the tree so I can enjoy something normal."

Having taken care of the rose bushes and the walkway Sam had slung his backpack onto his shoulder and started to leave before the words penetrated. He had no choice but to walk into Mrs. Flannery's house and take care of the tinsel. For his part, Jürgen decided the newspaper should write about up-timer decorations and how their tinsel contained no silver, to deter at least a few other break-ins and make less work for the already over-stretched police. He was happy, too, because he had good gossip:

Mrs. Flannery allowed a person into her house. On purpose. Invited, even. If anyone believed something so outlandish.

As Sam got ready to leave, Mrs. Flannery stopped him with an unexpected question. "Do you still live with your cousin Krystal?" After he nodded, she handed him a bag. "Please give this her and tell her I expect to see her properly dressed for mass next Sunday, and every Sunday after that."

Sam was too confused to do anything except agree and give Krystal the bag when he saw her that evening. Krystal was equally confused to be given a vintage-style dress with a matching belt and a note. The label clearly proved the dress was home-made, but it was equally clearly high-quality. This was by far the nicest dress she had ever owned, and not just because she didn't like wearing dresses.

Miss Reed,

I'm sure you know that I am not accustomed to doing things like this, but I cannot abide seeing young women come to mass looking like hoydens. Your great-grandparents have assured me that you plan on coming more frequently but have little time for leisure activities, including shopping, given your work and study schedule.

Since you have the excuse that your church clothes did not come through the Ring of Fire with you, and Sam is such a help with my roses, I am enclosing a dress for you to wear to church. Since I did not have your measurements, it will almost certainly be loose. The enclosed belt will ensure it fits properly. Please wear these items to mass going forward and be sure that your appearance is neat and tidy, since I have gone to the effort of ensuring you have an appropriate dress to wear.

—Irene Flannery

"Well, I'll be dipped in shit. Mrs. Flannery is acting like an honest-to-God human being. It's almost like she has feelings."

"Are you really going to wear that dress, Krys?" Sam asked.

"Of course. It's not like I want to show up to church in scrubs or a sweatshirt, and I don't have any other church clothes. I would be embarrassed if everything went back to normal during mass and I was wearing worn out sneakers and a '1999 Orientation Fairmont State' t-shirt. But now I need to find church *shoes*. None of the three and a half pairs of shoes that came through with me are dress shoes." Krystal was wearing her new sneakers when the Ring happened. A bag on the back seat of her car held her new nursing shoes and old sneakers, which, along with one water shoe wedged under the seat, constituted all the shoes she brought with her down-time. "Bethel's old boots fit me, so maybe she can give me some old church shoes, too."

The next afternoon, Sam biked out to visit Grannie B and Grandpa Eli. "Mrs. Flannery let me into her house a few days ago. Her living room looked like a set from *Austin Powers*. Why did anyone ever think disgusting green kitchens and shag carpeting looked good? And she gave Krystal a dress to wear to mass."

"Irene let you in her house? And she made Krystal a dress? Perhaps we should ask them to check and see if she's had a stroke." Grannie B grinned at her own joke. "She hasn't wanted people in her house since, well, ever really, but she started getting bad after they got new furniture in the sixties. She hasn't bought any new furniture or major appliances since then. A lot of people buy their major furniture and appliances young and never replace them, but most people don't leave their home frozen in time. I recall hearing that when she replaced the worn-out shag carpeting a few years ago, she found someplace to install new shag carpeting. Hard to believe she thinks she has such great style! Honestly, I thought that was just a mean-spirited rumor, but I guess not. Does Irene still cover the sofa and chairs with plastic? I bet she used that old machine Patrick gave her not too long before he died to make Krystal's dress. Either that or her mama's old machine."

"I don't know if she *made* her a dress, but she definitely *gave* her a dress," Sam said.

Grannie B shook her head. "Trust me, Sam, if a dress came from Irene Flannery, she made it. She was always the best in our sewing club, and she took more of the sewing correspondence courses than anyone else. She prided herself on never wearing store-bought clothing." Grannie B had always been more than a little envious of Irene's sewing skills, but her curiosity about the house got the better of her. "What did the house look like? We haven't been inside in decades."

"The living room had an ugly gold patterned sofa and orange chairs, covered in plastic like you guessed," Sam said. "A giant console record player with records from people like Elvis and some group called 'Peter, Paul, and Marla' sat under the window. But everything was super clean, and I told her the house looked nice, so she didn't yell at me again. Krys likes the dress. She said she'll wear it to mass, but she needs church shoes to go with her new church dress."

"It's 'Peter, Paul and Mary', not Marla. They were famous back in the sixties. I forgot how much Irene liked folk music back in the day. She used to go to Fairmont to buy the newest records. Patrick bought her that big old console record player when they got married. She couldn't carry a tune in a bucket, though. That's why she ended up cleaning the church instead of in the choir." Grannie B looked a bit sad. "She tried joining the choir, it just didn't work out for her."

CHAPTER 6

Krystal preferred utilitarian clothing that rarely netted her any compliments, but not for Sunday mass this week. If all dresses were as comfortable as the one Mrs. Flannery made her, she might wear them more often. It had pockets. Not tiny things that barely held a tissue, not awkwardly placed annoyances, and not semi-useless back pockets that ended up with a hole in the bottom, so things fell out. Actual pockets that were just a bit bigger than her hands, sewn into the side seams of the dress so they were easy to reach, with some kind of odd seam that wouldn't rip out easily. In short, genuinely useful pockets.

The dress itself was soft, warm, comforting dark green flannel, with a coordinating jacket. It reached the middle of her calves, so her legs stayed warmer than with her short up-time skirts (down-timers were scandalized), with short, cuffed sleeves and was loose enough to not need a zipper or buttons. Twisting around to try to reach a zipper in the back was such a pain! Combined with the long-sleeved bolero jacket, easily worn under a warmer coat, the outfit would be comfortable almost all year, depending on how Krystal wore it. She also didn't have the constant problem of her shirt coming untucked and the simple wrap belt kept cold air from shooting up her back. All in all, her new dress was much more comfortable than she ever expected from church clothes. But still, with all the snow and cold, Krystal opted to follow the current style and skip the church shoes, instead wearing her boots and jeans under the dress for warmth. Being generally oblivious to fashion, she was surprised by the compliments she received on her new dress.

At the end of the service, Krystal went to find Mrs. Flannery. She looked quite pleased to see Krystal wearing the dress, and even more pleased to overhear the compliments Krystal received as she walked toward her. "Thank you so much, Mrs. Flannery. I've never liked dresses, but this one feels wonderful, and has real pockets to boot! It's a lot more practical than I expected."

She snorted. "Young lady, women didn't wear dresses for millennia without making sure they were practical! But I can understand how, if you are judging them by the standard of some mall-store, low-end piece of sweatshop garbage, you might think that. When women still made their own clothing, they decided how big their pockets needed to be and make the whole outfit fit their body instead of making-due with some ill-fitting... Never mind. I'm glad you appreciate it. I look forward to seeing you wear that dress many more Sundays." With that, Mrs. Flannery nodded and walked away.

When they got home, Krystal asked Sam to take a picture of her in the new dress for her parents, jeans and all.

***

As the Christmas Eve carolers from St. Mary's started progressing from their street to the next one, Anna Maria pulled her husband aside. "Heinrich, it would be a kindness for you to stay with *Frau* and *Herr* Reed, so they don't get sick in the cold. Perhaps have some hot *Glüwein* waiting for us when we get home? We will call when we leave the Parish Hall to come home." With a kiss, she ran off to catch up to the other carolers.

Grandpa Eli gave Heinrich a conspiratorial grin as they walked up the sidewalk. "When I was a boy, the children's choir director sat me down and looked me straight in the eye and said, 'Eli, there are a lot of ways to serve the Lord. Singing in the choir is not the best way for you to serve the Lord.' Since that day, I have sung quietly when I'm not alone in the shower or the car. Looks like someone may think similarly of your singing."

Heinrich grinned back ruefully. "I may have heard something like this a time or two before I learned to sing not so loud. My good wife married me even after she heard me sing, so I knew right away that she was a tolerant woman with a good sense of humor!" With a shrug of his shoulders, "But I do not mind missing caroling and staying in the warm house to make *Glüwein* with my American friends!"

Sam, Krystal, Agatha, Gisela, Dietrich, and Anna Maria were all laughing and smiling as they stomped the snow off their boots on the front porch. As soon as they peeled off their layers inside the house, they were handed steaming mugs of *Glüwein* to warm them from the inside out. It smelled like Christmas.

The German tradition was to open presents on Christmas Eve, not Christmas Day. Since Christmas Eve was a busy day with caroling, mass, baking, and all kinds of activities, the Schulte family agreed to only open one gift on Christmas Eve. In truth, they weren't sure why the Americans thought opening gifts would take so long. Sam and Krystal were the last to open their gifts on Christmas Eve. Krystal had a stethoscope and blood pressure cuff. Sam had a manga comic book.

Grannie B spoke softly, "Sophia bought you other things, but these were your most special presents. Grandpa Eli and I decided to do what Sam suggested and keep the others for other years so you can still have a little bit of them with you at Christmas." Krystal looked up sharply at that, brows starting to knot together. Grannie B sighed. "If they don't come back, child. If they do come back, they can give them to you all at once themselves. If you decide you want them all, you can open them any time you want. But for now, this is what we thought was best."

At bedtime, Grannie B heard Krystal crying herself to sleep. Perhaps she was starting to see that her parents really weren't coming back.

One could hope.

The next morning, Grannie B and Grandpa Eli woke up in their old bedroom, like they had for nearly fifty years. Aiming to be the first to get up, they went downstairs as quietly as they could to make a Christmas surprise for everyone. "You heat up the water, Eli, while I get out the mugs and measure out the mix. We can each have a mug while we wait, to make sure it's still good, of course, if you don't wake everyone up galumphing about." That last was said with a bit of a twinkle in her voice.

As they turned the corner from the steps into the kitchen, Krystal looked up from her mug of herbal tea and gave them a questioning look. "And just what is it you are trying to hide from the rest of us?"

Grannie B grinned. "Swiss Miss!! With mini marshmallows, no less. We found a container packed in with the ornaments. We want it to be a Christmas surprise for everyone. But there's plenty for us to have a mug before everyone else comes down." Before Grannie B finished, Krystal was putting the kettle on to boil and pulling out mugs. Unfortunately for their plan, the kettle's whistle woke everyone up. It sounded like cattle thumping around upstairs and down the steps into the kitchen, where they made everyone wait until they were all gathered together to see what was under the tree.

Once everyone had their hot chocolate, Grannie B, Grandpa Eli, Heinrich, and Anna Maria went in to sit near the Christmas tree. Expecting only the one gift they had opened the day before, Heinrich and Anna Maria's kids (Agatha, Gisela, and Dietrich) were amazed to find more gifts under the tree. For Krystal and Sam, the small number of presents they each had was a stark reminder that their loving parents, home, and friends were all left up-time. (Sam's father was down-time, but he wasn't a loving parent.)

After the presents under the tree were opened, Grannie B and Grandpa Eli each pulled out one more. "Krystal and Sam, we know most of your clothing and all your stuff was left up-time." They handed each one a gift. "With a little help from Heinrich and Anna Maria, we found these in the attic for you."

Krystal gasped in surprise. Grannie B had been wearing her Scotty dog scarf for at least fifty years. "I can't take it, Grannie B. It's your favorite! Everything will go back to normal soon and I'll have my own things again."

"No matter what you think, we don't know when *or if* things will go back the way they were." Grannie B's response was firm. "Even if they do, I'm quite happy to stay inside my nice warm assisted living facility. I don't need it anymore. You most decidedly *do*."

Now it was Grandpa Eli's turn to give Sam a gift. His box was a whole lot bigger. When Sam started to rip into the wrapping paper, everyone shouted at him to make him slow down and remove it carefully, so it could be reused. When Sam finally opened the box, he held up a motorcycle jacket, clearly confused.

"Believe it or not, Grannie B and I had a lot of fun back in the day. I had a motorcycle when I met her, mostly because I could afford and it and also because, well, never mind the other reason. But Grannie B liked it almost as much as I did, never mind what she tells you."

"Back up a minute, Gramps. You rode a motorcycle? Why didn't we ever hear about it? And where is it now?"

Grannie B butted in, afraid this was headed toward Sam wanting a motorcycle. "Yes, he rode one of those pestiferous machines, until he had an accident and totaled it. He still has a limp when the weather changes from that infernal machine. Most of it went to the junkyard, and some of it went to his friends who didn't have wives to reign in their crazy streak."

"She's not entirely wrong, just mostly wrong. She had as much fun on it as I did, but wreck it I did, and broke my leg pretty badly in the process.

Since we had kids by then, there was no way I could afford to repair or replace it once the frame was bent. It was wrecked. So, crazy streak or no crazy streak, I had to let it go. But I kept the jacket until now, and I've made sure to take care of the leather, so it isn't dried out. Now it's your turn to take care of it, kiddo. Take care of it–and wear it. You never know, maybe someday the National Guard will give you a motorcycle to ride!" He was old, but not stupid. Grandpa Eli moved out of range before Grannie B could whack him with her purse for suggesting Sam ride a motorcycle. Even if it *was* a lot of fun.

And of course, Krystal took a few pictures for her parents.

PART 2
1632

Bethanne Kim

CHAPTER 7

January 1632

Justin agreed to work the New Year's Eve into New Year's Morning shift at the Emergency Room because holidays counted double so he would be able to have two free afternoons. The LPN teachers were clearly stretched thin in (re)designing their classes, with much of the progression seemingly based on what they guessed they might need to treat next. In early fall, they learned about treating burns, smoke inhalation, and "carbon monoxide poisoning", which he still didn't understand, before people started using fires to heat their homes in the winter. Before Christmas, it was food poisoning and treating patients who ate spoiled food, and handling cold-related injuries, like frostbite.

With the heavy snowfall tonight, he expected a quiet evening, which he planned to spend studying the women in the hospital. It was better than studying German medical terms, especially when the women dressed so scandalously. A few peaceful hours later, the nurses' station phone rang and the whole place erupted into action. Unsure what was happening, Justin, melted back into his chair, hoping to avoid notice.

"Young man, bring all the gurneys and wheelchairs you can find to the emergency entrance." The orderly had been given a lot to do in a short time. "You work here, yes? Then work!"

Unhappy at having an orderly order him around, Justin started to balk until he saw Nurse Mary Pat Flanagan, Director MacDonald's right hand, watching him. Not wanting another lecture from her, he did as requested. As he finished and headed back to his chair, she intercepted him. "Justin, prepare each bay in the emergency room for burn victims, as quickly as possible. We are about to get a lot of people with burns."

"How bad are the burns? How many people? Was there a fire? Where was it? How many patients do you think I will be treating?"

Out of patience, Mary Pat turned and practically snarled. "You can do what I tell you, and what anyone else on staff tells you, including the orderlies. You are a student, not a doctor, nurse, or other staff member. We all need to work now, not waste time asking questions." She turned to a nearby nurse's aide and asked her to call all the students in to help with the emergency.

Hours later, Mary Pat called the students into the break room where pizza, fresh bread, and small beer awaited them. "Director MacDonald and I couldn't be prouder of how you have helped this evening. No one enjoys debriding burns, and dressing the smaller burns with honey without making a sticky mess took some getting used to, but you are all handling it like pros. Your work made a real difference tonight, for the hospital, the patients, and the families. We even have a few new treatments, thanks to suggestions we received, such as using honey for burns and 'tape' to hold gauze in place."

Mikki was clearly ready to drop from exhaustion but still sharp as a tack. "Quick question. That 'tape' is fabric that was woven, not cut, into thin strips. Why do they call it tape?"

"I always wondered that when I had to use 'bias tape' for sewing. Tape is defined as 'a narrow flexible strip of band such as adhesive tape or magnetic tape (cassette).' And be happy that they helped us out with that. Like the honey, it let us stretch our other resources. Speaking of honey, we tried putting honey on the back of some of the tape to make it sticky. It's an experiment. If it works, we may have a makeshift, and reusable, replacement for paper tape. Now, let's dig into this pizza, then go home and *sleep*!"

Sam shook the snow flurries off his coat and hat before going inside to talk to Krystal. "The Refugee Center is sending over a new family to live with us. You need to let them use Grannie B and Grandpa Eli's old bedroom since the other bedrooms are still being used. Don't get mad! I know you believe they are coming back, but Aunt Sophia and Uncle Donnie Joe aren't here right now, and Grannie B and Grandpa Eli need the extra rent money. The new family was living in one of those houses that burnt down on New Year's Eve, so they won't pay much, but it's better than nothing. They are planning to build their own house, but they need a place to stay until it's warm enough outside for building. They agreed to do some work on the garage, too, in exchange for staying here. If your parents come back and these folks are still here, we can kick them out. Okay?"

It was not 'okay' with Krystal. No matter what anyone else said, she still believed her old life might come back. She didn't say a word as she stood up, left the room, put on all her outdoor layers, then slammed the door on her way out. If bike tires could squeal, hers would've squealed as she turned onto their street from the driveway, grateful they had only had flurries and not a real storm that week.

She thought about going to St. Mary's and talking to Father Larry, but he was busy with all the new Catholics in town. Besides, the best people she knew to help her calm down when she was this good and mad were Grannie B and Grandpa Eli, even if it was a lot further to the assisted living home than to St. Mary's. By the time she got there, she was calmer, thanks to the exercise, but she still had to make a decision. "Grannie B, I know my parents are still out there. I can't give up on seeing them again. You know I can't. And my friends at college! But mostly Mom and Dad, and all my grandparents, and all my relatives on Mom's side. I can't give someone else the last bedroom. Where will they stay when they get here? It's like I don't believe I'll see them again if I do that!" By now, Krystal was practically crying in frustration, anger, fear, and all the other emotions she tried to keep hidden away.

"Baby girl, what would your parents want?"

"What?"

"It's a simple question, my not-so-little-great-grandbaby. If you could call your parents and ask, would they want our old bedroom to be kept empty waiting for them, or would they want you to let a family whose home just burnt down, with what little they owned in it, use the room?"

Krystal tensed up, then let out a big sigh. She finally had an answer she could live with. "Since they can't use it, they would want someone in need to use it. Thank you, Grannie B."

"Besides, I heard the only person in town who isn't taking in refugees is Jimmy Dick Shaver. You do not want to be like Jimmy Dick. That boy has been trouble since Ike was President." Grandpa Eli liked to add his two cents. "If they bring chickens, promise to bring me to see them. I miss having chickens and fresh eggs at the house, and I miss having the milkman deliver milk. The old coop was still in the garage when we moved here. Pretty sure the milkman was dead, though."

"Eli, Krystal just told you a bad fire burnt up all their things and here you are fussing about chickens and milkmen. But he's not wrong about the chickens or the chicken coop, Krys, it was there. And chickens do a good job of eating all kinds of bugs, especially ticks. You should try to get some chickens. Kids love running around after chickens."

Poor as it was, the housing that burnt down was an improvement over having nothing. Moving into the house with Krystal and Sam was a miracle to Gretchen Dieter and her family, even if it had only been one day so far. "Agatha."

"Yes, *Frau* Dieter?"

"It is *Fräulein* Krystal. She cries so hard again. We stay in our room to not make her sad, but we still hear her."

"It's not you. Really. She misses her parents and family that were left up-time. And every time I try to talk to her, she ends up feeling worse, so it's definitely not you. I'll ask *Mutti* to talk to her this time."

"Krystal." Anna Maria knocked gently, then opened the door and entered slowly. "What is it, child?" As she sat on the bed and held Krystal, gently stroking her hair, Krystal gradually quieted from the violent sobbing only a devastatingly deep loss causes. Her worries and hurt spilled out. Losing loved ones and home were easily understood and clear immediately after the Ring. Others had taken longer to come into focus but were starting to hit her harder. The distress of knowing she would lose patients to diseases, like tetanus, that most people had forgotten up-time. The frustration of knowing that cowpox could reduce the threat of smallpox but being unable to do anything with the knowledge. The plague. The horror of how commonplace torture, rape, and murder were down-time. Guilt over living in a home full of someone else's things. Worry about

Grannie B and Grandpa Eli without up-time medicine. The stresses seemed to multiply daily.

"Sometimes I feel like everything gets me down. I miss blue Doritos and soda. Kurt and I had plans to see *Shanghai Noon*, and now I'll never see that or understand why he likes, liked, whatever, Jackie Chan so much. And Julie Marie, my best friend in the whole world, and I planned to see *Coyote Ugly* for her birthday in August. It's all gone! My life is just…gone, and I have no idea how to fix it." Tears streamed down her cheeks again and she started hyperventilating.

"Shhh, you need to calm." Anna Maria rubbed Krystal's back while pushing her head down between her knees. "This will help. It's hard, but try to slow your breathing. It may take a minute. You panicked a bit. It's okay. You're fine. Your body will feel better in a few minutes. Feelings may take longer, but your body will feel better soon." She continued talking, rubbing her back, and generally helping Krystal calm down until she was back to the neighborhood of normal.

"Thank you, Anna Maria. I feel better now. Really. Yesterday, I promised Grannie B and Sam to let a second family move in here, into the master bedroom, the room I had been saving for my parents. The one I haven't let the Schultes' use. They both said that if Mom and Dad show up, whoever the new folks are, they'll move out, but I know that isn't true. I know they don't believe I'll see my parents again. No one believes it. Letting *Frau* Dieter and her family stay there feels like I'm giving up on them and my whole old life up-time. My parents wouldn't ever give up on me."

Seeing tears welling up in her eyes again, Anna Maria rushed to stop that train of thought before she had another panic attack to contend with. "No, no! Your parents won't think you gave up on them. You still have to live your life. That's what parents want for their children: to live a happy life. I promise you that any family will move out if your parents arrive. If they don't want to move, my family will help make sure they do. Now, before you cry again, I believe Gisela is baking. Let's go sneak a sample. It smells like she is baking fresh bread, and you can have a nice cup of chamomile tea with it." At the word "sample", Krystal forgot all her cares for a few minutes.

✳ ✳ ✳

Like all the nurses, Beulah MacDonald, Director of Nursing, was a busy woman. Too busy, really, to take time to talk to a former-and-possibly-future student, but helping a struggling youngster was so much more enjoyable than paperwork, and everyone could see Krystal Reed was struggling even more since the fire. "Come into my office and talk to me. Are you upset about your family, child? Are you missing them?"

"No. Yes. That's not what this is about. *Frau* Banz and her son died. They were living in that awful shanty town that burnt down. When they moved out of refugee housing, they said they were going there. I had heard it was dangerous and I should have tried harder to get them to move. It's my fault they died." When she saw Mathias Heydman after the fire, Krystal thought his whole family was safe. When she found out about his wife and newborn, the news devastated her.

"No. Stop that *right now*. You are not even slightly to blame. You warned *Frau* Banz, but her determination to move out of refugee housing immediately was too great. Her husband agreed, or they wouldn't have been there. The fire department couldn't determine the exact cause, but the poor construction and dangerous conditions were, to us up-timers, as plain as the drink or cigarette Wooly always had in his hand. Wooly, God rest his soul, bears responsibility for the construction and generally unsafe conditions. *Frau* Banz and her husband bear responsibility for choosing to live there, *especially* after you tried to warn her. You do not. You tried to show her the danger, which is more than most would have done, *and* you have taken one of the families into your own home." She looked severe as only a strong-willed old woman can.

"Yes, ma'am." She paused. "But that's not how it feels."

"You did nothing wrong and that's a fact, not a feeling. If you truly feel like you owe that family something, figure out a way to help ensure other families don't have to endure something like this. Not today, though. A project like that bears thinking on for a while, so take your time. I know you want to be an RN, not 'just' an LPN when we get that program set up. I understand why you dropped out last fall, but all your work with the well-baby clinic, the residents at the Bowers, the Refugee Center, *and* the pharmacy mean that you are extremely well prepared now. I would love to see you as part of the incoming class next year. In fact, talking to you about it was already on my to-do list for the spring. Is that something you might be interested in?"

Deep breath. "Yes, ma'am. I want to try again. Working with Ursula, Nurse Sims, and Doctor Sims on the well-baby clinic has helped me a lot. I'm getting comfortable with herbal remedies now, so I won't be as worried about it next year. Thank you for allowing me to return. Do I need to take any exams or fill out any paperwork?"

"Fantastic! No paperwork or anything. You were already accepted. If you are interested, I'm going to recommend you join our teams that go out into the surrounding communities to provide general medical care, not just the well-baby clinics. Experiencing different areas will help you figure out what kind of nursing you want to specialize in. With all that experience, you will be starting ahead of your classmates." Beulah was pleased that Krystal was receptive to her suggestions. Privately, she also hoped Krystal would share her experiences with her classmates, allowing them to see more facets of nursing and medical care.

"Unfortunately, it's time for my next appointment. You should remember Justin Marbury from your original class. Please show him in as you leave."

"Mr. Marbury, what can I do for you?"

"*Frau* MacDonald, I appreciate the 'opportunities' you believe you have given me, but the events on New Year's Eve were the final straw. I am a gentleman. I will not take orders from underlings like these 'orderlies'. I quit your program."

Beulah frowned at the disrespect in his tone and the form of address. "It is Director MacDonald to you, young man, and you should be talking to Director Szymanski, not me. However, I will relay your resignation to her. Your instructors have noted your struggles to fit in so this is not the surprise you might think it is. If you change your mind, please let us know. What are your plans now?" *Please, Lord, don't let him change his mind! I know we need trained people, but he's such a condescending little prick!*

"For the next few months, I will do research at the libraries here. The moment the weather allows, I will return to England any way I can." Justin was pleased with himself for not letting his feelings show. These jumped-up 'nurses' thought they were so special! As if they had any medical knowledge or skills worthy of a gentleman and future doctor.

"Before you leave, please stop back. We could use your thoughts on how we can improve the program for down-timers. You can use the time to refine your thoughts on the matter. If there is nothing else you need, I will let your instructors know." Dismissed and relieved to be out of the program, Justin took his leave.

Bethanne Kim

CHAPTER 8

Agatha felt more than a little uncomfortable, but she was more worried about her friend Krystal than she was uncomfortable talking to her about how distressed she was, so she steeled herself and rushed through what she had to say. "Krystal, when we got here, we were all worried and scared and upset and we'd lost almost everything we had and everything was new and different and we couldn't understand anything and we didn't know what to do, didn't know what we could do." She ran out of breath and had to slow down a bit. "We didn't even know how or where to go to the bathroom because there weren't any outhouses, and we were inside buildings without chamber pots and such. So, it's not like we don't understand at all how you feel. It's different, but not entirely different. When we were at the Refugee Center, before we came here, a lady named Caroline talked to us and told us different things to do to help ourselves feel better. I don't remember all of them, but I remember she said to start every day by listing three things we were grateful for. She also told us something about breathing and emptying our minds, but I didn't understand that. Can you do that, Krystal? Can you think of three things every day in the here-and-now that you are grateful for?"

The sheer volume and speed of the words that had just fountained out of her normally quiet friend and housemate overwhelmed Krystal a bit. "I am grateful for a friend like you. I am grateful for Grandpa Eli and Grannie B's house. I am grateful for…"

Agatha gave her a hug and whispered, "You can do it! You got two right away. You can think of one more."

Krystal shivered a bit. "I am grateful for still having central heat, even if it is turned down a bit from other years."

"You up-timers like buildings too hot inside in the winter, and too cold inside in the summer! Let's start coming up with the things we are grateful for together, every morning. Is okay with you? I would like to start doing this too, telling God how I am grateful for what he has given me and my family."

"Up-time, a famous woman on TV name Oprah Winfrey talked about gratitude journals a lot. If you write down what you are grateful for, then on hard days, you can go back and look at things you have been grateful for. If you would like, I'll find a journal for you, too, and we can keep gratitude journals together. I'm fairly sure I saw some blank ones around."

Agatha gave a small squeal of joy. "Yes!"

February 1632

Krystal finally admitted it to herself. Grannie B and Grandpa Eli's tenants weren't coming back. Even if the world went back to normal, after nearly a year, they would have a new home somewhere else, newlyweds with a new baby. With help and encouragement from Grannie B and Agatha, she started packing their nursery-in-progress. The stack of thank you cards, and pile of wedding-shower cards and gifts gave away that they were expecting to get married sometime around the Ring of Fire. The baby furniture, maternity clothing, and other nursery items, added to the ultrasound image on the vanity, showed a baby was expected not too long after that. Whatever happened, they clearly weren't coming back to this house and the Schulte family could really use the space it would free up in their room. It was time to box up the rest of their personal items and find a corner to store them in.

When things went back to normal, she could still return it all to them. The government may have said that owners could keep anything left in their home, storage unit, store, or whatever, but Krystal didn't think that was entirely all right. What happened when they came back? It was one thing for toiletries, medicine, food, and other things that expired, but another thing, in her mind, for clothing and things that wouldn't go bad. They had already eaten most of the food, used the toiletries, and given the government a lot of things from the garage like oil and car parts. The bedrooms were the last places she had to clean out and pack.

As she emptied a drawer, Krystal's hands started shaking, a vein in her head started bulging, and she blew up. "Those BASTARDS! Those scum-sucking, evil, misogynistic, woman-hating, sadistic, perverted corporate BASTARDS! They knew–KNEW–those...*things* weren't doing a thing and they MADE US WEAR THEM!" By the end, Krystal was screaming. "Those unholy motherless pieces of shit knew how to make them–KNEW–and chose not to." She was too furious to stay in the house, much less continue cleaning.

Her rant continued, unabated, as she threw open the bedroom door and stormed downstairs. "Those lazy SOBs claimed they had to be made that way for 'support'. Liars! If I could find one of them, I'd make the sadistic bastard wear a codpiece made of salted leather and edged with pointy little stones and wires with pokey ends, and nothing underneath it to spare his delicate flesh. See how the sick son of a..." Krystal's voice finally started fade away once she went outside, but everyone avoided her on the sidewalk. The epic rant clearly wasn't quite over.

Sam started to ask Grannie B what the problem was, but she looked almost as angry and was muttering in Italian as she left (always a *very* bad sign), so he just shut his door again. Finally, after she clomped out the front door too, Sam risked asking Agatha, who simply looked confused.

"Truly, I do not know. We were going through the clothings of the woman who lived here before the Ring and was expecting a child. Krystal picked up some bosom holders. She looked surprised by how they felt. She scrunched them into a ball several times. She told *Frau* Reed something about them not having wires in them. They both looked at them closely, scrunched them some more, then became very angry. I do not understand why bosom holders would have wires, and I even less understand why bosom holders *not* having wires would make them so very angry."

At lunch the next day, Sam told everyone at the table what had happened. The guys and down-timers were all as confused as he was. The up-time girls were split. The ones with less impressive bosoms didn't seem as upset. But a few were muttering to themselves and looked angry. He concluded this was not the humorous incident he thought. In fact, it was a dangerous topic that he should not mention where any other up-time female could hear him. Especially ones with impressive bosoms. In the interest of his safety, Sam wanted to know why this was such a dangerous topic so he could stay far, far away from it in the future, but it took a good deal of thought to figure out who would be safe to ask. Since the men he asked were also clueless, he needed a female. Sam finally decided the best person to ask was his Aunt Bethel, just very carefully and after clearing it with Uncle Raymond. She wasn't happy about it, either, but at least she didn't start yelling. She just got a "regular" bra to show him the difference.

"This is called an underwire bra because there are wires that go under the breast. Any woman who doesn't have teeny tiny bosoms was forced to wear these infernal underwires most of the time, up-time, because that's how every company made bras, especially for larger cup sizes, which means bigger bosoms." Bethel had figured out that saying 'bosoms' instead of 'breasts' caused less snickering and embarrassment with up-time males, especially teenage ones. "They were not comfortable, and still aren't. Women wear them all the time so it's the kind of thing everyone got used to, but they still hurt sometimes, especially at the end of the day or when the fit isn't exactly right, and the fit is never exactly right. The ends of the wires poke sometimes. We're not talking stiletto-heels-all-day uncomfortable, but at least you can slip out of uncomfortable shoes when you sat down.

"All the bra companies claimed underwire was the only way to support the weight of heavier, larger, bosoms. I'm using past tense because underwires have been around longer than most women in this town have worn bras, but no one can manufacture them anymore because you need elastic, which means rubber, and we all know that isn't available here and now. Most of us are still wearing them, at least until they get too beat up, stretched, and worn out to keep wearing.

"What Krystal found was a nursing bra. They support much larger breasts, and ones that are full of milk for a nursing child, so they are bigger and weigh *a lot* more than non-nursing breasts. This nursing bra doesn't have underwires, so it shows that they were, in fact, lying sons-a-bitches and lazy to boot. My guess is the wires caused some kind of health issue for nursing moms so they couldn't be lazy and throw underwires in and be done with it. There was never a need for women to wear these blasted underwires. That's one plus for being down-time: no one will be manufacturing another underwire bra anytime soon. I'll miss the elastic on my up-time bras, but not those…things. They were harder to manufacture, admittedly, but it was entirely doable. And they never, ever, gave us a choice." She started looking angry but took a few deep breaths to calm herself.

"I have to admit, I'm only a little surprised by your visit. Krystal came over to see me after she left your house, Grannie B trailing after her, and they were both still steaming. I didn't nurse your cousins, so I never had nursing bras and didn't realize how different they are, so seeing those made me angry too. Uncle Raymond was unfortunate enough to be in the room and just asked, 'so, why don't you do something about it? Make your own bras that don't hurt.' Since none of us had an answer for it, Krystal plans to ask Nils to help her find someone to design a new garment to replace both underwires and corsets or bodys or stays or whatever they are calling what down-time women wear. Once she finds someone, Grannie B wants to help get a company started to make them. Hopefully, we'll have comfortable bras to replace our old, stretched, worn-out up-time ones *soon.*"

"One last question. How did they get stretched out of shape?"

"The elastic. Over time, with washings and wear, the elastic stretched and they wore out. And sometimes the underwires would pop through the end of the channels that held them and that *really* was uncomfortable. Painful, even."

Sam never asked another woman about underwires. Ever.

CHAPTER 9

"**N**urse Sims, what can I help you with today?" Raymond had been a patient of Old Doc Sims and his wife from the day he moved to Grantville until the day they retired and Doc Adams took over.

"What I'd really like is some bluing for my hair, but I don't expect you have any of that left. Doctor Sims and I heard you have an herbalist working for you now and decided we would like to see for ourselves. Maybe learn a few new things."

"As it so happens, we still have a bottle or two. I'll grab you one from the back. *Frau* Ursula Durer is our new herbalist. If you can wait until she takes a break, I will introduce you. Until then, I believe you know my niece, Krystal. Excuse me." Raymond ducked into the back room.

"Krystal, sweetie, Doctor Sims and I want you to know we appreciate your help with the well-baby clinics. Your skill with the patients has been such a blessing for us." Nurse Sims hands felt soft and dry as only an old lady's can as she patted Krystal's cheek, reminding her a bit of her Nana.

"Thank you, ma'am, but I should thank you. All of this," she waved airily around, "is hard but I like being around the babies and new moms. It feels like there's a point to what I'm doing. I've lost track of how many people have told me you are the first doctor they ever trusted, and sometimes they mean you, Mrs. Sims, and not Doctor Sims. As much as I hate being here sometimes, it feels good to help people like that."

Doctor Sims looked at her with pursed lips for a minute, considering. "Lass, would you care to learn a touch of midwifery?" The suggestion surprised her. For that matter, he surprised her by speaking up at all. His wife did most of the talking with the students.

"I...guess so? What do you want to teach me? I'm planning to rejoin the LPN program in the fall, and I am helping with some of the other general medicine clinics now."

"Me? No, not me. You aren't a nurse yet, much less a medical student. Besides, delivering babies is a young person's work. The hours are long, the patients are cranky, and my wife doesn't like cleaning blood and bodily fluids off my clothing." Alice cuffed his head gently at that, but she laughed too. "There is a new midwife in town, and I've heard she could use an assistant. Even experienced nurses are having a bit of refresher on their midwifery skills. You might get some good experience from her."

As they spoke, another women walked up, clearly quite pregnant. "Doctor Sims and *Frau* Sims?"

"Yes. Do you need help? Is it time for the baby? If so, it looks like it's quite early and we'll need to get you to the hospital."

A happy little laugh. "No, I don't ask for you, you ask for me. I am *Frau* Durer. *Herr* Little said you wish to meet me about healing people with plants."

"My husband, Doctor Sims, he's a medical doctor not a dentist like our son, and I run a well-baby clinic and are hoping you can share some remedies with us. We know the up-time way things were done. We are old dogs, but we want to learn some new tricks, specifically for treating new mothers and babies. Can you help us?"

When he returned, Raymond found Krystal had left and the other three were deep in conversation. He had a bad feeling that the pharmacy was about to lose their herbalist. He let them chat as long as he could, but finally had to speak up. "Excuse me, folks, but it's getting late. You might want to continue this at home, or at the Gardens." Having been intent on their conversation, they all looked surprised at how late it had gotten but agreed to continue the conversation in a few days, when Curt could join his wife at the Sims' home.

As they strolled home, Alice spoke first. "What do you think about *Frau* Durer, JT?" She was the only one who ever called John Thompson Sims "JT".

"You know what I think, mother. We need an herbalist on staff for the well-baby clinic. A pregnant down-timer who works at an up-timer pharmacy is about as gold-plated as we are likely to find. I just don't want to make any of our local pharmacists angry, so we need to talk to them before we even think about making an offer to *Frau* Durer."

"We will take care of it on Monday so we can make her an offer before the next clinic." JT saw no reason to argue with his wife's logic, so they kept holding hands and walking.

✳ ✳ ✳

Every winter since 1959, Irene had taken a few of her roses over early in the morning one Sunday to tuck them into the altar flowers before anyone else arrived. That was the reason she started cleaning at the church all those years ago: they gave her keys to let herself in and no one else was there to bother her. When people placed altar flowers, they normally said who they were in honor of, but she didn't like to talk about her little stillborn John Francis, and she definitely didn't want to talk about her other baby, the one she didn't have in her teens. Those discussions were between her and the Almighty, so she donated the flowers anonymously.

After her Patrick passed in 1971, she donated altar flowers in his name on the Sunday closest to their Valentine's Day anniversary. No one needed to know it was for her babies, too. It worked out nicely that the roses she grew for her first baby were purple, like Lenten vestments. She hadn't missed tucking her roses into the altar flowers in all those many years. A little thing like being thrown back through time and space wouldn't stop her this year.

When Irene and Patrick married in 1958, he turned the old mud room into a mini greenhouse for her. (It was an unusually long mud room with a lot of windows.) Her most prized flowers in there were still her roses. Even in the dead of winter, she always kept the space warm enough for her precious flowers to bloom. With all the troubles of the past year, she'd had a hard time of it this winter, but she had managed to coax a few small blossoms to come forth to tuck into the altar flowers.

She cut them carefully, leaving the longest possible stems, then removed the thorns, as she had every winter since John Francis was born. She gently wrapped the angled bases of the stems in damp cloth so they wouldn't get thirsty on the short walk to the church, now that she couldn't drive over with them safe and warm in her car. This early in the day, most people wouldn't be at St. Mary's yet, not even Father Mazzare and the new curate. It was also bitterly cold, and the sidewalks were icy, so she had to be as careful with the blooms as she was with her footsteps.

Before the Ring of Fire, she always went home for a time after tucking her roses into the altar flowers and before the service started, but walking on icy sidewalks was hard and dangerous at her age, after she placed the roses and sat a few moments in prayer for her lost family, she wiped away a few tears, pushed down the feelings of sadness, and started to bustle about with little clean up tasks. With all the newcomers, there were always things to clean and straighten in the church. The new curate's wife—and what a scandal that was!—seemed to be trying to take her place, so Mrs.

Flannery made sure Father Mazzare saw her hard work and didn't write her off as a useless old woman.

March 1632

"Uncle Raymond, I'm giving you my two-week notice for the pharmacy. The well-baby clinics have been going so well that we are going to start doing a traveling version of them for the next few months and, of course, Ursula is going to be a mom soon." Krystal didn't realize she was holding her breath waiting for his reply until she let it out.

He gave her a hug. "I wondered if this might happen with Ursula due soon. Congrats! How will this whole thing work? Are you still taking the LPN course this fall?"

It was going far better than she had expected. "Yes, I'm still taking the course. Doctor Sims and Nurse Sims will keep running the clinics here in Grantville. Ursula and I will be traveling around to different towns after her baby is born and she recovers a bit. The Sims are sending a local midwife with me the first few weeks while we figure things out. The Sims' want us to find some others we can train to do well-baby clinics, probably local mid-wives which is why they are sending one with me, so as many people as possible have one near them. I need help, especially at first, because my German is still a work-in-progress, and so is my knowledge of herbal remedies. Should we keep an eye out for another herbalist who might want to move to Grantville?"

The Grantville pharmacists, doctors, and nurses had wrestled with this question for months. They needed the help and the knowledge, but they didn't want the local communities to lose their best source of medical care for it. Now, Raymond couldn't wriggle out of giving an answer. "If you meet an herbalist who really wants to move to Grantville, visit us, or study here for a bit, send them here. What we don't want to do, on purpose or by accident, is to take away the only medical caregiver for a community, so work hard to make sure you don't do that. We want to share what we have with them, not take from them. Catch me up on what you have been doing, how it's been received, and what your mobile version will do."

"Hmm. You know Doc Sims and his wife started running these clinics shortly after the Battle of the Crapper, which the other doctors really appreciated. People were afraid at first and didn't want to do it, then Gretchen marched all the little ones with her over and people stopped arguing. Of course, she moved out so her showing up was a one-time deal, but it made an impression. Lately, we've had more people coming who don't live in the Refugee Center. They saw how much Leahy helped the burn victims. Combined with reassurances from people who lived in the Refugee Center, they are trying the well-baby clinic. Not all come back, but some do. Especially the ones who live with or work directly for up-timers, who sometimes straight-up order them to get their kids regular checkups."

"Good summery. Now, tell me how it's *doing*?"

Krystal looked confused. "Well? One of our first patients came back two weeks ago. Before this year, she lost three babies to winter sicknesses. I can't even imagine. She said she listened to what we said and this one didn't even get a sniffle. Another mom, one we put on bedrest, gave birth to her first baby before the big snowstorm in January. She wouldn't tell us how many she had lost before that, but it must have been more than a one or two. Her baby was little and small, but not too much. She is so grateful to us, and the little girl is so darn cute! They named her Alice for Nurse Sims and kept her in a kettle with warm bricks and soft blankets during the coldest days."

"It sounds like it's doing good. Are you enjoying it?"

Krystal looked surprised. "You know what, I am. I really am. Those babies probably wouldn't be alive without our program, and they aren't the only ones. Sometimes, at the Refugee Center, we clean the injuries of people who were attacked. It really upsets me, and I hate doing it. The well-baby clinic is the opposite, for me."

If she had looked, Krystal would have seen her Uncle Raymond's face relax just a little bit, then almost melt with relief before reforming to neutral. This was the first time she sounded like she was adapting to her new world. He finally had some hope that, with time, she would be okay again.

Bethanne Kim

CHAPTER 10

"**K**rys, we need to do it! You're not an ostrich. Get your head out of the sand." Sam's anger was palpable.

"No, Sam, we don't 'need to do it', you just think we do. They could come back anytime. We didn't get any warning when we were sent down-time, we won't get any warning when we get sent back up-time." Krystal was equally angry.

"Really? We need to keep every single thing the Clevengers' left in this house before the Ring of Fire?" Krystal nodded yes. "Really? Then why did you eat their eggs? What happened to the milk and the rest of the food in the refrigerator?"

"That's different! Food spoils. Shoes and furniture are different and it's just not right to get rid of their stuff. There is space to store it, and they'll be back." Krystal looked mulish again. Nearly ten months after the Ring of Fire, she was no longer positive things would go back to the way they were before, but she wasn't ready to admit it yet.

Grandpa Eli and Grannie B's house pre-dated plumbing. It was built with an outhouse, not a bathroom. When they added indoor plumbing, they turned the first-floor bedroom into a bathroom, which meant it was crazy-big for a bathroom. With the attic already full of Grandpa Eli and Grannie B's things and all that extra space in the bathroom, the Clevengers' personal things were stored at one end of the bathroom until the world went back to normal, which Krystal still insisted it would.

"Their clothing doesn't *need* to go anywhere yet, but why won't you go through the toiletries and that stuff? Some of it must be going bad soon, and those boxes are just taking up space we could use. Did it occur to you that they have a new place to live by now? Do you think they have gone without brushing their teeth or getting cold medicine for this long?" Krystal managed to glare harder at Sam. "Fine. Whatever." Not wanting the windows to break from the force of her glare, he grabbed his bike and headed out.

In addition to mowing Mrs. Flannery's lawn, he took care of her rose bushes and other flowers. Before the Ring of Fire, his younger half-brother Donny had done it, but Sam met Mrs. Flannery's very particular standards better. Everyone seemed surprised a teenage boy was good with flowers, but his chores had always included gardening, and he had figured out that girls were impressed when he gave them otherwise-expensive flowers that he had grown. Besides, biology class was much more interesting than diagramming sentences in English. (Why, oh why, did he have to get the one teacher who still insisted on teaching them how to diagram sentences?) There wasn't much gardening to do in the middle of winter, but Mrs. Flannery had a few things in a sunroom at the back of her house and he hoped to start growing some herbs and vegetables there. If it worked, they would have a nice start on the growing season. He wouldn't have believed it a year ago, but the thought of a garden-fresh tomato made his mouth water.

Krystal sat on the toilet looking around the overly-large bathroom, remembering the argument with Sam. *All that stuff does take a lot of space we could use for something else.* Then she let out a big sigh of realization. *It has been more than almost ten months. Sam's right. Even if things go back to normal, anyone who lived in Grantville and was left up-time will have a new place to live by now. I know they could still come back, but some of that stuff is going to go bad. Make-up supposedly expires, and toiletries definitely expire, so I should go through that junk before it explodes and makes a mess or something. Agatha will be so happy. I hope Ms. Clevenger isn't mad that I took the silver comb and brush from her vanity set. She clearly never used them!*

After washing her hands, Krystal opened the door in case anyone else needed to use the bathroom, her mind continuing to wander as she started emptying Marquise Clevenger's vanity, which sat with the boxes at the far end of the bathroom, planning on moving it to her own room. *I still don't understand why Grannie B and Grandpa Eli just turned a whole bedroom into a bathroom. They could have a little bedroom or a nice size storage room if they used half the space for it. A normal-size bathroom would heat up faster, too.*

She took her time emptying the vanity, deciding what to sell, what to keep, and what to repack for the Clevengers. Only expiring and inexpensive, easily replaced (up-time) items went in the sell pile. Replacing hairbands was much easier than replacing a favorite sweater, up-time. Down-time, hairbands were a limited and valuable commodity indeed. Since her own things were all left up-time, Krystal kept some make-up, brushes, and other small items (including all the hairbands but none of the scrunchies). Most of it just wasn't her style (or coloring) on the rare occasions she wore full make-up, so it went into a box of junk for Agatha to sell or throw out. The things she repacked for Marquise went into a box with her other possessions, including the ultrasound images stuck into the edge of the vanity mirror.

Agatha loved it when Krystal brought her boxes like this of 'things to sell'. As she looked through this one, Agatha's eyes just about popped out of her head. The "sell" items included make-up, make-up brushes, perfume, elastic scrunchies, plastic barrettes, hair scissors (who needs four pairs of them outside of a salon?), hair dye, and two small mirrors. "Do you know how much this is worth?"

"No, that's why I asked you to sell it."

Since her family moved in with Krystal and Sam in July 1631, Agatha and Krystal had grown close. Despite being slightly younger than Krystal, Agatha was firm. "Too much. There will be too much extra money. Just the hair color could pay the bills for two months. My parents are putting our little money into this new 'OPM'. You will do this too."

"I will?" Agatha's firmness amused Krystal. Not surprised, but amused.

"Yes. You will. My parents have discussed it. You are good with healing people, but not good with money, and Sam is too young to care for his money without help. You are also busy with your jobs, and you will be going back to school to be a nurse. You do not have parents to help, either of you. My parents will help with this. You will put your money into OPM."

Krystal couldn't argue with that. If it got the Schultes to stop fussing about her financial future (and Sam's), she would start happily start an "OPM" (Other People's Money) mutual fund account. She really did not want one more lecture on her lack of a dowry. She and Sam both signed the paperwork the next day, including permission for the Schultes to deposit money into their accounts. To use a phrase Grannie B liked, Krystal figured it would be a good place for her 'pin money'.

CHAPTER 11

Grannie B stayed after mass to help Hannelore clear the altar. She was coming more regularly since she had gotten Krystal to start coming, to set a good example. Hannelore was the wife of the new curate at St. Mary's. As downright bizarre as having a married curate was to her and the other up-timers, it did seem better than what they had being doing: living in sin, his children with her officially bastards. This way was much better, and the down-timers all seemed to think it was normal.

After working in silence for a few minutes, Hannelore spoke up. "Why does this Mrs. Flannery hate me? I have done nothing to her that I know of."

Grannie B chuckled. "You are not the first person to ask that exact question. Irene McClanahan Flannery has been hating on people for eighty years. Mostly it's because she purely is an unpleasant human being, but sometimes it's because she has a very high opinion of herself, and a very low opinion of everyone else."

Hannelore considered this. "She could have been in the motion pictures. I have heard her say this. She must have been very talented and beautiful for a 'talent scout' to promise to make her a star in your movies."

Grannie B laughed sadly. "Well, yes, Hannelore, she has been saying that since the late thirties. She was very pretty, but the great and mighty talent scout she talks about was a flim-flam man. A liar and a cheat. He

93

went from town to town, convincing pretty, gullible girls like Irene McClanahan (her name before she married) that he was a talent scout. He was a bad man who left many of them in a family way in a time when... Let me put it this way, it would be like an American Puritan's unmarried daughter being in a family way. You've heard enough about them to know how bad that would be, right?" Hannelore nodded. "Irene was lucky that all he left her with was a good story. I think she knows, buried deep in that tough walnut that passes for her heart, that it could've gone differently, but no one ever saw a reason to argue with her about it. It's lucky for her that he didn't leave her in a family way like we later heard he did with those other girls. Who knows? Maybe he really was a talent scout and would've made her star. Maybe that contract just got lost in the mail. But we all know that if she had gotten a contract from Hollywood, she would've been gone like a shot. Becoming a schoolteacher in rural Appalachia was a hard pill for a woman with such a high opinion of herself to swallow."

They worked quietly for a few minutes before Hannelore spoke again. "So, she sees me and thinks of what might have happened."

"I don't think it's quite as simple as that, Hannelore. Priests in our time were not supposed to have marital-type relations, ever. They didn't have wives or mistresses or children. If they did, it was a huge scandal, and definitely not accepted by the parish. They had to leave the priesthood if that happened. For her, you and your Gus are a scandal, but she is even more scandalized that everyone else isn't scandalized along with her, if that makes any sense. She was always a bit unforgiving when it came to those things. She spent most of her life alone and that doesn't make a person able to bend enough to understand how others might do things differently."

"But she was married. Did her husband die?"

"Yes, there was a car accident. She really did love him very much, but they were only married for thirteen years. When a person has lived over eighty years, thirteen years isn't very much, especially when it was more than three decades ago."

Hannelore paused in her polishing the wood as she worked out how to say what was bothering her. "When we were cleaning one Sunday, I took the roses from the altar and gave them to people at the Refugee Center because they have nothing pretty in their lives. When she heard that, she was terribly angry. So angry she just glared at me and left. She did not even clean that day and she has been angrier since then. Was I not supposed to give them away? Father Larry said we should take them to the Refugee Center."

"You did right. Don't you worry about Irene Flannery. Everyone knows what she's like, bless her heart. If anything, it will make people like you a bit more to know you survived cleaning the church with her. Most people won't do anything where they have to work with her."

April 1632

As Father Mazzare swung the door into the Parish Hall open, Grannie B quite clearly heard Irene Flannery screaming "you WHORE" before she apparently saw the good father and abruptly went as quiet as a proverbial church mouse.

Knowing Irene as well as she did, Grannie B turned around and sat down on a bench outside to wait until Irene came out, certain it would only be a few minutes.

"What do you want, Barbara? Come to gloat that they want that whore Hannelore to clean the church instead of me? That I'm not even useful to clean toilets now?"

Grannie B stood up to follow her outside. "Irene McClanahan, you were born a drama queen, and you'll die a drama queen. And you are closer to one than the other, so calm yourself down before you have a stroke or a heart attack. We both know you have been an anti-social, cantankerous bitch since your Patrick died–you know it's true so don't pretend you are shocked and offended—but you have been, let's just say a bit *more* of that since the world changed. Now this, inside a church no less. Spill."

Irene walked in silence, steering them both toward a side street neither of them had ever used often. She stopped halfway down it. "That's the house, Barb. I know my parents thought I went to Fairmont or somewhere like that, but I didn't. I just walked over a few blocks away. The 'back-alley doctor' was a classmate's mom. She moved here from Columbus, that's where she started 'helping' girls in my situation, and they moved back there after only a year or two. That was almost 65 years ago." Grannie B was shocked. All these years they had been wrong about what happened with the "Hollywood agent"/flim-flam man. She couldn't imagine going through what Irene must have when she realized she was young, single, and pregnant in West Virginia during the Great Depression. And even worse, how alone and afraid she must have felt after she ended the pregnancy.

"I planted a rose bush out at my grandparents' house to remember. It's still there, I guess. It was there when they took us and brought us here. I don't know if it would've been a boy or a girl. I don't even know if it would've lived. I didn't have a choice, not with the first one. I couldn't keep it, no matter what I wanted. Our little John Francis didn't take one single breath when he was born. Do you remember that? Not one breath. His grave was left up-time, too, right beside my Patrick. I can't even visit their graves." Angrily, "It's not right!" Tears filled her eyes to overflowing as she started to sob. "It's just not right." Grannie B reached out and held Irene until she pulled away.

"I would go cut roses from the bush I planted, to remember. I couldn't keep the baby, not then, not when he left me like that, alone. But I never wanted to forget. That's why I always had roses in my house and in my classroom. Once Patrick and I had a house, I made cuttings from it and planted them in our yard, but it isn't the same. That bush is the one I planted, right after. When my body healed enough from what that butcher did to me. After my grandparents died and they sold the house, everyone was too scared of me to say I couldn't cut the roses. Their fear made sure they took good care of the bush, too, so I wouldn't get mad at them.

"And now I don't have those roses to remember, and no one else knows why they were there. Why they mattered. Now someone will cut down my baby's rose bush and it will be gone forever." The tears dripped off her cheeks as Grannie B handed her the last purse size pack of Kleenex she had.

"But I never forgot. I always put flowers in the sanctuary on the anniversary of when it happened. Even last year, after we came here. I have a bush in my breakfast nook, so I can see the flowers year-round and I like to put them in the church in early Lent. After the services were over for the day, when I went to get the flowers, they were gone already. They told me later that Hannelore had taken them. I don't know what she did with them, but she took my baby's flowers." Tears welled up in her eyes again.

They stood side by side, awkwardly, looking at the back of a rather unremarkable old house. Grannie B finally broke the silence. "Thank you, Irene. I understand now. I never knew. Never even suspected. No one else may understand, but I do, and Eli will too. This is your personal business. You've spent decades perfecting your reputation as a curmudgeon on top of all those years as a schoolmarm scaring kids. Don't think you don't still have most of the town scared of you!" That brought a small, watery smile to Irene's lips, but it couldn't make it the whole way to her eyes.

"We can't help about the bush that was left behind, but we'll help protect the ones in your yard as long as we are still here. Eli and I won't tell anyone. Friends might be stretching things a bit, but Eli and I are here for you. Not too many left that have been around as long as we have, so we need to stick together. And those roses you had in the church? Father Mazzare had asked Hannelore to take the flowers from the church over to the Refugee Center, so they have something pretty to look at. I know it hurt you when they were gone, but some scared young girls and children had their day made just a little better because of your baby's flowers going over there."

Grannie B took a hankie out of her purse and started dabbing Irene's face. "There now! That's much better. If you had sunglasses and a scarf, no one would even know you had been crying." Irene brightened up a bit and pulled those items out of her own purse.

Now that Irene was calm and looked presentable, Grannie B wanted to head back. "I'm still older than you, Irene, and I'm tired. Let's go back to St. Vincent's. St. Mary's. Darn it, it's not right changing a name after a century! A person can't be expected to remember a name change after that long." In a rare display of friendship, Grannie B held out her elbow to walk back arm-in-arm with Irene, who agreed whole-heartedly that changing the name from St. Vincent's to St. Mary's was just plain wrong, even if the man wasn't technically a saint yet.

"Barb, please don't tell Eli. I said I would take that secret to the grave, and you are the only person I have told. It's embarrassing enough that you know. Having a man know would be so much worse."

"Whatever you want, Irene. It's your secret, not mine, but we are here for you. Eli was Patrick's friend, you know, just as I've been yours."

As they neared Irene's house, Grannie B shared a thought that might help keep the peace. "Why not use this as an excuse to stop cleaning and spend more time on your yard? You may be able to get a few more rose bushes started out of the ones you have. Start selling them all over the place, then your baby's bush will live forever. Sam can help you with it. Did you know he won first place at the county fair for his roses? It's not something he brags about, being a teenage boy and all, but he makes a mean rosehip tea, and his sugared violets are better than grandma made."

Mrs. Flannery's head dropped to her chest, eyes squeezed shut. When she looked up at Grannie B again, gratitude briefly shone from her eyes. "That's a lovely idea, Barbara. I just may do that. I remember both my babies with the roses, but Patrick planted that lilac tree when we were waiting for our John Francis. Now go home and leave me alone." With that, she wearily trudged up the driveway to her front porch, where she stopped and stared at her flowerbed as Grannie B made her way the short distance back to St. Mary's.

CHAPTER 12

*I*t's been nearly a year and I can't keep wearing the same things. My socks have holes, I'm sick of my three t-shirts, and my jeans are too valuable to keep wearing. I have to figure something out. Krystal was having a fashion emergency, but she didn't have any girlfriends in this universe to help her out. As she was getting ready to go to the Freedom Arches for a study group, she started down the steps and realized the answer was staring her in the face in that family portrait gallery in the stairwell: Marquise seemed to have good taste and be in the general ballpark of the right size. And her entire wardrobe was in boxes.

She won't mind. It's not like they're coming back. Krystal reasoned, not quite ready to connect the dots to realize that her life was not coming back either. Within an hour, her wardrobe was revitalized, except for shoes.

❋ ❋ ❋

Mrs. Flannery hated to admit it, even to herself, but ten years ago, she wouldn't have lost her temper like that with the young whore cleaning the church. Using that kind of language in the church was unseemly. In all her years as a schoolteacher, she had managed to never use that kind of language in front of children or families, no matter how much they deserved it. Now she had embarrassed herself in front of Father Flannery and Barbara Reed. What's worse, Barb might be right. Maybe it was time to stop cleaning the church and let someone younger take over, even a woman of dubious enough morals to have children out of wedlock and marry a man of God who was meant to be celibate. Spending more time on her own yard didn't sound all that bad.

To add insult to injury, Irene's arthritic knees decided she should find someone to help with her flowers, and not only the outside ones. She became lost in her own thoughts. *Sam is taking good care of the flowerbeds. Maybe it's time to let him help inside, too. He didn't muck up anything at Christmas, after all, and he could move the heavy plants, like that ridiculous Bird of Paradise. I should have gotten rid of the silly thing when it grew too big for the breakfast nook table. But ridiculous or not, small tree now or not, it's still the last thing my Patrick gave me.*

Irene decided. Sam would begin by helping her with the rose cuttings she had started in the fall. They should be planted soon, and her arthritis assured her that she was too old for digging in barely thawing dirt. In a month or two, he could help her start propagating more roses from her bushes. Sam could certainly help her with those things. She decided to make him a decent suit since his things were left up-time. Being seen talking to someone so inappropriately dressed at mass embarrassed her.

She had always been proud of her garden, and very particular. Most of the flowers were in shades of purple, yellow, and white, which she found soothing. Over the years, she had almost forgotten that she originally chose those colors because, along with green, they could be used for a boy or a girl, and she never knew if that first baby would've been a boy or a girl. Irene was certain her purple roses were the only ones in town, which meant they were the only ones still in existence. Her yellow roses might not be the only ones in existence, but they must be the best smelling ones, based on all the people who kept traipsing through her yard to smell them.

She made up her mind. Sam would start helping her with all her flowers the next time he came over.

May 1632

Mary Frances Flannery was worried enough to take a trip out to the Bowers Assisted Living Center. Her Aunt Irene had barely spoken to her husband's family since the mid-eighties, but they were the closest family Irene had left on either side of the Ring and they tried to keep an eye on her, from a bit of a distance. Most people would rejoice to see an older relative turn over a new leaf, but Irene Flannery wasn't a "new leaf" kind of person. Seeing her doing nice things was down-right worrisome. The best, and only, person anyone knew to talk to about Irene Flannery was Barbara Reed, and she lived at the Bowers, so Mary Frances was visiting the Bowers.

"Barbara, I feel unkind asking about this, but I'm worried about Aunt Irene. I saw your great-granddaughter Krystal wearing a dress Aunt Irene had clearly made over the winter, and now Sam has a suit she made. Now, either they stole the clothing, which they didn't do because Irene wasn't yelling and screaming, or Aunt Irene made it for them. Since she always refused to sew for money, those were gifts. When was the last time you saw her give something to anyone for no reason?"

Grannie B started to answer, then sat there, stumped. After a minute, Grandpa Eli startled them both by answering. "1958. She and Patrick were newly married, and she was so happy to be in a family way. Most people wouldn't guess it, but she did like kids, as long as they weren't messing with her flowers. That's why she taught in a rural school. She got to teach 'em from kindergarten the whole way through eighth grade and really watch them grow up. She always wanted some of her own. Anyway, Donnie Joe was a baby, and she gave us a little coat for him. Irene being Irene, she said it wasn't quite up to the quality she wanted for her own baby, but she sewed one of those labels of hers in it, and she only does that when she likes something. That's what Patrick told me, anyway. And that was the last time I saw her do something nice like that until she gave Krystal the dress at

Christmas. Funny coincidence that the last person she gave something to was Krystal's own daddy."

"I knew it! There's something wrong with her. Do you think it's a tumor? Or a psychiatric problem? Aunt Irene hasn't listened to me in years. Can you convince her to visit a doctor?" Mary Frances was genuinely worried that her aunt might be unwell. With everything else happening in the world, having to live with and care for the old termagant made her top-ten list of "things I don't want to do". (The list also included having actual marauders in her home.) But family is family, and Aunt Irene was Uncle Patrick's widow, so if push came to shove, she'd do it. Well, if a really *strong* push came to a really *strong* shove.

Grannie B and Grandpa Eli had lived at the Bowers for several years now. This wasn't the first time they had seen an older person soften up a bit, usually toward the end of their time. "No one will ever argue that Irene has *nothing* wrong with her, but there's no need to worry too much. She is still a terror. The police officers complain that some weeks she calls them three times about people touching her flowers, and you heard about the fuss she made at the church over the new curate and his wife." Since the "fuss" was more of a screaming match, this news very much reassured Mary Frances.

$$* \quad * \quad *$$

As Bethel and Raymond strolled through the park, enjoying the first flowers of spring, the smell of fresh-cut grass, and the sight of dozens of people enjoying a day that was practically perfect in every way, they saw Krystal on a bench, staring into the distance. "Hey, kiddo! How are you doing this fine day? Your Aunt and I were stretching our legs after spending most of the winter cooped up inside."

Krystal glanced at them, tears glinting in her eyes. "My Mom and I used to go to the botanical gardens in Pittsburgh every spring. Those gardens were amazing. There were so many flowers and plants from all over the world! When I was little, I thought I wanted to work with flowers because of the Phipps Conservatory. Mom and I started an herb garden together. That was our special thing every year, and every year we brought a new flower, herb, bush, *something*, home for our garden. Only a few survived that first year, before Mom took over from me. That's what convinced me I probably shouldn't try to work with plants. I kill them. But this place, this little garden, hardly has anything. Nothing interesting. Just plain old roses, azaleas, and other dime-a-dozen plants. And it's so small. There is hardly room to move! The year before we came back here, someone gave West Virginia land to start a botanical garden near Morgantown. Mom and I were so excited to go there on Mother's Day. But I wasn't there for Mother's Day, and I'm not there again this year, and I may not be ever again. And this is the only public 'garden' in Grantville. It's pathetic."

Her aunt and uncle couldn't help having their good mood deflated by all she had said, but they were determined not to let her get them down. "You don't need to do anything now, but why don't you think about starting a botanical garden later? You could start inventorying who has what plants and asking anyone who travels far to bring back other things for you. Whenever you finish nursing school, well, you'll probably still be busy, but you can start looking for a place to put it. What do you think? You could name it in honor of your mom."

For the first time in a very long time, hope bloomed in Krystal's eyes for a minute as she thought about it, before fading away. "Well, I can think about it, but I don't have time and it will take a lot of money. That would be a huge project."

"Just think about it, keep the idea in the back of your mind. Maybe someday we'll have a new capital city in need of just such a garden. Mrs. Flannery might help. We all know how much she loves her flowers. Okay?" Krystal nodded, mostly so they would leave her alone, but the idea stuck with her in spite of herself.

CHAPTER 13

June 1632

Mrs. Flannery called Sam inside for a cool glass of lemonade after he finished with the yardwork. He still wasn't clear how he had ended up doing so much gardening for and with Mrs. Flannery, but some of the other kids had much worse jobs and she kept surprising him with things, like lemonade on a hot afternoon and a suit. (He still had no clue why she made him a suit but turning down such very nice–and free–suit would be stupid, so he had no complaints.)

Even after months of helping her with the plants in her small greenhouse sunroom, he hadn't noticed the little lemon tree growing in the corner. It had just enough fruit for a refreshing pitcher of lemonade. Sam didn't even try to keep himself from examining the little tree. Before he realized it, he and Mrs. Flannery were discussing propagating it so more people could have their own little lemon trees. People worried about the common scourge of scurvy, especially on boats. Citrus helped prevent scurvy, so Mrs. Flannery's little lemon tree might really help a lot of people. Living with a future nurse could be educational. To his surprise, Mrs. Flannery loved the idea and agreed that if they figured out a way to grow these little lemon trees on boats, he might make a fortune. Or at least a tidy little profit. She pulled out an old planter so he could get started right away.

A few hours later, he realized she had said he would make money, not including herself in it. For someone as cantankerous as Mrs. Flannery, that struck him as oddly selfless. Now that he thought back on it, she hadn't yelled at him much over the past few months. Apparently, she tolerated him now. He didn't want to go so far as to say she liked him, or any other person, but it was headed in that direction.

July 1632

"You didn't do half-bad, boy. Those rose bushes might make it, and the new lemon tree isn't dead yet. Don't go getting lazy or cocky now. You have to keep on doing it." That was the highest praise she had given anyone in years. Decades, even. "I'm thinking of sending one of my bushes to this Swedish king himself one of these days. Then everybody else will want them too and I won't have to worry about my roses disappearing. I'd send Gustavus Adolphus that darn Bird of Paradise if anyone other than my Patrick gave it to me. Maybe when I'm dead you can send it to him."

Sam wasn't used to hearing compliments like that from her, but he was comfortable giving her his own thoughts and opinions now. "Unless he forbids other people from having them so he's the only one that has them, but he doesn't sound like that kind of king."

"Hmmmm. That does bear thinking on. Maybe we should go the other direction. Have these Committees of Corresponding do something with them. They seem to be everywhere." Irene had never been a fast mover, and old age didn't change that. When she died in the Croat Raid, she was still considering.

August 1632

"Who do they think they are, ordering me to leave my house? I'll stay here until I decide it's time to go." By the time the Croats were within a few blocks, Mrs. Flannery was in a towering rage. Mrs. Flannery in a joyous and light-hearted mood scared the tar out of people. Mrs. Flannery in a rage could stop a rampaging Viking in his tracks. Having received absolution from Father Mazzare over the phone mere minutes earlier, she had no worry over her own soul, especially since she had lived a spotless life, but she was certain the monsters headed toward her could have no such assurance.

She watched the Croat mercenaries tearing through the neighborhood, wreaking havoc on lawns, lawn furniture, shutters, and anything else they could grab quickly and destroy. They were clearly on a mission with a tight timeline. But she was on her own mission, and she would defend her rose bushes, her lawn, and her home no matter the cost to her. Irene Flannery stared stonily at the ones coming toward her home with a gaze that had stopped countless men, women, and children in their tracks. As the mercenaries advanced toward her, she started hissing at them. Literal hisses, which weirded them out as much as it had decades of small children. She genuinely sounded a lot like a snake ready to strike. No one knew why she did it, even she didn't know, but it worked so she hadn't questioned it in decades, generations even. Right now, she was so knotted up with anger that she couldn't think past it to the very real danger she was in.

"You are horrible little man-children. God will punish you for what you have done." She hissed as they froze in surprise. Most hadn't been spoken to like this since they actually were children, if ever. "God will smite you and yours, He will..." The word "smite" broke the spell. Unlike the little boys she was used to catching in her yard, these were grown, battle-hardened men. They were very used to being threatened with hellfire and brimstone, and smiting. Seconds later, she lay dying in a pool of her own blood. Determined, as always, to do things on her own terms, Irene Flannery dragged her body to her rose bushes, determined in death as in life to protect the flowers she had planted for the children she never got to love.

✳ ✳ ✳

Krystal was visiting Grannie B and Grandpa Eli when word arrived about a raiding party in town. Most of the able-bodied adults and teens worked to ensure everyone's safety, but it was more than Krystal could take. When they told her to go to another room, she would follow people or go if led, but she wouldn't (couldn't) do any more than follow exact instructions. Once the staff told everyone it was a false alarm and they were safe (but the town had been attacked), Grandpa Eli called Bethel to pick up Krystal and take her home.

Bethel arrived to find Krystal sitting in a chair, knees pulled up to her chest as she stared out the window, silently watching. When Bethel told her they were going home, she stood up and placidly walked out with her. As they got closer to town, Bethel noticed Krystal's thousand-yard stare as they passed the walking wounded. Some were uninjured refugees wearing rags stained with blood from others, but the visual impact was the same.

Krystal started speaking, her voice hollow. "This is our life now, isn't it? I mean, it's really our life? When I graduate, I won't just be in a hospital or doctor's office tending to patients. I'll be going to their houses, their businesses, their battlefields—which might also be their houses and their businesses—to heal them. I will know them. I thought I would work in a hospital somewhere like Pittsburgh, or at least Winchester, maybe a giant city like New York. I wouldn't have known my patients before they arrived, and I wouldn't have seen them again once they left. They would have been strangers, almost all of them. Now, some of them will be. But a lot of them won't be." Krystal was taking a big step to accepting her new reality.

"I don't know. Things are changing all the time, but I don't believe they can go back to 'before' after all that has happened. More cities are building hospitals modeled on ours. People have started to come to Grantville from all over Germany, though. It isn't just people from the Ring area. It seems like working at Leahy will be like working at Johns Hopkins or the Mayo Clinic up-time: people coming from all over the world (or Europe, in this case) for the best care, plus a clinic for locals." As the wife of one of the town's few pharmacists, Bethel had a better idea than most the direction medical care was headed in Grantville, and that it was headed that direction with all the decorum and stateliness of a loaded freight train on a downhill with no brakes.

After a minute, Bethel continued talking. "I don't know if you heard, but they think Mrs. Flannery died. They haven't found her body yet, but she refused to leave her house and she isn't yelling at any of the people walking through her yard, so she is presumed dead." Like most people in Grantville, Bethel had been yelled at enough by Irene Flannery to not be overly broken up about her death, so Krystal's response surprised her.

"Really? That's sad. Sam will miss her. Well, maybe not miss her-miss her, but he seemed to kind of like doing her yard work and now he'll have to find a new after-school job. Mrs. Flannery and Grannie B were kind of friends, so she'll miss her too. In a way."

"I'm glad to hear that. I'll be honest, I didn't think anyone would even kind-of, sort-of miss the old battle-axe, and it's a little bit heartbreaking when a person dies and no one cares at all. Let's get you home. I bet Gisela baked something tasty today. She is talented in the kitchen! If she were up-time, I bet she'd end up a famous five-star chef with her own TV show and bakery."

"Thanks Aunt Bethel, but I'm better than I was. I want to help. I'm going over to Leahy now, not home. I'm sure all the new LPNs are helping. But please save something from Gisela for me and I'll eat it later."

CHAPTER 14

September 1632

"Father Larry, if I could have a moment." In deference to what she called her advanced age and decrepitude, Father Larry Mazzare met with Grannie B to hear what she had to say. "Eli and I thought about coming to Irene's funeral, but the weather was just too cold and wet for oldsters like us. You don't have to look so surprised. She was never an easy woman and frenemies was always the best description for how we got along, but friend is part of that word. You didn't know her when she was a girl. I wish I could say she was sweet and everybody loved her, but I won't lie to a priest. She was sharp-tongued from the first word that came out of her mouth, and I'd be willing to bet the last words out of her mouth were too. For most kids, their first word is mom, or yes, maybe no. I'm fairly sure Irene's first word was 'bad', or maybe 'mad'. It was a long time ago and the memory has faded. Some people pretend they don't care what others think. For Irene, she really didn't care, except for a few people like her Patrick. She doted on that man. Everyone else could go pound sand for all she cared, but she was always different with him."

"But you're a busy man so I'll move toward the point. Irene might have been alone, but it was her choice. It was no failing of the church. The church was her refuge. I was there after the fight with Hannelore, and I listened to her rage. When she had the spit and vinegar over that incident out, I suggested that she 'take the out' and spend more time on her yard since it had a lot of meaning for her. She was old, tired, and cranky, but she didn't feel unwelcome at St. Mary's. She was just ticked off as only Irene McClanahan Flannery, with that legendary Irish temper of hers, could be.

"She wouldn't have wanted a big wake and funeral. People not liking her suited her just fine and pretending otherwise after she died wouldn't have suited her. The woman was nothing if not honest to a fault. Other people might have been sad that you had to ask strangers to carry her coffin to the burial site, and that there were no mourners. Irene would have been pleased to be buried with no unnecessary people there. Don't ever think otherwise. Some people just want to live and die alone, or as close to it as they can get, and Irene was one of them. You did good by Irene Flannery, Father, real good." Seeing his bowed head, Grannie B patted his hand comfortingly.

Father Mazzare kept his head bowed in prayer for a minute after she finished. When he raised it, he looked more at peace than he had since the Croat Raid. "Thank you for that, Mrs. Reed. It does help. I hope her soul is at peace now." He took another minute to contemplate the odd twists and turns God sometimes takes before saying goodbye to a smiling Grannie B and continuing about his business.

Chief Frost knocked on the front door. "Sam, I need to talk to you, son."

Krystal opened the door and motioned the Chief into the living room where she and Sam sat down to listen. He was there for Sam not her, but she figured she should listen since, at nineteen-almost-twenty (in three months), Krystal was an adult, unlike Sam. The Chief delayed the conversation a moment longer by stopping to smell the spectacular vase of yellow and lavender roses next to the door. "It's Mrs. Flannery."

Sam tensed at the name. "She said I could take a few flowers sometimes, as long as I didn't hurt the bushes. I didn't steal anything. And she died and Father Larry buried her. They said she wouldn't leave her yard and was yelling at the Croats, so they killed her. So how is she still complaining about me when she's dead?"

Dan Frost looked amused for a moment before his expression turned serious again. "Well, son, if anyone could register a complaint from beyond the grave, it would surely be Irene Flannery, but that isn't what this is about. She left everything she had, including her houses and her flowers, to you. She originally left it to St. Mary's, but then she got mad and changed her will."

"The closest person to a friend Mrs. Flannery had was your Grannie B. She told her lawyer that since Grannie B was even older than her, and you 'didn't completely mess up the flowerbeds' and 'took particular care of her rose bushes', she decided to leave everything to you. There are two requirements that come with it. You have to keep spreading starts from her rose bushes, and other plants when you can, as far and wide as you can, and you need to use any profits from selling the roses to help unwed mothers. The lawyer said she wanted the help to be specifically for unwed Catholic mothers, but her lawyer is a Lutheran and he left the word 'Catholic' out of the final will so that part isn't binding. She told him that your Grannie B and Grandpa Eli can explain about the rose bushes 'because Barb's probably told Eli by now, even though she said she wouldn't.' Can you agree to that?"

"Uh, I guess. Sure. Wait. I really inherited a house from Mrs. Flannery?"

"Yes, you really did. You're only seventeen and up-time you would've needed someone else to be in charge until you're eighteen, but it's only a few months, so I don't think anyone will object if you just take everything now. There are too many other things to worry about."

Sam and Krystal stared at him, open-mouthed, gawping like fish. "Well, I guess that's all kids. While you are deciding what you want to do with the houses, call Lamb's Commercial Properties. They can help you find tenants or move in, or whatever you want to do, and they understand the situation. You might want to talk to your Grannie B and Grandpa Eli for some advice. I'll let myself out. I wouldn't wait too long to at least take a look, though. The Croats could've damaged something as they rampaged through."

Without thinking, Krystal said, "My parents and his mom can give him their advice as soon as they get back." Even in her own head, she sounded less than sure, like she didn't entirely believe it herself after more than a year. Knowing that Krystal was in some denial about her parents and Sam's mom being left up-time for good, the Chief simply waved goodbye and left.

Twenty minutes later, Sam broke the silence. "I don't want to move. This is my home now."

Krystal nodded, looking bemused. "Two years ago, everyone was sooo worried about Y2K. Now, Julie Sims is a married, pregnant Baroness, and her parents are happy about the whole thing. You own a house. Jeff Higgins is married with a whole big family and a famous wife. Mr. Trout was killed in battle with actual swords in the gym. And we have a sort-of-not-quite Emperor. No one expected the year to go this way. Although, to be fair, someone started a betting pool a few years ago on how Mrs. Flannery would die. 'Shot in her front yard while yelling at someone' was the second favorite, after the odds-on favorite 'rage-induced heart-attack'. So, the only real surprise is that her killers had swords and armor instead of a hunting rifle."

Two days later, they were discussing Sam's inheritance with "Bunny" Lamb of Lamb's Commercial Properties. "You need to decide which property you want to live in, or if you are going to rent them both out. Mrs. Flannery started renting out the old McClanahan property before your parents were born, so that one is easy to keep as a rental. You can sell some of Irene's things to help pay for utilities and any repairs you may need to make after the raid, if you need, but the rental income should cover all the costs. I don't think the Croats damaged either house but with all the other things going on, we didn't check yet. You're very lucky that Irene owned both of them outright, no loans."

Sam was confused. "I thought I just inherited Mrs. Flannery's house. Who are the McClanahans?" Krystal had brought her camera along to get a picture of Sam entering his new house for the first time for her parents and his mom. Instead, she snapped a picture of a confused Sam with Mrs. Lamb in the background.

Mrs. Lamb looked pleased. Not many people took her picture anymore. "The McClanahan's were Mrs. Flannery's parents, and she inherited their house/store. It hasn't been used as a store in over half a century but converting the front room back would be easy enough, if anyone wanted to. The way downtown is going now, I'm surprised it hasn't already happened. Two or three families are living there right now. One is a Danish tailor with a son about your age. He's working as a general laborer—the dad not the son—because we don't need tailors here. Good tenants, no problems. Two other families moved on when they found a farm lease they could afford. There aren't enough rooms to rent in town, so finding new tenants is no problem. If you want to turn the front room back into a store, just let me know. That's a different pool of tenants."

She looked at their increasing confusion. "I guess most people under sixty hardly know a thing about Irene Flannery. The McClanahan's house was also their store. The first-floor front room housed a nice general store her daddy's family ran for generations. Her daddy kept the store going until he died in 1938. Irene was only eighteen. After that, her mama threw herself into the herb garden and turning the storefront into part of the house to district herself. Five years later, she passed too. By then, Irene had finished normal school and started teaching."

"She was a bit older than me, but everyone said Irene was the prettiest girl in town when she was young, especially since her parents liked to give her new ribbons and pretty things from their store. As their only living child, she inherited the house. She could never bring herself to sell the place, even though it was too big for her alone. She had boarders until she married Patrick Flannery and moved in with him. We've managed it since then. It's a cute little house."

Sam absorbed this new information before blurting out, "I want to stay with Krys until I graduate and join the National Guard."

"That's fine, whatever you want. Like I said, just let me know when and which house. What about Mrs. Flannery's things?"

"With school, I don't have time to go through all her junk right now. Can you have someone put her stuff into the attic or somewhere out of the way?"

Mrs. Lamb kept her priorities in order. She approved of Sam's choice to continue renting the properties, which, not coincidentally, provided her with continuing income. "I think we can make those things happen, son. I think Irene picked just the right person to inherit her houses, and her roses. I'm busy today, but how about we go look at the houses in a few days?" Seeing his nod, she made a note in her calendar.

The next day, Grannie B and Grandpa Eli called Sam and Krystal and asked them to come out to the Bowers to update them about Sam's inheritance. They were more than a little surprised to find out Mrs. Flannery had left him two houses, which apparently settled an old bet between the two of them.

Grandpa Eli rummaged around and gave his beaming bride a dime, looking a bit sheepish. "I said Irene sold the house when she married Patrick, and your Grannie B disagreed. When we made the bet, a dime was worth a bit more, and made of real silver. But Irene never stepped foot in that house after she got married! Not once. Didn't make a bit of sense if she still owned it. As for you, young man, what are you doing with *two* houses?"

"Nothing. They told me Mrs. Lamb can find renters and take care of everything, like she does for all those properties Jimmy Dick owns. I'm not moving, at least not until after I graduate from high school next spring. After that, maybe I'll change my mind."

Grannie B was having none of it. "Young man, you have been living with your cousin in our house for well over a year, using a room we could be renting out. As long as you needed it, we were glad to help. But you now have not one but two houses, so you don't need to stay in our house. Pick one and move there. By the end of the month. Clear?" Sam was clear.

Grandpa Eli was annoyed with Grannie B. It was his house too and he was *not* clear on Sam needing to move out. He gave her a short glare before re-assuring his great-grandson. "We don't mind if you take a little more time to decide where you want to live, son, and to let your tenants get comfortable with the changes, if they need to. Don't let your Grannie B chase you out, you lost enough in the Ring and senior year is always a busy time in high school. Now that we settled that, what do you plan on doing after graduation next spring?"

119

"Join the National Guard! This world is a dangerous place, and I want to protect Grantville and our allies, like you did for the US and our allies in WWII." Grandpa Eli looked proud enough to burst at that.

Krystal looked up. "I don't think your mom will approve. You know she wanted you to go to college and study chemistry."

"I still want to study chemistry someday, but we all hear about the things that Tilly, Horne, and all those vermin are doing in war. Even the 'good guys'! Two years ago, I didn't know one girl who had been raped, or a kid who had seen a family member killed in front of them. Heck, I didn't know a kid with a family member who had been murdered when they *weren't* close enough to see! Now? Who knows how many? It's a lot. Before the Ring of Fire, poor people still had a house, clothing, shoes, a phone, plumbing, central heating, electricity, school for the kids. Now, people who literally only have the clothing on their back are all over the place, and most of the kids can't even do the most basic reading and writing."

Grannie B looked at her, gently. "And if no one comes back before he graduates, Krys, what then? Where can he go to college for up-time chemistry? Honey, I know how much you are holding onto your hopes, and I can't say for sure you aren't right, but it's been over a year. Even if we somehow 'go back', we can't ever really go back. Too many people are dead, and Sam's right, most of us have seen things that changed us too much. Are you the same person you were that afternoon? Do you think your up-time nursing classmates would understand if you forgot and washed your rubber gloves to re-use them? What would your teachers say if you gave 'tear fabric strips and boil them' as the first steps in bandaging a wound? You need to start accepting that we may not see any of those people again, and that, if we do, we might not ever fully fit in again." Krystal got a mulish look her family knew too well on her face but nodded rather than argue (again) about it. Today was about Sam, not her, and, to be honest, the more time passed, the harder it was to believe life would ever go back.

"Mrs. Flannery said I have to keep making starts from the rose bushes and selling them, and to use any profits to help unwed mothers, especially Catholics. She said you could explain."

Grannie B nodded, suddenly looking incredibly sad. "When Irene was a bit younger than you are now, a flim-flam man—a con artist with a shiny new car—rolled into town, made her feel special, promised her the world, got her in a family way, then disappeared. Things were different back then. Being a single mother ruined a young woman's future. Irene had no way out, so she ended the pregnancy. If she had had the baby and given it up for adoption, people still would've known and ruined her future. Sometimes girls went out of town to 'visit relatives' and people suspected the girl was having a baby, but Irene had no one to go visit. It would have been obvious. She was terrified of what would happen if anyone found out. People wouldn't have been kind to her. She kept that secret her whole life. When I found out, she made me promise not to tell anyone, including Eli." Everyone in the room was clearly surprised. She had kept her secret well.

"She never talked about what happened, but she wanted less to do with other people after that summer. Most of us thought she felt even more full of herself because a 'Hollywood agent'—the flim-flam man—said she could be a movie star. But after I saw how sad she still was a few months ago when she finally told me what happened, I think she always regretted it, even though she didn't have many choices back then, especially after she lost the other baby with Patrick. Their little John Francis was stillborn. Those rose bushes are how she remembers both her babies. They are her personal memorial for them. That's why they matter so much, and that's why she wants to make sure they don't die, even after she did."

Hearing that story, and having lost so many loved ones himself, inspired Sam to make saving and spreading those flowers a mission. It also gave him a new name for the lavender roses. Whatever their name was up-time, they would now be the John Francis Flannery rose.

CHAPTER 15

"**U**rsula, I am tired. This is the most tired I have ever been in my entire life." Krystal had just finished her first full week of the LPN program with a healthy dose of helping people at the Refugee Center during her "free time."

Ursula considered Krystal as they walked. "You have had an easy life."

Krystal swelled up with indignation, then deflated almost as quickly. "Yeah, well, compared to what most down-timers have lived through. What is the plan for the traveling well-baby clinic without me?"

Ursula scrunched up her face like she something smelled bad. "I made a mistake. I asked Nurse Washaw about this. I meant to ask if the new LPNs could help, but she started biting my head off before I finished. She used fancier words, but her message was that it was 'beneath her' and I should ask people 'whose time is less valuable'. She looked ready to go on, then snapped her mouth shut and left. Director MacDonald walked up behind me just after that and asked if there was a problem. Everyone knows Nurse Washaw is unpleasant, but I did ask about LPNs for the well-baby clinics. Director MacDonald will ask for volunteers but said not to expect anything."

A few minutes later, Ursula picked up the thread of the conversation. "Why do you think Doctor Sims and his wife asked to talk to us today?

Krystal shrugged, chewing her bottom lip as they walked the final half block in silence.

The Sims were relaxing on the sunlit porch glider with lemonade as the two young women walked up. Alice rose first. "Come inside, my dears. Would either of you like a lemonade? We've been rationing our Country Time, so we still have a bit left. No? Make yourselves comfortable in the living room while I bring you each a glass of water, then."

"Not wishing to be rude, I hope this is not too long a conversation. My little Florence needs to nurse soon but I didn't want to wake her from her nap when I left." Ursula looked a bit embarrassed to bring it up.

"Of course. If you don't mind, how did you choose her name? It's an unusual choice. Being a nurse, it reminds me of Florence Nightingale." Alice had wanted to ask for months but didn't want to be nosy. Curiosity finally got the better of her.

Ursula beamed "Yes! I have read the book *The Lady with the Lamp*. This Florence Nightingale is someone I would be honored to have my child be like. She helped many and made new opportunities for women, even when powerful men did not want it. She is a good model for our new times." She shrugged. "And this name makes it easy for her to know when someone calls to her. I have never heard of another person named Florence."

As his wife settled Ursula and Krystal, Doctor Sims settled himself into his own favorite chair and polished his glasses. "Ursula, you need at least one more pair of hands to help when you are out of town now that Krystal is a nursing student, especially now that your little Florence is starting to roll around and may crawl soon. Mrs. Sims and I have talked about this. As long as the weather holds, the two of us will travel with you for rounds. It will do us good to get out and see what some of these villages are really like, and I can treat patients who need a doctor."

Ursula spoke up first. "This is a wonderful surprise! Thank you. I spoke to Director MacDonald about getting some LPNs, but this is much better. What about after the weather turns? Will we keep going during the winter?"

Alice replied. "Given how hard the winters are, almost certainly not, but let's get through the fall for now. During our visits, Doctor Sims will be evaluating what their health needs are, what else we need to be doing, and what information, supplies, and equipment are most needed. We can spend the winter months working on a plan to deliver on those needs. I have an unrelated question for you, Ursula. At your house, I saw a small box that looks like a loom on the table. What is it for?"

For some reason, the question amused Ursula. "It is a loom, for making tape. Everyone uses so much and it's easy enough for small children and old people, so we just keep a loom in the house and make our own tape. It's one of the first chores given to small children." She held out the ties on her cap. "Cap strings, apron strings, holding up plants, holding up stockings, tape is used for everything around the house."

Doc Sims grinned. "So, this 'tape' is down-time duct tape. You use it for everything. Interesting. The hospital could use a regular supply of it. Do you think the folks at the Refugee Center could help out?"

"Put some small looms out with the necessary supplies and women will put their kids to work on it to get them 'out of their hair'. The residents at Bowers could make it, too. It might even be a good exercise for hand and arm rehab, now that I think on it."

Alice cocked her head. "Could we do the same at the clinic? Set out a few small looms and the children weave tape for us, and occupy them, while the other children and mothers are cared for? That might give us enough for our own needs and any extra can be shared." They all agreed this was a splendid idea, just as soon as they could get the looms.

Within a week of Ursula mentioning it to a few friends, grateful down-timers donated the first few looms. Soon after, some clever person created a pattern so the tapes had crosses on them. Once Lothlorien got wind of the new pattern, the clinic received a special lot of bright red thread to make the new "red cross" pattern. It didn't take long for tourists to start asking to buy the new genuine "red cross tape" as a souvenir. And so, a side business was born, giving the well-baby clinic enough profit to pay for its own supplies and equipment.

CHAPTER 16

October 1632

Sam had put it off for as long as he could. Krystal was out of patience with him. "Just unlock the door. It's your house and your stuff, Sam." She even gave him a small push forward. "Now."

Krystal and Sam looked through the basement and first floor of Mrs. Flannery's house quickly before checking out the upstairs, where they ran into a small problem. Sam called downstairs to their great-grandparents Grannie B and Grandpa Eli, "This door is locked. Do we need a skeleton key or something?"

Grannie B and Grandpa Eli tensed up when they saw which door was locked. Grandpa Eli reached into the hall closed and pulled a key from a hook hidden high up in it, something he remembered seeing Patrick Flannery do over forty years earlier. As he put the key in the lock and forced it to turn, he and Grannie B both looked grim. The door clearly hadn't been opened in an extraordinarily long time, maybe even more than forty years.

Tears filled their eyes as they took in the room, but Krystal and Sam were confused. The layer of dust in an otherwise spotless house. The calendar that read "1958". The layette. The crib. The toys. The neat rows of dusty but otherwise-pristine bottles. The room made no sense in childless, neatness-obsessed Irene Flannery's home. Krystal started taking pictures, trying to not waste what remained of her precious up-time film. Her parents wouldn't believe this unless they saw it.

As she took it in, Grannie B started sobbing, clutching Eli's shirt and burying her head in his chest as they held onto one another like they were drowning. The first words Krystal and Sam could understand were Grannie B asking him over and over, "Did you know? Did Patrick tell you? Did you know about this?"

He kept shaking his head, no, too stunned to speak at first. Finally, he said, "Patrick said she was having a hard time. Right up to the end, he said she was having a hard time and never really accepted what happened. But I never thought he meant this." Worried about their great-grandparents now, Sam made tea while Krystal guided them out of the nursery and downstairs. After they calmed down enough to talk, they took turns telling the story.

"When Irene was young, she was the prettiest girl in town, there was no denying it and she knew it. She could have had any boy, but she set her cap for Patrick Flannery. He was eight years older than her and not interested in a 'little girl'. He went away to college, then started working in Pittsburgh after he graduated. He came home when Irene was about 15. He hadn't seen her for years and she was a beauty by then. She was still too young, but she had plenty of beaus, including a man from Hollywood. A 'talent scout', he said, but flim-flam man was the truth of it. Patrick left right around the time she took up with that him, trusting person that she was back then.

"Not long after, that flim-flam man left town, telling Irene and her parents that he would send a contract for her to come to Hollywood. She started eating and sleeping more, but we all thought she was depressed waiting for the contract. No one else knew it, but her time of the month didn't come. People think morning sickness is always the give-away. It isn't, but more people seem to notice that. Hardly anyone realized what happened with Irene, even her own parents. Not until after, at least. A back-alley doctor 'helped' Irene because the only other choice was to have the baby, and Irene couldn't do that, not as a single girl in the Great Depression, but the 'doctor' was a hack, figuratively and literally. She cut Irene up inside real bad. That's how her parents found out, because she was so hurt after it. They had to take her to the hospital in Fairmont. The doctors didn't think she could get pregnant again, and she almost didn't. I don't think Patrick ever knew anything about that first baby. It was a big secret. I suspected, but I didn't know for sure until Irene told me just a few months ago, after that big fight with Hannelore at the church.

"When Patrick's parents died, he inherited their house and came home. I don't think he planned to stay, but Irene was still waiting for him, and the age difference just wasn't as much of a problem anymore. Twelve years old is too young when you're twenty. Thirty-seven is just fine when you are forty-five. She never found anyone else she liked, or maybe she just couldn't find anyone who would put up with her high opinion of herself. They eloped in 1958, which came as a surprise to everyone. Most people never even knew that Irene and Patrick were expecting a baby, especially so soon after they got married, but it does explain why they finally tied the knot. Your Grandpa Eli and Patrick were friends, though, so we both knew.

"You kids didn't see it before the Ring, but having a baby is hard, dangerous work, and not just for the momma. It's hard for the baby too. Irene and Patrick weren't young then, and their baby was born too early. They called me to help because I was a midwife during the war, and I'm as close a friend as Irene ever had. She always trusted me more than most people. Their little John Francis Flannery was tiny thing. His whole little body fit in my hand. He never took even a single breath. We cleaned him up and let her hold him, but he was gone before he even arrived. Irene and Patrick just cried and cried until we took him so the Father could prepare him to be buried. Something broke in them both that day. After that, they just clung to each other and hardly talked to anyone else unless they had to. Irene went back to teaching, but she was always a bit more bitter after that. Instead of trying to impress people, she shut out everyone except her Patrick. Then he had that car accident back in seventy-one. He always used to tell her 'a bit of 'shine won't hurt me none' but it must have kept him from seeing that black ice." Everyone was silent for a minute after that.

"Since Patrick died, she hasn't invited a soul into that house unless something had to be fixed, until she left those refugees move in and then she had Sam come in to help with her Christmas tree. Sam, you look a bit like her Patrick might have when he was younger. Not like he did look, mind you, but like he had a brother or something, so maybe she likes you—liked you—because she saw a bit of her John Francis in you, Sam. They were so hoping it would be a boy, and it would have been just like her to decorate it that way, sure she would get what she wanted, even though we didn't know, back then, until a baby was born if it would be a boy or girl, or sometimes even if there would be more than one."

"After John Francis died, she must have just locked the door and never touched a thing, not even the calendar. There are still diapers stacked up in the corner next to a diaper pail, waiting. I wish we had known how bad it was. Maybe we could've helped them. I always knew losing that baby tore her up inside, but..." Grannie B's voice faded off. "There are a lot of ways to lose people. Irene lost part of herself when she lost that first baby, and she lost another big chunk when they lost John Patrick. I think she lost most of what she still had left after her Patrick died, the soft, kind parts. She was always a lot to take even as a toddler, but she could be fun, too, until she lost them both. I know it may not make sense to you, Krystal, but that's part of why I worry so much about you hanging on to your belief that everyone we left up-time will come back to us. I saw what pining for something, someone, lost did to Irene and it will break my heart if it happens to you, Krystal Marie."

What can you say after a story like that? Krystal and Sam couldn't think of a thing. After a while, Grandpa Eli broke the silence. "We have to do something now. Irene wouldn't want the room to be a mess like that, so we'll start with dusting, but not today. And that means you kids will start with dusting. We'll figure out what to do with the rest of it later, but you should lock it up for now and make a plan for what to do with all those things."

CHAPTER 17

His backside still figuratively stinging from Grannie B kicking his butt out (even if Grandpa Eli did say he could stay), Sam decided to live in Mrs. Flannery's house. Living with Krystal was kind of nice, but his real home had stayed up-time with his mom. Besides, taking care of the flowers would be easier and the Flannery house had two bathrooms compared to the one (admittedly enormous) bathroom in Krystal's house and the single (tiny) bathroom in the McClanahan home.

Once he made the decision, he had to choose a room, clean it out, and move his own stuff in, all while keeping up with his classes, taking care of the flowers, and figuring out what else he needed to do around the house. Since most of his friends were high school seniors like him, they didn't have any free time either, especially the ones dating or active in clubs. Not to be mean, but he needed to find someone unpopular enough to have a lot of free time and broke enough to help him for a small paycheck. Help came in the very unexpected form of Hans Jorgensen. Hans and his father were the Danish tenants in the McClanahan house that Mrs. Lamb had mentioned. Hans had free time because he had no friends and refused to join anything. He was almost a young, Lutheran version of Mrs. Flannery. More importantly, he was strong and willing to work cheap while helping to clean out Mrs. Flannery's first floor sewing room. Everything was boxed up and ready to move before he got there.

"You Americans have a lot of stuff. Too much clothing." As a tailor's son and (one-time) apprentice tailor, Hans felt strongly on this point. The glut of American clothing, followed by the disaster American sewing machines caused for down-time tailors, had destroyed the tailoring business. As if being chased out of their home by marauding armies wasn't bad enough, his father, a master in the tailor's guild, was forced to work as a common laborer because Grantville didn't "need" tailors. Luckily for them, Mrs. Flannery didn't listen to her property manager any more than she listened to anyone else. It kept their rent low while she lived. With a new owner, it would almost certainly go up now. Being nice to the new owner was just good sense.

As Hans and Sam took a short rest after moving a cabinet into the garage, one box fell and spilled out its contents. Looking through the stuff as he repacked it, Hans saw a small plastic oval with the magical word "Singer." Suspiciously, expecting things to somehow get worse, he asked, "Is this a tiny sewing machine?"

Sam looked in the box. "Naw, it's just stuff to use with your machine. My ex-step-grandmother had a box of stuff kind of like that for her machine and so does anyone I ever knew who had a sewing machine, including my mom and Grannie B."

"Why would Mrs. Flannery have had these things, but no sewing machine?" Hans knew people didn't like him because he was always angry, but he didn't care. He didn't understand why no one else seemed to be outraged when artists like his father lost their livelihoods to machines. How did they not see it was wrong? Did they not care about people like him? He had a solid future before the Americans and their sewing machines. Now he did not. He was an artist with fabric, like his father. Chemistry and science didn't interest him like they did Sam. If you gave Hans a length of fabric, he could imagine a coat or a suit made of it. If you gave him fabric scraps, he could find a way to use them. He could look at a person and know what color would look best on them and, sometimes, he listened and watched when his father taught the journeymen how to disguise physical flaws on people. He had even started learning local sumptuary laws to help keep people from breaking them. Not being able to sew wounded his artistic soul even more than having to look at all the horrible up-time "fashion" at school.

Too tired to explain a sewing machine cabinet, Sam simply opened it to let Hans see for himself. "It's not quite like the Higgins machine. This looks like my grandma's machine, so it's probably about forty years old. That's a lot newer than the Higgins machine. Sewing was Mrs. Flannery's hobby." He expected to see some surprise at the machine in the cabinet, not tears being quickly brushed away.

Hans almost whispered to himself, but Sam was close enough to hear him in the quiet garage. "If we had this, my father could work again. We could be tailors." Since they were classmates, Sam was used to seeing Hans angry. Seeing him like this threw Sam for a loop, but his mom had taught him to help others when he could, and this was a place he could help.

"Uh, I'm just storing it. I didn't even own a sewing machine until this week. If your dad and you want to use it, you can rent this one from me. The little box of stuff and everything." Unable to ignore or believe this stroke of good luck, Hans took the news to his father, Nils Jorgensen. Being a practical and experienced businessman, Nils knew an offer this good couldn't be true, but he had nothing to lose by checking and a great deal to gain. If nothing else, maybe it would get Hans to do something other than mope and be angry. Idle hands have ever been the devil's workshop, and Han's hands were far too idle since he wasn't an apprentice anymore.

The next day, Nils stood with Hans, looking at the up-time sewing machine in the Flannery garage while he tried not to crush the brim of his hat as he listened to Sam talk. "Last night, I asked my one-time step-grandmother Delia Higgins about renting you the machine." Seeing their surprised, half-hopeful, half-fearful expressions, he laughed. "Yes, that Delia Higgins, the one with the dolls for the Higgins Sewing Machine Co., the same sewing machines that you hate so much, Hans. All I asked her for was a bit of advice. I don't need the machine and you do. It's not complicated to use, and we have electricity here, so that works well. Some of the Barbies were there, so you're lucky they aren't trying to take a piece of this. What they suggested is bigger than I had planned, but that guy Johan who works for them was nodding like he loved the idea, and he's not stupid about clothing the way girls can be. He said to tell you it's a good idea."

Nils had heard Johan talking at the Thuringian Gardens. He was not a man to back foolishness and everyone knew the Barbies were rich, which made Nils listen a little more seriously to what Sam said, even though he was too young to have any real understanding of business, and he spoke too much and too quickly. It can be hard to trust a person like that, but Nils had limited options, so he tried.

When Sam finally told him the full offer, it was too much to believe. It simply couldn't be true. The boy, young man, technically, offered to let them use not one but *two* sewing machines and the whole house they lived in for the business. No rent. Not a pfennig. Miracles like this did not happen to people like him. Nils was trying to work out how they planned to steal the business from him when it dawned on him: The boy had already told him the trap.

"I am a grown man, an experienced master tailor and businessman. I heard about the children running the Higgins Sewing Machine Company and these 'Barbies'. I will not work for a child. If you decide to rent either machine, I will try to find the money." Red-faced, Nils bowed stiffly, turned, and started stalking out in a huff before Sam picked his jaw up off the floor, but not, unfortunately, before he started laughing so hard he could barely breathe and offended both Nils and Hans.

Before they walked out the door, Sam managed to contain himself enough to speak. "No, good God, no I won't try to run your business. I barely know anything about clothing from the twentieth century. There is no chance of me trying to run it!" The casual blasphemy offended Nils, but with no other options to restart his business, he turned around and waited.

After a few minutes, Sam finally stopped laughing and wiped the last of the tears from his eyes. Still red-faced, Nils stood just inside the door, arms crossed on his chest, foot tapping impatiently, glaring while the man-child who claimed to want to help him start a business, but couldn't control his own emotions, slowly pulled himself together.

"You will own more than half–fifty-one percent–so I can't tell you what to do. You will be the boss, not me. The part I contribute will be the building, the sewing machines, anything that goes with the sewing machines, and maybe some up-time ideas and connections. Krystal and I found some old sheets you can use to make the first few outfits with genuine up-time material. That should bring in enough money to pay some other start-up costs." Sam went on to explain that he'd be a silent partner, but that he talked a lot so he wouldn't really be 'silent' per se. But no matter how long he nattered away, the final decisions would be Nils'.

Simultaneously relieved and confused, Nils didn't want to look a gift horse in the mouth. "No rent for the whole building and also for two sewing machines? And the house has electricity for the machines?" He wanted to be sure he didn't misunderstand. "If we do not have to pay rent for the whole building, we can add journeymen and apprentices immediately. I know good men who want to work our trade again. They can stay in the house and work on the new Grantville fortifications and road work just enough to buy food until the business is strong enough to only be tailors. Hans, you can leave school now and be an apprentice again!"

Nils quickly realized that Sam understood how needed he was. As owner of the house and sewing machines, he could force a few decisions, if he cared enough to threaten to leave. No matter what his view about school were before the Ring of Fire, he wouldn't let the apprentices in his company drop out. Including Hans. They could work, but they would also stay in school and maintain their grades. Sam would not budge on this, and they really did need his house and sewing machines rent-free, so Hans and the other apprentices stayed in school.

Hans and Sam were now Entrepreneurs, one of the newest and most popular cliques at the high school. With his new social clout, Sam got a few other kids to help him with Mrs. Flannery's flowers at the old McClanahan house, especially the herb garden. Now that they were Entrepreneurs, other Entrepreneurs dragged Sam and Hans to Helene Gundelfinger's lectures, where they heard all kinds of ideas they brought back to Nils.

"I kind of forgot about Mrs. Lamb mentioning it, but after our meeting today, when Hans and I walked in the front door, the one facing the street, it hit me. This house was a general store for decades, a place that sold a little bit of everything people needed, and the family lived behind and above the shop. You can make it a store again! Not just a shop where you work. Make the front room a bigger shop where people can come in and look at what you are selling, see examples, and maybe pick out patterns, fabric, and whatever else they need to decide for you to make them an outfit. What do you think?" Sam and Hans were talking over each other to get this whole idea out because they were so excited, especially Hans.

Nils was not so excited.

Hans wasn't so easily put off. "Papa, you can start a tailor shop making up-time inspired clothing for down-timers, putting samples in the front window. You won't be the only one, of course, but being right here in Grantville, we could make a lot of money from visitors. Unlike other shops, we live in the home of a famous person. Dead, but famous. I think people will remember the names of the up-timers the Croats killed since there were so few."

Nils started slowly nodding his head, furiously re-thinking the layout of the house. "The large bedroom, that can be for the journeymen. The apprentices can still sleep downstairs near the steps so no one can break in. It is not a bad idea. But I still do not have money. There will be no money left for bills or food if we go spending money to make this front room fancy and make garments when people haven't ordered them. We will not waste the largest room by making it an up-time style store."

Hans and Sam didn't give up. None of them wanted to go into debt for it, but it took several weeks for Nils to convince them that they really didn't have the funds to do it immediately. They all finally agreed that they would do this when there wasn't a war close to Grantville or in danger of heading that way. But they could start working on it slowly, as they had cash on hand to pay for improvements.

* * *

Krystal had a rare afternoon off and decided to spend it cleaning out and packing the nursery in Mrs. Flannery's house. No one would look for here there so she would have a truly quiet afternoon. She opened the windows and aired out the room, which was musty and dusty after being locked and closed for more than forty years. She cleaned and boxed the children's toys and books. She emptied the dresser and moved on to the small wardrobe where she found a tiny coat identical to one her father wore as a child. Grannie B had a picture of him wearing it in her house that had moved with her to assisted living, and she had seen the actual coat in a cedar chest in her parents' bedroom.

Two hours later, Sam arrived at his new home after school to find Krystal still sitting in the middle of the floor in the nursery, clutching that little coat to her chest, silently crying, and clearly in need of a box of tissues or a pile of hankies. Totally out of his depth, Sam called their Aunt Bethel for help, then went in to try to find out what had gone wrong.

Krystal finally lifted her head and asked Sam to stop talking. "It's not any of those things, Sam, and it's not something you can 'fix'. I want my parents back. I need my parents! I'm not ready to have them gone. Or my grandparents. I still had three of them before the Ring of Fire and I miss them every single day. Julie Marie and I have been best friends since we were toddlers, and now she's gone. My house is gone. Everything is *gone*. Nursing school was supposed to be my ticket out of West Virginia. Now I'm stuck somewhere even more back-woods than up-time West Virginia, which is just freaking unbelievable. As I packed nasty old lady Flannery's nursery, I found a jacket exactly like one Dad wore as a toddler. Exactly! And it brought everything back, times ten. I. Want. To. Go. Home!" By the end, she was angry instead of sad.

Bethel heard part of her rant as she rushed into the house and up the steps, peeling off her sweater as she went. When she walked into the room, she simply hugged Krystal, then held on tight until she relaxed and returned the hug. Now that the hot flash had passed, she put her sweater back on, until the next one. "Honey, we all feel that to some degree. There isn't a person here, well not many, who wouldn't rather be home in 2001 in the good ol' US of A. Don't you think for a minute that you are alone in feeling that way! But if you just sit here on the floor, you'll die. You have to move and do things, whether you want to or not. You can grieve, you should grieve, but you can move while you do it." Krystal looked pissed at that. Bethel stood and held out her hand. "Come on. Upsy daisy. We are going to put that coat somewhere for safe-keeping and keep on boxing up what is in here, now that you've made such a good start. We will put it all somewhere for safe-keeping."

Just as Krystal thought they were finally done cleaning, Bethel opened a small closet under the eaves. On the plus side, nothing fell out. On the negative side, it had been insulation and who knows what else before the mice, raccoons, and other critters used it for their homes and the passing of years left it compacted tight. There was a nasty biohazard of a mess to clean up and possibly some roof repairs to go along with it. They looked at each other and burst into laughter. On the face of it, there was not a durn thing funny about it, but somehow, the juxtaposition of that horrible closet full of critter droppings, nests, old insulation, and other unidentifiable bits and pieces with the once again neat and tidy nursery was too much. So, they laughed.

It was too late in the day to deal with a biohazard that size, so they shut the little door and went home for a nice, hot Epsom salts bath. The closet had been like that for years, possibly decades. A few days, or weeks, more or less wouldn't hurt a thing.

Bethanne Kim

CHAPTER 18

November 1632

With the weather getting cooler and outdoor garden chores winding down, Sam had to start thinking about how to spread Mrs. Flannery's flowers farther afield than just to his friends and family. Seeking inspiration, he started walking and looking at other people's yards. At the park, he sat on a bench and stared at the flowers until Johan from the Freedom Arches sat down next to him and started talking, in German.

"So, they asked me to figure out a way to help these young unmarried mothers, camp followers, and widows, but I don't know what to do. Anything I think of takes money we don't have. Jobs do not grow on trees. They are asking too much of a simple farmer's son." Johan didn't expect the up-timer to understand his German. He was venting, so you can imagine his surprise when Sam's head popped up and he started responding in badly accented German.

"But what if they do grow on bushes! Your dad was a farmer, right? So, jobs might grow on bushes. Johan, we are going to do great things together." Sam's response confused Johan even more. Farmer's grow crops, not bushes or jobs. "Mrs. Flannery's Flowers, Johan! She told me to make sure more are grown and sent all over the place. These women can learn how to make new ones from branches off existing bushes, then sell them. They can ship them out all over the place like the Dutch did with tulip bulbs and keep the profits. It's what Mrs. F wanted and it's perfect!" Johan still didn't understand what the crazy up-timer was talking about, but he nodded politely.

* * *

Living in Krystal's house, Heinrich Schulte couldn't help knowing about the new tailor business Sam was involved in and his new business partner, Nils Jorgensen. Having observed Sam and Krystal both since they moved into the house sixteen months ago, Heinrich knew the boy was no better with his money than any of the up-timers. Wanting to meet the Jorgensen family and be sure they weren't taking advantage of Sam's up-timer naivety, he arranged a meeting with Nils Jorgensen at the McClanahan house where he lived, which also allowed him to see a little of the new tailoring business.

"I must say, Master Jorgensen, I am relieved that you are doing right by young Sam." Nils bristled at Heinrich's words. "Please do not take offense. These Americans are not careful with their money. They do not understand the world well, and I wished to make sure you would be careful for the young man where he will not be careful for himself, as my family has tried to do for him and Krystal."

This got Nils' attention. "You have the right of that. He was ready to pack two perfectly functional sewing machines into storage and let who knows what happen to them! Thanks to my Hans, they are now making him money. Or will soon. What have you done for them?" The last question was suspicious.

"Simple. My daughter and wife sell things they would throw away as worthless or sell for almost nothing. Krystal and Sam each receive a small amount of the profit. The funny thing is that they think we give them most of the sales price!" Seeing Nils start to get angry, Heinrich waved his worries away as if they were nothing. "We are not stealing from the youngsters. Each one has an 'OPM' account. They assume there is only a small amount in the account, and we see no reason to change that view. Krystal calls this her 'pin money', which always makes *Frau* Reed smile, but that is where most of the money from the sales goes. We keep a small percentage for our work selling things, a little more when we do more work like cleaning or altering an item, and almost all of that is in our own OPM accounts. The profits from selling things is not a fortune but it grows steadily. Already, it is enough to allow them to settle down and marry sooner in life, even without what Sam inherited."

Nils remained suspicious because he was suspicious by nature. "What is this OPM?"

"It's like owning tiny pieces of many businesses. When the businesses do well, people with shares in the OPM (Other People's Money) mutual fund do well. If they don't, people with OPM shares can lose money, but by owning pieces of so many businesses, the danger from one or two doing badly is very small. My wife and I have permission to make deposits into Sam and Krystal's accounts. We should talk to Sam so you can deposit into his account as well. When we go to sign the paperwork for that, they can explain more and answer your questions. I think it is not good for a young person to know they have too much money. But it is good for us to know to help them. And it is good for you to know that he can perhaps help more if the new business needs it. He can also invest in other things without having to take money from the tailoring business."

A man of few words, Heinrich had said what he needed to, so with an abrupt nod of his head, he left and headed to the library, leaving Nils with a lot to think on. Perhaps, when the business became profitable, Nils would investigate this 'OPM' for his own family.

✶ ✶ ✶

As Doctor Sims, Nurse Sims, Ursula, and Krystal finished cleaning after the clinic closed, their conversation moved to the stormfront moving in and the future of the mobile clinic. "Ladies, as much as Nurse Sims and I have enjoyed traveling around with *Frau* Durer, the mobile clinics are definitely at an end until spring. Krystal, the three of us spoke extensively during our travels and reached some decisions, which the Leahy staff agree with. First and foremost, regular mobile clinics are suspended during the winter. Second, weather permitting, we will have larger mid-winter clinics in several of the larger villages. Families can gather there from outlying areas to get their babies checked and for other general healthcare needs."

Krystal looked doubtful. "They don't seem all that excited when we come to them. Why would they travel to us? It sounds like a lot of work for not very many interested people."

To her surprise, Ursula answered. "They won't come to see us. Seeing us will be a side effect. They will come to see friends from other villages, because winter is boring and lonely, and because other vendors will show up too, once they know a group of people are getting together. It will be a bit of a mid-winter mini-fair when everyone is sick of being home and wants to see their friends. Or passing acquaintances. Or really anyone who isn't their family, close neighbor, or wanting to kill them or steal from them. You'll see. It'll work."

December 1632

"How should we name this 'LLC' *Frau* Gundelfinger told you to make? A business name is usually the master's name and trade, but an American-sounding name could make us more money." Nils didn't want to tell a couple of kids, but he really did want his name in the business name. Seeing your name on a shop sign, showing it was your business, felt good. He had worked hard to become a master and earn that right. He was disappointed when they didn't immediately and enthusiastically say, "Jorgensen Tailoring!"

"*Frau* Gundelfinger said you can use anything you want for the LLC name. You have to use that with the government and banks and stuff, but you can use another name for the actual business or businesses you run." Hans and Sam were both confident on this point. Nils, on the other hand, found the American ways could be very confusing, even for a seasoned businessman, and wasn't quite so sure.

"How about JRs LLC?" Sam pronounced it "juniors", which made no sense to Nils and Hans. "Junior, like the abbreviation JR-for Jorgensen and Reed. It's perfect!"

Since it did include his name, Nils agreed. JRs LLC was formed and open by the end of the month. Irene Flannery would have been astounded to see her family home turned into a genuine fashion emporium. Her mama would have been proud.

✳ ✳ ✳

Sam hadn't forgotten his November discussion with Johan from the Freedom Arches about flowers and helping single mothers through the CoC. When the teachers started to lighten the class workload a bit before the Christmas holiday, he went to the Freedom Arches to start his search in earnest for someone to help him spread the purple John Francis Flannery rose and ensure its continued existence. "Do you have any young mothers here who are farmers' daughters or widows? I need help with my garden, especially my flowers. In return, they can live in my house rent-free. But it's super important that they are good with flowers and like working with them."

Johan remembered the American from the park a month earlier. He couldn't quite believe the young man was still going on about helping unmarried mothers with flowers, but that's Americans for you. *Verrückt.* "*Ja, Fräulein* Gerandt. She has two young children. Camp follower most recently but born a burgher's daughter and spent much time on a farm as well. With no family left alive to help with the *kinder*, working is hard for her. She earns some small amount by making herbal remedies her *Mutti* taught her. She will help you with your flowers, happily. Is now good?" When Sam nodded, Johan gestured to a server. "Please fetch Elsa Gerandt. Tell her we have found a new home for her, so to bring her children and all their things." He shook his head. Verrückt *American hiring someone to help with gardening in December.*

Sam planned to start talking to someone that afternoon, not have them move in, but he didn't know how to back out of it now, and he did have a spare room upstairs, so Elsa and her children moved in that afternoon, exactly when he had planned on going to hang out with friends. Unoccupied since the Croat Raid, the room was very much not up to seventeenth century German housekeeping standards. Elsa tsk-tsked and went to cleaning with a will, shooing him out of the room. Her toddler, Ernst, joined in with a dust-rag he swiped at things. Five-year-old Katherine took things more seriously. The areas she swiped with a rag ended up slightly cleaner when she finished, not smudged and covered in fingerprints like Ernst's did. Like most down-time women, Elsa was entranced by spray bottles and how much easier they made cleaning, and some gardening tasks. From that day forward, she was rarely without at least one spray bottle at home, and often enough when she wasn't at home.

Like a lot of camp followers, Elsa was full of surprises. Her English wasn't bad. Understandable, if rudimentary. She had cleaned the kitchen counters and stovetop, and pronounced the oven (unused since Irene Flannery had purchased a microwave and a toaster oven when they were new-fangled gadgets) "satisfactory" by the time Sam woke up and came downstairs the next morning. "What would you like? It is not fitting for me to take anything from the cold box without asking first." She did not want to anger him her first day in the house.

"It's called a refrigerator. I don't cook. I'll tell you what, if you cook for me, I'll pay for your food as well as mine. That's a square deal. Use whatever you need in the fridge and buy whatever food you need for me and your family." Sam was pleased with himself for this idea. He never wanted to eat scrambled eggs and carrot sticks again. The people who rented the other bedroom were rarely home except to sleep and never cooked at the house. Since he was a terrible cook, the idea of having an in-house chef thrilled him, as insanely extravagant as it felt.

"Is refrigerator or fridge?" Elsa liked to be clear on things.

"Either. Fridge is an abbreviation for refrigerator."

"Ah. *Verstehe*. Is good deal for me. I take it. You say what you like and hate, I make you food. But no saying to me you hate all vegetables. Too many Americans say, 'I only eat potatoes.' This is not good for you. Too much meat, and potatoes are animal food." Elsa liked French fries as much as the next person, but still looked askance at most ways to eat potatoes. After a lifetime of knowing them as animal food, humans eating potatoes felt wrong. "I cook vegetables, you eat vegetables." Unlike when his mom cooked for him, Elsa left no wiggle room on this point, and up-time junk food was only a memory now, so Sam ate vegetables. If his mom could've seen his 1632 diet, she would've fallen over in shock.

"And in the spring, you help me grow vegetables, Elsa. Maybe even raise a few chickens for eggs."

December 30, 1632

"Happy birthday Krys!" Agatha Schulte was practically bouncing up and down on her toes, a small present in her hands, another on the table beside her.

"Thanks, Agatha."

Seeing tears well up in Krystal's eyes confused Agatha. "I thought up-timers celebrated the anniversary of their birth as a happy day and gave gifts?"

"We do, but it makes me miss my parents and friends all over again. I'm starting to forget what it was like before. I've stopped expecting any of them to walk through the door. My parents would've given me something amazing as a present. It wouldn't have been expensive because we weren't rich, but Mom would've found something perfect, something I never even thought of."

"Last year," Krystal continued "was the first year my parents and grandparents weren't here for my birthday. Next year is my twenty-first birthday, which was a big deal up-time. This year, it's just a birthday. One of many that will all blend together someday. It isn't my first one without them, and I'm feeling like it won't be the last one. It feels like I already had my last, well, anything with them. My last birthday, drive, fight, hug, phone call, card, *anything*. I don't really believe they'll be here next year when I turn twenty-one, or when I get married, have a kid, any of that. They just won't be here."

"I heard that before you were twenty-one, they wouldn't let you drink any alcohol, even beer. Is that true? Even after years of living around up-timers, some of your customs are strange. Why would anyone have such a rule about beer?" Agatha had lived in Grantville long enough to know it was true, but she wanted to distract and cheer up her friend.

Krystal laughed. "It's true, and I can't explain it now. I never really understood it and I definitely don't now. Grandpa Eli used to make dandelion wine and he taught my daddy how to do it. Every June for years, Daddy had me gathering dandelion heads from everywhere I could find them so he could make his wine, but nowhere they put chemicals on them!" She sighed deeply. "They really aren't coming back, are they?"

Agatha looked at her sadly. "You know the answer in your heart. You said it yourself, you don't expect them to walk back through the door anymore."

"Yeah, I guess I do." She paused a moment. "Ever since the first hours after we came though I've been taking pictures to show Mom and Dad when they got here. I only have a few pictures left on my last roll of up-time film. Looks like it's time to stop taking pictures for them. I'll take the last few shots this afternoon, then pack it away."

Agatha wanted to cheer her up. "Please, open your presents. This one first." By now, everyone in the house and some of her family had gathered to wish her happy birthday, but the two gifts Agatha had brought stood out because they were wrapped in precious up-time wrapping paper. After carefully opening the first one so the wrapping paper could be reused, Krystal started crying. Agatha grabbed her gift and put it on the table to avoid damage from her tears. Sam picked it up, gently, "It's beautiful, cuz, she really captured you." That just made her cry more.

"Who is the Sonia Shea who drew this?" asked Agatha.

"That's her mom's maiden name," answered Grandpa Eli. "She was a gifted artist, just not quite gifted enough to earn a living from it, which is a tough place to be. Like Tom Simpson and pro-ball. Almost, but not quite. But the family treasures what she made, and she always signed things with her maiden name. This drawing of the family was one of the Christmas gifts she had put aside for Krystal last year."

Sam went to find a frame while Krystal enjoyed a nice calming cup of hot rosehip tea. After a few minutes, she opened the wrapped gift from Grannie B and gasped. "Why are you giving me this? It's part of you."

"My momma gave it to me when I married your Grandpa Eli. I'm not young anymore, missy, and I want to be sure you get this from me. It would pain me to look down from heaven and see that someone else had it or, even worse, that it was lost or put in a box."

Krystal had never seen Grannie B without the small cross. It was one of her most prized possessions, like her rosary. This cross had The Lord's Prayer written inside. There was a tiny magnifying glass in the middle of the cross that let you read it. Even when you couldn't see it under layers of clothing, Grannie B always wore it. It was practically part of her. As she put it on, Krystal stopped thinking about who and what was left behind and started to enjoy what she had now.

For perhaps the first time, she started to truly accept that things were never going back to "before". Like Grannie B had told Sam and her, there are a lot of ways to lose people. Losing people to death somehow made it easier to accept losing people to time, or God, or whatever it was. Admitting they were left up-time and were gone forever.

PART 3
1633

CHAPTER 19

January 1633

"Sam, is very cold." Elsa worried. It was what she did. Her family joked that she came into the world with a furrowed brow.

"Elsa, it's January in the Little Ice Age. I don't expect balmy." After barely a month, the worrying and fussing already annoyed Sam. Hiring her to help without interviewing anyone else might have been a real mistake.

"I live near here my whole life. Is very cold for *Januar*. Is bad for plants. This glass room will maybe become too cold for them. They should maybe move." Looking at Sam's face, Elsa had a sinking feeling he wasn't understanding and that she wouldn't be able to make him understand.

"Plants can handle it, Elsa. They are used to winter. We don't need to move anything. And if I don't leave right now, I'll be late for school." It was Sam's house and his rules, but Elsa still moved the little lemon tree and the Bird of Paradise. They were the only ones to come through the Ring of Fire and she wouldn't forgive herself if they died. If she moved all the plants, Sam would notice. Moving only the two was safer. Perhaps he wouldn't notice if she only moved the two.

* * *

A born worrier, as she saw it, Krystal had three choices. First, be a chicken and lose the opportunity. Second, take the risk and end up sick from stress, again. Third, ask for help. Having tried the first two at different times, she went for option three. "Mr. Pridmore, I'm hoping you can help me. I would like to sell my car but I'm not sure who can help me get the most for it."

Her beloved little car had sat on blocks in the garage, fluids drained and storage-prepped, courtesy of Sam and his buddies, for over eighteen months. It was time to let it go and move on with her life using the money it would bring in. Admitting to herself that she would never again drive it had been hard. Committing to selling it had felt almost impossible. Asking Mr. Pridmore to help find a facilitator for that sale came as a relief. Soon, it would be done. Her biggest link to her former life would soon be undeniably and irretrievably gone.

Krystal went home and cried herself to sleep, but when at knock on her door woke up her, she was more at peace than she had been since before the Ring of Fire. "I'm napping. Go away."

"You are awake. It is me. Ursula."

"I know your voice, Ursula, and it's my day off. Go away."

"The Doctor Sims and Nurse Sims talked with me this afternoon. It is about the mid-winter clinics."

"Nooooo. Let me sleep, you sadist." Having heard this complaint and the accompanying groaning before, Ursula waited for Krystal to pull the pillow off her head and open the door, more dramatic (at home) every month as she gradually returned to her pre-Ring of Fire self. "Enter."

"It's getting bigger every day! The LPN program is sending the entire class along with some of the teachers! The Sanitation Commission is sending people. The Committee of Correspondence informed us they will be keeping us safe, which also means the CoC will be recruiting. The Grange wants to give small classes on what farmers can do in winter to improve their crops. The 4-H is looking to start some new groups. A few business owners are sending 'recruiters' to look for new employees. Reporters are coming. It is going to be huge!" Her excitement bubbled over and Krystal got caught up in the excitement. This just might work!

"But how? Aren't they all different weeks? Will they keep giving everyone time off for it?"

Ursula made a see-saw motion with her hands. "We will start out with the closest big town and make a big circle to hit the four Doctor Sims wants us to visit, changing towns about every two days, depending on how many people show up. If the weather looks like it's getting bad, we head back to Grantville and resume our regular lives, then go out again when it clears. They think it's really important and are counting it as clinical time. The doctors and teachers will also try to teach you while we are traveling between towns, but that probably won't work out as well as they are hoping."

February 1633

"I'm one hundred percent sure this is the coldest week in the entire history of Grantville, not including any of the last six weeks. The temperature is tied with every day for the last six weeks. I can't believe we forgot to move the rose bush starts when the cold snap started!" Seeing one of Elsa's eyebrows shoot up before she could stop it embarrassed Sam into being more honest. "Okay. I didn't believe we needed to move them. You saw the need. But I've never seen a plant die from cold inside a greenhouse or sunroom before! I guess all the old single-pane windows let the room get too cold." There were only two rose starts that hadn't been killed by the weeks of bitter cold, and one of them seemed to be losing the battle.

As a grown woman, Elsa understood what would happen next. "When must we leave? If we can stay until the cold is less bad, I will do extra work for you. The Freedom Arches can find you a new helper." When something went wrong, a kind boss fired the worker; unkind bosses did worse things. Sam seemed kind. People foolish enough to warn the boss before things went wrong always had it worse. Bosses and lords never forgot that sort of thing. When that happened, they usually warned other potential bosses the person was trouble. That meant having to travel far for a new job. Elsa was worried about how far she would have to go because the American radio could send the message far indeed. She should never have said anything.

Hearing that, Sam felt confused and stricken. "You're quitting? Why? Is someone paying you more? I've tried to be fair in what I'm paying you. I thought the room and board would be worth a lot to you. Is it the money? Did something happen that you didn't tell me?" Elsa wouldn't believe, couldn't believe, that Sam wanted her to stay. After ten minutes, she still didn't believe it in her heart, but she accepted that she could stay, for now. Until he changed his mind.

Ten minutes wasn't nearly long enough to convince Elsa that Sam appreciated her help in telling him he should do something differently. It was, however, long enough to convince Sam that someone else needed to be heading this effort. He didn't have time to deal with this, and he would have even less time once he graduated and joined the National Guard in just a few months.

March 1633

"Master Jorgensen, you are a master craftsman, but you are a businessman too. You can see how fast the small items like caps sell out, and you know how popular the game bags are. We can't keep the small things in the store with all the people coming through Grantville who want souvenirs. You need to hire more workers to keep them in stock." As a forty-nine percent owner of JRs LLC, Sam felt entitled to an opinion.

As a master tailor and the majority owner, Nils Jorgensen was not inclined to listen to a high school senior, even if he did own the building and sewing machines. "Juniors is a quality shop! We will not just churn out small items like caps and pencil cases. They can buy these from a lesser shop. We make as many as we make. This is final. You will leave now. Go play with your friends."

Clearly, convincing Nils to expand would be a long-term project, but Sam wasn't going to give up. His goal was to convince him before he graduated from high school and started in the National Guard. Clearly, Nils still viewed him as a kid. It might be time to enlist some family to help, adults like Grannie B or Aunt Bethel.

* * *

Elsa worked hard. The up-time house was so warm with no drafts! American complaints that the house was cold made no sense. Her children hadn't gotten sick all winter, except for some colds, and wasn't that a miracle! She did not want to lose her job and have to move, so Elsa worked hard. In January, young Sam had declared that four of the rose starts were dead, but Elsa was determined. Two of them were all dead, as Sam had thought. But two were only mostly dead in January. In two months, Elsa nursed those two mostly-dead rose starts plus one sickly one back to

159

health, to her immense pride. When she showed the four healthy rose starts to Sam, he picked her up in a hug and swung her around in a circle in his delight that they still had four to work with.

Now was the time to start hardening them to the outside weather, bringing them one step closer to having four more John Francis Flannery rose bushes in the world. Elsa found spots for all four pots to spend the warm days outside in the sunshine, then she brought them all in from the cold at night until the weather warmed up enough for them to be outside all the time. Now she had to get Sam to sit still long enough to decide where the four rose bushes should be started. If he didn't decide soon, she would have to but she wasn't in charge so that wasn't fitting. She had to figure out a way to make him choose. It finally dawned on her. There are two ways to motivate any teenage male in any time or place.

"Elsa? I can smell the fresh bread and bacon. Where is my breakfast?"

"You tell me where to put the rose bushes, and I tell you where to find your breakfast."

"No fair!" This was met with silence and a stone-cold glare. "Fine. Plant them at St. Mary's."

"Is good for two bushes, but is better to put the other two somewhere else. Increase the chance of them living."

"Outside the Gardens."

"Where people will throw up in them? You think this is good way to honor *Frau* Flannery?" Elsa looked downright shocked.

"Fair point. I'll think better while I'm eating."

"Hmmm. Fine. I give you bread. But no bacon!"

As he finished his bread, Sam looked up at Elsa. "We should plant them at the Bowers Assisted Living Center. Most of the people who knew her when she was young who are still alive are out there, including Grannie B and Grandpa Eli."

Elsa beamed at him. "That is perfect. I knew you could find this answer! You have earned the bacon. *Frau* Flannery will be happy with this when she looks down from heaven."

Irene Flannery was probably sniffing in disdain that things weren't being done to her standards as she looked down, but secretly pleased as punch. Never a pleasant person, Mrs. Flannery had always been a pious woman who helped others (whether they wanted her help or not), so she was probably (almost certainly) looking down at them, not up, from the afterlife. But the better and longer people knew her, the more most of them believed it could've gone either way. Even Father Larry had moments of doubt about Irene Flannery's ultimate fate, especially around the time of her epic shouting match with Hannelore.

April 1633

"Master Jorgensen, seriously, you need to hire more apprentices just to make the small things. Have them make some buttons or hooks or something with this new casein plastic people are talking about, as well as making traditional buttons. Or hire someone unskilled to make buttons with a Juniors logo that we can sell. I'm just the silent partner, but there has to be something we can do. I remember that up-time, sometimes companies would have different divisions to do different things. Maybe have Juniors focus on apprentice work and small items, and a new division focus on fancier things."

It had started well in the fall but the resumption of war in the spring made business harder, as war tends to do. Nils couldn't find any top-quality English wool at all, just now, and the linen quality was equally disappointing. The leather, at least, met with his approval. But most of the clothing items one made with good leather—breeches, dresses, buff coats, etc.—weren't in high demand in Grantville and he didn't want to go back to making saddles, no matter how high the demand. Even as an apprentice, he had detested that part of the business. In fact, part of the reason he chose the masters he worked for as a journeyman was that they did little of that kind of work, with the end result that he was terrible at it. Even without the pestiferous young Sam reminding him every other week, Nils knew full well that the things selling well were the small and simple ones. The ones made by apprentices. A few by journeyman, mostly skorts, but not enough. Almost nothing that required a master tailor like himself. Yes, he had some work with all the visitors to town, but not enough. Not nearly enough to keep him busy. So, Nils spent too much time brooding.

Hans was glad his father wasn't a drinking man.

CHAPTER 20

Grannie B and Grandpa Eli didn't leave the assisted living center much anymore. They were getting more forgetful and Grannie B's health had started to fail. Her asthma inhalers were a distant memory. She had fared better than a lot of people because her recently refilled up-time allergy shots stretched to last through most of 1631 and Krystal found one or two old inhalers tossed in boxes in the attic, but she was still an allergy-induced asthmatic closer to ninety than eighty.

The springtime blooming of molds and trees alike had always been hard for Grannie B, but the allergy shots, antihistamines, and inhaler had made her symptoms bearable. The start of 1632 wasn't bad, but she was clearly struggling by winter. With all her medications gone, the coughing made a good night's sleep hard to come by, which left her tired. Elsa made her a lovely herbal tea that helped some but there was no real substitute for her medications. Herbal solutions were enough to help some people, but her problems, and her age, were simply too great.

Grandpa Eli worried about her. At a moment when she looked particularly miserable, holding a hankie up to her face, a memory stirred in Grandpa Eli. "Barb, didn't you tell me your mama made you wear a mask outside when you were a girl?" She nodded, miserable. "And they helped?" She nodded again. "You hated wearing them because other kids made fun of you, but most of the old folks here can't see far enough to notice, and the rest won't remember what happened five minutes later. Is it time to try again?"

Grannie B perked up for a minute, then drooped again. "It's a good idea, Eli, but where would we get the material? It can't be thick like wool. Mom always insisted on two layers. Doctors wore masks with several layers of gauze. But an allergy mask definitely has to be thick enough to keep the pollen out, thin enough to breathe through, and fitted enough to keep the darn pollen out. I'd feel better with a mask that has two layers since that's what my mom made me. No, it's a nice thought, but we can't just run out and buy them, now can we?"

Grandpa Eli remembered the military doctors and nurses wearing masks similar to her description and decided now was the time for them to make a come-back, and not just for hospitals and doctors. This might be a very profitable little business for someone. He kissed his lovely bride on the top of her head, then rested his head against hers.

* * *

"Mrs. Lamb, you may not remember me, but you are managing the houses my cousin Sam inherited from Mrs. Flannery."

"Of course I remember you, Krystal! Welcome, what brings you to Lamb Commercial Properties today?" Bunny beamed at her, always happy to have a potential new client.

"I sold my car and I want to buy real estate with the money. It should be enough for a down payment, I hope. I have a little bit of money in an OPM account too, if I need to use that."

Bunny started taking notes. "What about your grandparents' house? Will they be renting it out entirely now? Or are you looking to buy a commercial property?"

"Sorry about that. I was unclear. I know I've hurt some feelings saying it, but I never wanted to stay in Grantville my whole life, and I still don't. Magdeburg is the new capital and closest big city. With all the building and rebuilding going on, I would like to buy something there that I can live in later. I've always wanted to live in a big city and Magdeburg is definitely on its way. Nothing too fancy, but I would prefer to at least know I will be able to get plumbing and electricity added in the next few years. Until then, it needs to be rented out for enough to cover the costs. Can you help?"

"Hmmmm. I have some contacts there. Let me know how much you have for a down payment, and I'll talk to Marlon Pridmore and realtors I know in Magdeburg. Hopefully, we can find something that will work for you. Any idea how long until you might want to live there?"

"I have to finish my nursing degree, so at least two years, but I have a feeling it will be quite a bit longer. Right now, making sure renters cover the mortgage and other costs, including a property manager or whatever down-timers call it, is more important than my ability to live there. I may not ever live in Magdeburg." Krystal gave a small shrug. "But having the option will be nice. Owning a house will make it my choice."

"Got it. Do you want to look first? If so, that will seriously limit your options. Most things sell sight unseen, half-finished, entirely still rubble, before they officially go on the market. That market is crazier than Grantville."

"The New Year's Eve fire still haunts me, so I really want to look before buying."

"Are you sure, sweetie? That fire haunts us all to some extent, but it's a long trip to Magdeburg. You're going to miss out on a lot of opportunities if you insist on looking in person first. It's your money, so it's your choice. Just let me know if you change your mind." Bunny had been in real estate long enough to know a mistake when she saw it, and to know when someone's mind was made up and no facts were going to change it.

* * *

Bowing to the inevitable, Nils took a trip to Augsburg. There simply were no suitable potential wives who interested him in Grantville. He needed a woman who understood the traditional tailoring business but was interested in adapting the up-time tools, techniques, and methods. If he didn't find someone in Augsburg, Jena and Magdeburg were next on his list. By the time he left the Guildmaster's office in Augsburg, he was already tired, but he had the names of four women to talk with.

One of the masters made the time to introduce him to the first two women that very afternoon. As they walked up to the first home, the woman of the house was red-faced and screaming as she chased an urchin away from the alley next to the boardinghouse she ran since losing her husband and children. "If you don't mind, I think perhaps this is not the best time for me to meet *Frau* Rasch. She seems to be having a hard afternoon." Nils knew his temper tended to run hot. Marrying a woman with a similar temperament seemed unwise.

Master Justinus Teubener sighed. "Ah, well, for some people, every afternoon, and evening and morning, is hard. But *Frau* Rasch has a good head for business. She is a shrewd negotiator, and she's not yet been outmaneuvered by a lawyer. In fairness, she's not one I'd want to spend all my days and nights with, so we shall continue our walk. *Frau* Kautz is much more amiable."

"That's good to hear. This is a lovely day for a stroll."

By the time they arrived at the tailor shop *Frau* Kautz's late husband had left their sons, both Justinus and Nils were grateful for the small beer she gave them each. "*Frau* Kautz, Master Jorgensen is a tailor with a new shop in Grantville. He and his teenage twins have lived there since just a few months after Grantville arrived. His wife died in childbirth shortly before they moved there. At the time, there were no opportunities for tailors, and it was not until this year that he could afford to remarry."

"Hmmm. So, you are looking for someone to help you with your business and to finish raising your children? I've children of my own to look after and this business will go to them. My son is nearly ready to take his master's exam and take over the business. It's doing quite well and I'm not sure I want to move as far as Grantville, but I'll be happy to talk to you some more." Nils determined two things about *Frau* Kautz before they left. First, she talked a great deal, although she didn't seem to miss a thing said around her. Second, she was a highly adequate cook. Not great, but not awful. If he were to marry her, he would neither starve nor grow stout from overeating. Marrying her bore consideration.

The next morning, Justinus was at the inn to pick him up shortly after breakfast. "*Frau* Zimmerman is young. Compared to some of the other women, she has little experience, but she is the daughter of a tailor as well as the widow of one. One morning he just didn't wake up, and they had no children. Tragic. It was six months ago and with no one to take over the shop or help her, she needs to move. She isn't keen to go back to her parents' home. Her parents, and their tempers, are well-known, so we've done our best to help her stay here as long as we can, but it can't last much longer. A betrothal would be a blessing for her."

Justinus rapped on the door. "*Frau* Zimmerman, I know this is a bit irregular, but I have a visitor from Grantville you should meet."

A fine-looking young woman with a distinctive, but clearly old and well-healed, scar across the back of her hand and a few pox scars near her hairline opened the door and gestured for them to enter. "Welcome, but I'm not sure how this small shop could interest someone from the future."

"Ah, well, someone from the future wouldn't be here for the reason I am, *Frau* Zimmerman. I live in Grantville but am not an up-timer. I am what we call 'an old Grantville hand'. More to the point, I am a master tailor who lost almost everything during the war years, including my wife, and am only now able to seriously contemplate becoming betrothed and remarrying." Nils saw no reason to beat around the bush.

Clara Zimmerman looked up sharply at that. "Perhaps we have something to discuss, after all."

Negotiations took longer than Nils had hoped, but less time than he had feared. By the end of the month, he and Clara Zimmerman reached an agreement and were officially betrothed. She sold her first husband's shop as her dowry and immediately moved to Grantville. By the end of May, the banns had been read and they were married.

CHAPTER 21

Half-deaf, Grandpa Eli made quite a bit of noise clumping up the stairs to visit Nils. "Mr. Jorgensen, if I might have a minute." Once they were seated, he went straight to the heart of the matter. "I would like you to make some masks for my Barbara. I think it will help with her allergies and asthma."

Everyone liked Grannie B, so there was no real chance of Nils saying no, but at the same time, such a simple project held no interest for him. He wanted to make sure they did things right, though, so he asked a lot of questions about what to make and how Grandpa Eli thought the masks should look and fit. "This not hard to do, although this is something we have not done before. We will make this for *Frau* Reed. She is Sam's *Oma*."

"Uh, actually, it could be a great side business. I know you want to focus on clothing, but nurses, doctors, orderlies, and a bunch of other people in the hospital could use them to stay safe from viruses, bacteria, and bodily fluids like blood. Up-time, we mostly used disposable masks, but those are gone. Other people with allergies could use them. Anyone in an area with plague. I really think masks could be a great little money-maker, and I'd really like it to help other allergy sufferers like my Barb."

"Hmmm. If we had another sewing machine, perhaps, but this is so simple. These masks barely require an apprentice much less someone with real skills. If I asked an apprentice, much less a journeyman, to focus on this, they would quickly become so bored they quit. But since we don't have another machine, we can't even try it. Not as a business project." Nils refused to waste a precious sewing machine making such a simple project, and he wanted his workers to become proficient with a sewing machine. Using up-time tools and techniques for their work was a point of pride (and marketing).

Grandpa Eli cleared his throat sheepishly. "I could help with that too. Barb's old sewing machine is still in our attic. She never wanted to rent it out, but if you need it to make masks to help her and other people—including Krystal since she's going into nursing—then I'll help you find it, with a few conditions. Save the profits to buy new machines. As soon as you have two new ones, bring back Barb's. In return, Krystal will be part-owner of the mask business, same as Sam is with Juniors." Grandpa Eli seemed embarrassed to have sat on something so valuable for so long.

Nils spent a few minutes turning the idea over in his mind. "*Ja.* Okay. Thinking on this, Sarah is an apprentice who will never make journeyman. Her fingers are much more nimble and her eyes much sharper than her mind. Sarah could make these because she does not mind doing the same thing over and over, and over. She can be a trial because she *wants* to do the same thing over and over, day after day, and our normal work has too much change for her. I was thinking I must send her away, but this is much better. I will make a pattern and we will try. If this project goes well, we can perhaps provide a job for others who are simple-minded like Sarah." Grandpa Eli grinned from ear to ear at the news. "No promises, mind you! But we will try."

May 1633

Sam usually stopped in at Juniors on Monday evenings, to check how the previous week had gone, and stayed for dinner. Today was Saturday.

Sam visiting on Saturday was unusual, and not in a good way, making Nils on edge before Sam said a word. Nils was none too happy to be told—not asked, told—that he would spend the next afternoon at the Bowers Assisted Living Center. Being told Grannie B requested his presence didn't help. They were spending as much time as they could on the silly mask project and he disliked being rushed. Getting something fitted around the nose was the tricky bit. People simply didn't normally need something made to fit their face that way, and masks moved a great deal when people talked. At least he had a few masks ready for her to try.

Grannie B didn't waste any time once they arrived. "Young man, there are a few things you need to understand about women's clothing." As a master tailor, Nils' immediate reaction was offense. No one had called him a young man in decades! And who knew more about clothing, women's or otherwise, than a tailor? Grannie B watched Nils' face getting redder and redder as she kept talking. "You know about how to make clothing, and about down-time fashion, but you don't know bupkis about *up-time* fashion. You are in Grantville now and you need to learn." By this point, he was beet-red and about to explode. "And you need to take that temper down a notch or three. I'm too old to waste time shillyshallying around the subject. I won't try to teach you how to be a master tailor, but that doesn't mean you can't learn a thing or two about fashion and women."

Nils broke in. "I know more than enough to make these masks! I am taking time to try different ways of making it, but the basic mask is simple enough for an apprentice to make it. You are insulting me." He threw the sample masks at her and turned to stalk out.

"Hold on everyone!" Grandpa Eli stepped in to calm things down. "Nils, the masks were a surprise. This is the first Barb's heard of 'em. She's trying to talk to you about Juniors. Barb, I asked Nils to make you some masks like you wore as a kid to help with your allergies. If it goes well, they may make and sell them to hospitals and whoever else needs 'em. But right now, it's an experiment."

Grannie B covered her surprise by picking up a mask to examine. "Thank you, Nils. You go ahead and take those lilacs Sam brought from Irene's house to the nurse's station while I see what I think of these new masks. Take a walk if you need to but come back here calmed down and don't take too long about it, young man." Unsure what else to do, Nils did as Grannie B instructed.

When he got back to the room, Grannie B jumped right into what she wanted to say. "First of all, I like the fit of this mask best. Second, one of the nurses came in. She liked one of the other ones. I gave her most of the other masks for her and the other nurses to wear and tell us what they think. Sort of an unofficial group of beta-testers. That means they are trying out your product and will give you feedback to improve it, including what not to change. I'll try going outside wearing the masks I kept this week and I'll let you know if it helped the next time you come out here.

"Now, back to my original point. Some of the other ladies out here and I have been keeping an eye on what you young men are doing in town. We may not get out much, but we read the papers and we get visitors. Our granddaughters and other younger women like the nurses tell us plenty, the sensible ones who like fashion, not the silly fashion-phobic ones like Krystal. Since Sam is my great-grandson, we all agreed I need to talk to you some and give you our advice.

"Nils, you have seen that our clothing is made of all kinds of different materials. A whole rainbow of materials. More kinds of fabric than anyone can remember the names and care recommendations for. Because of that, we put labels in the neck like this care label." Grannie B handed him one of her shirts to examine the label. "Most of our clothing had two labels, and the other one had the name of the clothing line, like the one to the left of the care label. Sometimes companies had more than one line of clothing.

They called each one a 'label'. Every label wanted to be, tried to be, different from others and to appeal to a specific group of women. There were also different labels for more expensive, and less expensive, clothing from the same designer. We think you need to keep Juniors and start a second label."

"You had too much clothing if you forgot who made it. I shall think on what you have said, but we are not changing the business." Nils changed his mind slowly, glacially even, and right now he thought Grannie B and her friends had gone soft in the head.

"Here's our idea, a bit more specifically. You keep Juniors and use it for simpler designs, which look best on younger women, and for accessories and the like. That means collars, cuffs, petticoats, bags, decorations, all that kind of thing. Start a second label and focus your personal efforts there. Make court dresses for the Grantville women who need them. Sew gloves and coats with gorgeous, and expensive, embroidery and details. Small and exclusive. But keep Juniors as a place to experiment, and a solid source of income. Juniors will bring in small amounts per sale, but *a lot* of sales. The new label would bring in a lot per sale, but not a lot of sales. Combined, you'll make enough to retire well and for your children to marry well."

They didn't agree to anything that day, or the next Sunday, but Grannie B and her friends (or the Bowers' Broads, as they called themselves) insisted that Nils, Sam, Hans, and Gebhard keep coming out on Sundays to learn more and explore this concept of 'labels' until they were convinced it was a good idea, or until they convinced the Bower Broads it wasn't.

The turning point came when the men found out that up-time "juniors" were clothing specifically designed for teenagers and young women. More importantly, it allowed them to experiment with style, color, and technique on clothing for "Juniors" and when they were happy with it, use what they learned for the premium label, all while making a profit. The apprentices and journeymen would focus on Juniors. The journeymen and Nils would work on the new label, which was what Grannie B suggested in the first place. With all the changes in materials and tools, Nils could live with this. Barely, but he could live with it.

CHAPTER 22

Sam and Elsa had planted two of the new rose bush starts at the Bowers, hoping Grannie B and Grandpa Eli would be able to enjoy them. They were still scrawny little sticks, but they did have some leaves for Grannie B to look at as she sat outside on a bench, enjoying the spring day, courtesy of her new mask. The mask helped, but she knew from experience that she would still pay for spending time outside, mask or no mask. She would suffer a bit less, and be able to stay out a bit longer, wearing the mask, but suffer she would.

Allergies suck.

After people started asking where she got her mask, she started an order list to give Nils on his next visit so he could fill the orders and collect payment. Sitting outside, enjoying the soft breeze, warm sunshine, and riotously colorful flowers was pure pleasure. It hadn't been all that long, but it felt like years since she had been able to simply sit outside and just enjoy existing. Whatever she ended up paying for it later, simply enjoying being outside and making these memories for later days was worth the cost. No one ever knows how many more days with perfect weather are left in their life, but Grannie B felt sure the number had become quite small for her.

* * *

Nils stomped into the kitchen. "It is time to end this mask-making nonsense. It is a waste. Sarah can go home where she belongs."

Clara looked up, alarmed. She knew Sarah's family did not want their simple-minded daughter back. As burghers, her presence embarrassed them. "Why? Isn't she doing good work? The masks I saw were well-made and she isn't complaining of boredom with the work. She has never caused problems before."

Snort. "No, no complaints—from Sarah. But if she doesn't have someone to talk with, she wanders off too often in search of a conversation. If someone sits there with her, she'll work all day. But she won't sit there alone, and she distracts the other workers if they are nearby with her chatter." Nils sighed deeply. "It's a pity. There are several groups who were about ready to order masks and now I don't think we can fill the orders."

"Keep her for one more month. Let me try to fix it. Do you still need someone to cut the pieces for the masks? If so, I'll hire someone for you, and I'll make sure they are clear the job may end in a month." Since this involved no work on his part, and he still wanted nothing to do with making masks, Nils found this solution ideal.

✳ ✳ ✳

"Is there anything you need of for the mobile clinics?" Stretched thin as they were, Garnet sincerely hoped the answer was "no", but knew better than to expect it would be.

"Now that you mention it, there is one thing. When we did the mid-winter clinics, there were some long wait-times, especially for the kids. Their moms would start gossiping but they didn't want the kids wandering too far with so many strangers around. The kids got bored. Ursula had some YA books with her that someone started reading to the kids. Historical novels were the most popular because the kids understood them better. There are a few we think should be republished including *The Door in the Wall* and *The Lady with the Lamp* about Florence Nightingale. We really want the second one to help get across the concept of nurses as caring professionals worthy of respect. It shows the difference one person can make, and how important hygiene and sanitation are to well-being." Ursula had borrowed those particular books from Krystal's Aunt Bethel, along with a biography of Milton S. Hershey and a set of books for children on mental health.

"That's a great idea! We are working with some publishers for the new textbooks. I'll make a note to see if they might want to start a sideline in children's books. I bet we can find some more around town if we ask."

"My Dad always said they bought him used books because they couldn't afford to buy enough new books for him and the library was too small, so almost all of his books were used. Which is a nice way of saying 'old'. Wherever they packed up their books, Grannie B and Grandpa Eli may have some good ones squirreled away. Aunt Bethel has a set of books on mental health issues for kids. I skimmed them and they seem pretty useless for down-time as they are, but someone may be able to rework them into something useful. The ideas aren't bad, but the book on TV viewing habits is pretty useless now. The one on how boys and girls are different and similar could be good. The one on trauma definitely needs to be reworked. Down-time kids still mostly think of a cast as a marvel that ensures they won't lose use of a limb, not something that keeps them from having fun. They've been through a lot more than those books imagine for a kid."

"We'll look into that too, eventually. Krystal, you are coming up with a lot of great ideas. I'm not the only one who is impressed. The nursing team discussed your ideas for continuing training after the LPN program and before the new nursing program starts and are going to implement most of them. Do you know if anyone else is interested in this?" At Krystal's nod, Garnet added to her notes. "Please get me a list of names. We will offer these opportunities to everyone in your class, and the one ahead of it, for that matter. First, an intensive on herbal remedies. Second, some classes on botany. Both of those will be more intensive over the summer and into the fall but will continue until we open the new school, and you start the new curriculum. Third, shadowing RNs and assisting with some of their tasks. Finally, rotations to learn more about each nursing specialty. Also, some additional information on down-time diseases you aren't familiar with, like pox, diphtheria, and tetanus."

"Great! I'll go tell the others." She started to bounce up out of her seat.

"Hold on there! We had a few ideas of our own." All the bounce went out of Krystal and she sank back into her seat. "An old-school down-time doctor will discuss standards of care as of the day before we arrived. That includes the expected roles of men and women, taboos, and pretty much anything that might get an up-timer in trouble with a strange down-timer. You will also learn about bloodletting, leaches, miasma, humors, and all that, well, nonsense to us. No one expects–or wants!–you to *use* any of it, but if you can understand the reasoning, it's easier to argue why a different way is better. I hear a new start-up is making masks. They can be presented as a way to fight against 'miasma' or bad smells, as an example."

"My grandparents are actually involved in that mask startup. I may end up getting some income from it, which could really help out. I'm buying a house in Magdeburg with money from selling my car. I kept trying to go see properties but finally gave up and listened to Mrs. Lamb. She told me to have someone I trust in Magdeburg make the decision for me and put in an offer. So, I really hope the masks are successful enough that I don't end up getting foreclosed on my new house before I even see it."

Krystal looked even more nervous than she sounded. "On the plus side, I'm told my new place came with tenants even though it wasn't finished until after they moved in. The plus side of buying in a city without enough housing."

"That's a good use of the limited resources you brought with you. I hope it all works out. In the meantime, get me that list of interested students. Please send in my next appointment on your way out."

June 1633

As he talked to women in his shop and around town, Nils realized that the old ladies were right. "Juniors" didn't have a strong meaning to a lot of women, even up-time ones, but generally sounded like something for younger people, to down-timers and up-timers alike. For Sam's high school graduation present, Nils told him that he agreed to start a second label. When you can't use your name, naming a business or part of a business isn't easy, so they focused on other details first, like what each "label" would focus on.

Nils hoped the Sunday visits with the Bowers' Broads would stop when Sam left for the National Guard and he started the second label, but it didn't. If anything, more women wanted to give their opinions now. He didn't particularly enjoy it, but he was smart enough to listen to them. The women had firm opinions on most thing related to fashion, including what the label name should be and what the label should make. Those firm opinions rarely matched, and the Bowers' Broads were often still arguing when the men from Juniors left, but there were a few things they were in complete agreement on. Most importantly to them, any faddish clothing had to be part of Juniors and the new label for more mature women would focus on classic styles that change slowly, very slowly.

"What does this 'faddish' mean?" Gebhard was curious.

"FAD is short for 'for a day' which is another way of saying clothing that goes out of style quickly." Seeing thunderclouds forming on Nils' face again, Grannie B hastened to reassure him. "No one thinks your clothing is faddish, Nils! And it doesn't mean low quality. Please. We are trying to give you up-time ideas to help you become more profitable, and keep your apprentices and journeymen working." Nils harrumphed at this, but the thunderclouds started to clear. "Up-time, fashion designers tried to convince women to buy new clothing every year. Most of us did buy some new clothing every year, but we didn't replace our entire wardrobe every year. However, most things would look out of style after a few years, even jeans, and then we would get rid of the old and buy new. Not all at once, of course, a few things every year. In five or *maybe* ten years, most things were hopelessly out of style, but some were 'classic' styles and those could remain in use for decades. When us ladies out here were younger, people restyled their old clothing, but no one has done that much for decades now. Clothing got so cheap it wasn't worth the effort of remaking anything, and most was so poorly made it didn't last well anyway. Down-time, it's clearly different. People hand their clothing down to younger or poorer people so the same garment can be worn for many years, decades even.

"Anyone buying something from Grantville will want something clearly new and different. You have complained about this yourself. They *expect* and even *desire* a bit of faddishness, so to speak. In this case, we really mean up-time style. Older women will want something a bit different with some up-time style, but not as daringly different as younger girls will want. Skorts for older women (we all see how popular those are!), dresses worn without stays or bodys for younger, daring ones. That sort of thing." The other women nodded their agreement to what Grannie B said. "And, of course, fabric using those wonderful, bright Lothlorien dyes! But, as Mary Brooks Picken always taught us, the brighter the colors, the younger the wearer should be. The second label should focus on deeper, saturated colors, leaving the bright colors for Juniors. Those 'classic' styles I mentioned should be the core of the new label."

✱ ✱ ✱

Elsa burst into the kitchen, surprising Sam with his head in the refrigerator looking for a snack. "The roses! They are blooming! I did not see the ones here last year, so I did not know. They are *purple*! Truly! I have never seen roses that are such a color."

Sam gave her a bit of side-eye while continuing to forage for lunch. "Uh, yeah, lavender, like I said. That's why we didn't want them to die–they are the only ones."

"So, this lavender means purple? I did not understand the word but there were many more words I did not understand then."

"Lavender is a light purple. Like lilacs. You saw the lilacs blooming in the spring. But back to the blooming part. That's great! So, the four we planted are all healthy? Did you check them all?"

"No. I did not go to Bowers today. I will if you wish. But the other two, the ones at St. Mary's, they are blooming so beautifully today, like the ones in the yard!"

"Nah, no need to go out. I can go visit Grandpa Eli and Grannie B tomorrow."

"Visiting Grannie B and Grandpa Eli, is it? Not the cute young nurse?" Sam turned bright red all the way up to his hairline. "*Ja*, I have noticed how you look at her. But she looks at you too, so have a pleasant visit with…your great-grandparents. And not the young nurse." Sam might not think about it, but Elsa never forgot that he was still her boss. She teased him sometimes, because it made him happy, but not too often and not when they were working. It was unseemly, even if he didn't realize he was part of the Adel.

July 1633

"It's been one month. How is Sarah doing with the masks?" Clara's smug tone showed she knew exactly how Sarah had been doing.

"Not a bit of a problem now. She stays and works all day and doesn't disturb the other workers a bit. I haven't met the new cutter, but I'm guessing that was the key," Nils replied.

"Indeed. Sarah just needed someone to talk with while she worked, to relieve the boredom. I get that way sometimes. But she needed someone at her mental level. Since the cutting is repetitive and boring, like the sewing, I found someone like Sarah who could master one simple task and do it over and over again, day after day. Ada lived near me in Augsburg, so I've known her family since before she was born. Her given name is Aldessa, but she couldn't pronounce that as a little one and called herself Ada. The name stuck. Now you need a second person doing sewing, possibly a third, to keep up with all the cutting! And possibly sound-proof walls so others aren't distracted by all the chatter from the group of them." She was quite pleased with her solution, and even more pleased to have found a way for Ada to work and support herself.

"You can see for yourself how much business we are getting for the masks. Now we must make another LLC for the mask company. I do not like naming businesses the up-timer way. It is too much work. *Fräulein* Reed suggested 'Medical Masks LLC' but that is a poor name" As much as something that plain pained Nils, he almost agreed out of sheer exhaustion over the whole naming issue. He really regretted taking Grandpa Eli's offer. He should have said the whole business had to belong to Krystal, not just a percentage.

He also needed to hire someone to run the mask business, and possibly another person or two for the sewing once he had more machines, just like Clara said. Knowing his family would not want for money was wonderful but keeping track of everything got harder every day. He couldn't wish for someone to do a better job with the business end of things than Clara, but she couldn't stretch to do a third business without more help. His daughter Eleonore was doing the business end of the mask company for now, but she would be a journeyman herself soon and leave to finish her studies. Then where would that leave them? Up a creek, that's where. So, he had to find someone, and they had to work well with his Clara, and with Sarah and Ada. Not everyone had the patience and understanding to work with the simple-minded.

"Miasma Masks!"

"What?" Nils was startled by his wife's outburst and missed what she actually said.

"We should call the company 'Miasma Masks'. The less modern doctors, and patients, will like that. Up-timers won't care one way or the other what we call them. Anyway, the name gets the spirit of the thing across: they keep out bad vapors and smells." Clara sounded quite pleased with herself.

Nils' relief showed as he gave her a huge hug. "Right you are! The paperwork for Miasma Masks LLC will be filed this very week. Our portion of the business will be in your name, not mine, which means you get to be responsible for the business now. You've been making some good suggestions for it, after all. So, you get to find a 'business manager' or whatever it is they are calling the person you need to help you run the business *and* hire the new employees you think it needs!"

"Punishment for a good turn, is it? I'll take it!" In truth, Clara couldn't believe her luck in this second marriage, and wouldn't really believe the new business was to be hers until she had paperwork with her name on it.

Having never wanted the mask business at any time, Nils was relieved to give the whole business to her and not have any further involvement in it. Making his new wife happy was a bonus. If they ever had a daughter together, that could be her dowry. Stranger things had happened in this odd new world.

CHAPTER 23

August 1633

Ursula twisted on the wagon seat until she had a clear view of Krystal's profile over her baby girl Florence's head. "Krystal Marie Reed. The way you were flirting with Johan was almost embarrassing!"

"I did not flirt with Johan!" Krystal was mortified and almost wailed her denial. "Not even an itty-bitty bit."

"Ooookay." The drawn-out syllable proved Ursula's disbelief.

"I didn't! He isn't cute at all, and definitely not my type. His sister has some real potential in biology, though, so I have been there a lot to help her with her science lessons."

"No, not Johan from the village this morning. I didn't think you even knew his name. *Johan!* The cute one."

"Johan the journeyman? He *is* muscular and healthy looking, no pox scars either, but I'm not sure I'd say cute. More 'manly' or 'strong'. 'Virile' even. Definitely attractive, but not cute. Also not my type. But nice to watch working." Krystal sort of faded out as she started thinking about Johan working shirtless at the forge.

"Not *that* Johan! How hard is it to think about which man you were flirting with?"

"You mean if I *had* been flirting? If I *had* been flirting, it would be easy. But I wasn't."

"Johan with the half-blind sister. Ringing a bell yet?" Ursula knocked on the side of her head as she said that.

Krystal turned pink. "I wasn't flirting! We just had a nice chat. I showed him some things from the big anatomy book we carry with us."

"Whatever you say." Noting the blush, Ursula smirked the whole way to the next town, where Johan the Elder lived with Hans the Younger, who was slightly older than Johan the Elder.

After riding in silence for ten minutes, Krystal broke the silence. "I hope the docs can do something for Sibylle's vision. Can you imagine? Twenty-one and nearly blind because she doesn't have glasses, and her vision a bit worse every year of her life. And I thought it was bad when I had to stop wearing contacts!"

"Johan Becker is a fine man. Much better than that friend of Sam's you 'had a crush on' last year. Also better than what you tell me of your up-timer boyfriend who was left behind."

"Skateboarding takes more skill than it sounds like. But, yeah, point taken. Those hard muscled baker's arms of Johan's are nothing to sneeze at. Did you like the croissants he made? He's working hard to have the skills of a master and it shows. I found a croissant recipe and brought it to him. He's almost mastered it."

"So that's where it came from! I heard people talking about them but no, Krystal, he doesn't share them with many people. Croissants are a lot of work, and you rate his best pastries. I get plain old rolls." Ursula smirked again. "Want to tell me again that there is no flirting? Before you decide to deny your interest in him three times, when are you going to bring Sibylle to see the eye doctor in Grantville? You have enough money to buy her a pair of glasses. She seems good with mental math, and we need someone to help with organizing the clinic. I'm sure other businesses could use help a few hours a week, so she'll earn enough to pay her way and repay you for her glasses, which she will probably feel she needs to do."

"I, um, hadn't really made any plans for that."

"Krystal, I saw the extra thick glasses you brought for her to try. I heard you mention getting glasses in Grantville to her parents. When are you going to arrange for her visit, and where is she going to stay?"

Sigh. "Fine. I'll talk to them next visit to try to set a date. I did bring up the Grantville eye doctor and glasses. They were excited about the idea but worried about the cost. She needs a job while she's there. If you think the clinic can use her, that will help. If we can find other places to hire her so she earns enough money to stay, she can come soon. I thought about having her stay with me, but I don't know if I'll have a free room, so I didn't want to volunteer. Happy?"

"What about Johan? Is he invited to 'keep his sister safe'?" Ursula grinned at her, then made a kissy face.

Krystal chose to ignore the whole comment and ask a question of her own. "How did you and Curt meet? You never told me."

"Changing the subject. Fair enough. When I was in the Refugee Center the first summer, we were in an English language class together and he was working on some of the new refugee housing. We saw each other a lot, started talking, then started practicing our English, and eventually got married. Since neither of us had any family to ask, the betrothal and marriage were fast and easy. No long, drawn-out negotiations. I never expected to be able to marry a master in any guild, much less a master mason, but he was a master without a business after Magdeburg, and we were both free to choose who we wanted." Ursula paused for a moment. "You up-timers truly do not understand what a blessing that is."

* * *

Mary Frances Flannery, Irene's niece by marriage, was visiting the Bowers one Sunday while the Bowers' Broads tried to convince the men from Juniors of something. Seeing an argument in the offing, Mary Frances butted in to ask a question that had been bothering her. "What are you doing with Aunt Irene's stash?" The men were confused. The women looked like they had forgotten the most obvious thing ever. "You know, her fabric stash? It may have been in the same room as her sewing machine, or maybe a closet or the basement, or all of those?" The men still looked blank, so she tried again. "Stacks or boxes of fabric, thread, bias tape, buttons, all the things you need to sew clothing, but mostly lots of fabric?"

Grannie B's asthma wasn't well-controlled at all anymore, so when she did speak, it sometimes came out gasping, like a fish out of water. "Good lord, she's right. We forgot all about Irene's stash." The other ladies all nodded in agreement, looking downright embarrassed at missing something obvious.

Before Grannie B stressed herself by trying to talk more, Mary Frances explained. "Anyone who crafts a lot, who genuinely enjoys it, like Aunt Irene did, has a stash of supplies for their hobby. For sewers, there will be fabric, thread, bias tape, buttons, and other notions. Aunt Irene definitely had a stash. For knitting and crocheting, it's yarn. That kind of thing." The men now looked highly skeptical. Fabric was expensive and even tailors only kept what they needed for business on hand.

Nils shrugged. "A few yards of material would be nice, but it won't make a difference."

"You *really* aren't understanding what we mean. When the one fabric store in Fairmont went out of business a few years ago, I watched her taking bags of fabric to her car. She filled the entire cart, and the store wasn't even at 75% off yet, so I'm sure she went back at least two more times. And not too long after Princess Di married Charles, I saw her buying bridal satin, that astoundingly embroidered and beaded eighties wedding lace, and tulle. She pretended she didn't recognize me, but I saw her at the cutting counter as clear as I see you standing here now. I can't for the life of me work out why she would've bought fifteen yards each of bridal satin and beaded lace, and twice that of tulle." Betty Ruth Snodgrass looked genuinely puzzled. Nils looked gob smacked.

Mary Frances looked like an old puzzle had been solved. "It's our Fran! She got married in eighty-four and Aunt Irene offered to make her a gown. She said she already had the fabric, but it never occurred to us that she would have bought fabric just to make Fran a gown. Fran already had a gown on order, though, so we politely declined. No wonder she seemed so mad at us after that! We never understood why she cut us out of her life then. How odd. Now I'm embarrassed. Aunt Irene was trying to be nice!"

Nils finally spoke, in a slightly strangled voice. "This stash, it would have thirty yards of uncut up-timer fabric, and another thirty of this tulle? Perhaps the famous polyester? I remember the auction for the denim fabric. We could use this?"

The Bowers' Broads started laughing and shaking their heads. Seeing his disappointment, Mary Frances spoke up. "She had thirty yards—of those two fabrics, plus the tulle. They are probably in a box together, somewhere, waiting for the right project. She'll have *at least* one hundred yards of fabric, and most dedicated seamstresses have hundreds of yards on hand, waiting for the right project plus a box or two of scraps from past projects. Realistically, as old and tight-fisted as Aunt Irene was, she for sure more than three hundred yards squirreled away somewhere. Especially if she hit that store-closing sale as hard as Mrs. Snodgrass thinks she did. Crafters try to avoid knowing exactly how much is in the stash so when our husbands ask, we honestly can't give a definite answer. As a widow with no family, Irene could've kept buying fabric and putting it aside for the perfect project, or just to enjoy looking at."

Nils collapsed onto the chair behind him, stunned into silence. He didn't move or speak until the staff shooed him out at dinner time. He couldn't comprehend having so much money you left hundreds of yards sitting around for years on end. So much you didn't bother counting how much was there. And now it belonged to Sam, who didn't even know it existed.

* * *

As she looked up and down the street outside the eye doctor's office wearing her new glasses, Sibylle slowly blinked. She cocked her head and blinked again. Then she looked consideringly at her brother Johan. "Why didn't you tell me how many colors the sky has?"

Now Johan blinked. "What? You were never completely blind. You saw better when you were little. You already knew that. Didn't you?"

"No. I can't remember ever seeing clearly past the end of a room, much less the whole way up to the sky. I knew sunrise and sunset had more colors, but not this many. And not so many shades of blue in the sky. Also, they say I can go to night classes at the high school. These glasses have changed my life. You go home if you want. I am staying in Grantville." Sibylle looked ready to argue.

Johan laughed. "No one ever thought you would leave Grantville once you got here, Sibylle. That's why *Mutti und Vatti* asked so many questions about the job for you, housing, and all those boring things. And they want me to spend a little time looking for more recipes like those croissants while you settle in. If you don't like it, come home with me. It would be fun to see the expressions on *Mutti und Vatti's* faces!"

Sibylle happily took her brother's arm and walked back to their temporary lodging with Ursula. Now that she had decided to stay in Grantville, she would move in with Krystal. Johan was going to live in a cheaper house with other young men. Every time someone suggested he move into Krystal's house too, he changed the subject. He was simply happy he no longer blushed when it was mentioned.

CHAPTER 24

September 1633

I rene Flannery's stash. They found it, packed away in the garage, the spare bedroom, the linen closet, and the basement. There was a bit in the nursery. Once he started recovering from the shock, Nils insisted they hire a security guard, selling some of the precious stash, if necessary, but Sam refused. The fabric was in his home and he didn't want a security guard "prowling around outside the bedroom." Nils reluctantly accepted this wasn't actually a business decision since Sam owned the fabric, not the business. That meant accepting Sam's choice, which left him uneasy.

Sam found an entire box of printed polyester from the seventies. Nils was disappointed that Mrs. Flannery's stash had more cotton than polyester, but not by much and the cotton was patterned, and the colors were either bright or deeply saturated, both extraordinarily expensive down-time. All the fabric from the nursery was printed, although there wasn't much yardage of any fabric.

Three days later, Officer Hans Schruer called Sam out of training. "Mr. Reed, we received a call about an attempted burglary at your house. We would like you to come with us, if you can be excused." Since training for the day was almost finished, Sam's instructors agreed. When they got to his house, he gaped in astonishment. The inside of the garage was strewn with fabric. Someone had clearly gone through Mrs. Flannery's stash for the most valuable fabrics.

"We got a call about two hours ago from your neighbor," Hans paused to flick through his notes to find her name, "Margaretha Kniess. Today is laundry day, and every time *Fräulein* Kniess came into the yard this morning to hang laundry, she heard your tenants in the garage. After lunch, as she removed dry items, she saw them piling boxes onto a cart. They have done this before, so she didn't think much about it, until they started piling their own things from the house on top. That's when she called us."

Fräulein Kniess nodded. "They were bad people. I heard them saying that all up-timers are rich, so rich they don't realize when things go missing, but I didn't think they were stealing from the person who gave them such a fine place to live. *Frau* Flannery was not a happy person to be near, and she should not have called them such names, but she was an up-timer. She treated them like people and didn't try to hurt them like many of us are used to. Now, since they steal from their family, other people will maybe think other refugees steal from the families we live with. They will make those Club 250 people look right." She looked ready to either cry or beat the snot out of her former neighbors. Things could go either way. "So, I call police."

Officer Schruer nodded his agreement and was none too gentle in handling the prisoners. "I'll need you to come down to the station and give a statement, *Fräulein. Herr* Reed, please list all the fabric they were trying to steal and anything else they might have taken. We would like Master Jorgensen to come down to the station as well. He can help value the fabric."

Nils walked into the police station to hear Sam arguing with the Chief of Police. "They just stole a bunch of old fabric! I don't want to ruin their lives over something that isn't worth that much."

Nils exploded. "Not worth that much?!? I could buy an entire shop in Paris with what that fabric is worth! Not just the shop, but everything to go in it. They stole, or tried to steal, *polyester,* not some cheap linen! And you aren't the one who 'ruined their lives'. They did that themselves. Didn't you hear the *Fräulein*? They stole from *Frau* Flannery before she died! They are liars and thieves."

Fräulein Kniess joined in. "You up-timers can be too trusting. Of course, some refugees will be liars and thieves, but even liars and thieves behave when they fear getting caught enough. If you do not punish those who show themselves to be such, you encourage others. Do you want your friends and neighbors, including me, to have their things stolen because letting the law handle these three makes you feel *sad*? Do you?" Sam quickly shook his head no. "Then do what the Chief and his officers tell you. This theft is not a small thing. They will be in jail for a long time. The others, they will not think Americans are quite as foolish and easy to steal from when this lot are punished."

By this point, Sam was looking down at his feet, wishing desperately that he had agreed to security guards when Nils suggested them. He was a soldier now, though, and he forced himself to admit he was wrong. "Master Jorgensen, you were right about the security. You can decide where to store the stash and how to guard it. Tell me what I need to do and how much I have to pay. I'll figure out what to do with it all later."

Nils looked proud at that. In the nearly-a-year since he met Sam, he had started to view him as almost-a-son. When they first met, Sam wouldn't have admitted that he was wrong, no matter how obvious his error. Nils still worried, though. "Officer, can we keep what happened quiet? If people know there is so much fabric there, others might try to steal it."

"Not entirely. The charges are publicly available, including what they were stealing, and we can do nothing about that. They won't mention how much additional fabric was at the house, but we can't change what these thieves have seen and will tell others. And since this entire conversation happened while the intrepid Betsy Springer, star reporter for the *Grantville Times* and *Grantville Inquisitor* was standing here, there is really no chance this will remain a secret." The Chief shrugged and looked like he felt bad for them but saw no wiggle room.

Nils and Sam both looked defeated, but Sam perked up after a minute, clearly having what he considered a brilliant idea. "Ms. Springer, you write for the *Inquisitor*, right? Could you write a story about Irene Flannery's house being made of fabric, just like the Hansel and Gretel witch had a house made of gingerbread? The furniture, the walls, even the wood were really made of fabric! Make it as outrageous and over the top as you can. It's brilliant! After that, no one will believe the real story!" Sam had a huge grin.

Betsy got a gleam in here eye that those who knew her recognized even before she held up her hands, spread apart as if she was reading a headline between them. "I can see it now: 'Local Woman Inspired Gingerbread Witch'. I love it! No, wait, make that the Gingerbread house, not witch. We don't want to accidentally start a real witch hunt."

The Chief quickly assumed a shocked expression. "The Hansel and Gretel witch was modeled on Irene Flannery?!? Well, I never! I do declare, that is the most shocking thing I have heard in years!" He then proceeded to fan himself with his hand, bat his eyelashes, and pretend he was about to faint dead away, to the hysterical laughter of everyone in the office. It was most out of character for him.

"Bless her heart!" At Betsy's comment, the up-timer's laughter redoubled, to the utter confusion of most of the down-timers.

"Seriously, though, kids, it's a good idea. Spread crazy rumors about what was there, then this story will come out, if Betsy and her editor agree, and before you know it, no one will believe a word these guys say about her having a ton of fabric. If anyone else has a stash, spread the word that I would appreciate them keeping it quiet to make our job easier." With that, the Chief turned and went back into his office and everyone else dispersed to go about their own business.

The days were already getting cooler. Grannie B and Grandpa Eli knew it was this darn Little Ice Age, but with the cold, they would have to stay inside more. Broken bones were doubly serious for the elderly now. As a result, they soaked up the sunlight every chance they could and enjoyed every flower that still bloomed. The John Francis rose bushes were producing their second, and almost certainly final, gorgeous blooms of the year. Grannie B pulled out scissors she had put in her bag for just this purpose and cut off one of the blooms to bring inside with her.

In her heart, she knew she wouldn't see another summer and she wanted to enjoy what time she had left. All summer, she had brought a flower here and a bud there into her room to enjoy. Undoubtedly bad for her allergies, which meant bad for her asthma, she couldn't bring herself to care. This close to the end, it wouldn't make much difference in how much time she had, but it made such a difference in how much joy she had. This rose would be the last she brought back to her room, though, and this would be the last time she came outside for a walk. It was getting too hard. She'd been using a walker for months now and had accepted it was time for a wheelchair. Her lungs weren't up to much anymore, but she had *so* wanted just one of these roses to keep. Irene was gone, but she was still here to remember, and remember she would, for whatever time she had left.

* * *

"Ladies, I promise you, this is what the police recommended, and not just for Mrs. Flannery's fabric. If anyone else has a stash, they should keep it secret. Since it's too late to keep Mrs. Flannery's a total secret, doing this will make sure no one believes the truth, and they likely won't believe the truth about anyone else's stash either, unless anyone is foolish enough to let other people see the real extent of it." Nils was used to talking to the Bowers' Broads and knew that while they respected his craftsmanship and his down-time business knowledge, they also thought he had a lot to learn about how things were done up-time. Sometimes they were right, but not always. This was one case where their innate prejudices (as old people, not as up-timers) were getting in the way.

"Nils is telling the truth. The chief told us to start rumors about her stash. They should start out close to the truth and keep getting more outrageous as often as we can until, in a few weeks or a month, the rumors get to 'she didn't have furniture, just stacks of material' or 'she had rolls of fabric to use in her fireplace' or 'the driveway and garage were covered with stacks and stacks of fabric'. The more outrageous, the better, because then even people from far away will (hopefully) not believe it. Later, when people say someone has 'boxes and boxes' of fabric, or 'hundreds of yards', no one will believe them. That's the idea anyway."

Grandpa Eli gave them a considering look. "If I understand you young men correctly, you are asking these fine, upstanding ladies to do some creative gossiping. Do I have that about right?" Nils and Eli paused, then nodded. "Ladies, do you agree to some extensive and creative gossiping, anywhere you might be for the next few weeks. Furthermore, will you enlist any crafters you know who have their own stashes to help with this misinformation campaign?"

Nurses and orderlies came rushing in when they heard the whooping and carrying on the ladies made in agreement with Grandpa Eli. "What is going on here, ladies? Is Eli being a trouble-maker again?"

At eighty-seven, Betty Ruth wasn't one to waste time. "Sam here told us what they found at Irene's Flannery's house. Turns out that she filled the entire guest room with nothing but fabric she hoarded for sewing! Not a stick of furniture in there. When that was full, she put more fabric in the garage and basement. I want to go see for myself. Who knows? Her basement might be stuffed so full of fabric you can't see the windows!"

Bethanne Kim

CHAPTER 25

October 1633

"**I** do not think a good Danish name like Jorgensen would help business right now. It is, as your Grandpa Eli says, time to 'shit or get off the pot.' We shall start this 'new label' you have been so pestiferous about this month. Please tell *Frau* Reed." When it was your own family name, admitting this was not easy, but a seasoned businessman like Nils Jorgensen knew how having the wrong name sometimes hurt a business, especially during war. It could also lead armed soldiers to your family and business if they didn't like "your kind", however they defined that.

"You could always change your name." As Donovan Reed's son, Sam had wanted to change his name more than once and was always amazed that his half-brother Donny (Donovan) Higgins didn't seem to hate the name he'd been saddled with. Nils' expression made Sam snort some small beer up his nose. "I guess that's not your first choice then! We could name it McClanahan's for the house, or Flannery's since Mrs. Flannery owned it."

"Or Irene's since that was her first name." When Hans and Sam snickered at her suggestion, it irritated Krystal. "What? It was."

The three of them started going back and forth with ideas while Nils was lost in thought. *Grantville Fashion: maybe, but kind of boring. Reed Style: reeds are plants, not clothing. Sam or Hans Clothiers: not a boy's name for a women's store. Krystal, Sonia, Michele: none feel right. Krystal's suggestion of Irene's isn't awful, but it doesn't describe the thing at all. The answer is so close! But we have to get it right this time. We can't keep adding more labels, no matter what* Frau Reed and her friends think.

"A business name is not a thing for boys to decide, including boys who are old enough to be journeymen or with enough money to buy a business. This is a thing for men to do, so I spoke with our journeymen, some masters I know, and some women who might be customers. This new label will be Flannery Fashions." Nils felt resigned, relieved, and resolved. "I will tell the Bowers' Broads when we go out this afternoon."

Krystal, Hans, and Sam looked at Nils, blinking, while they absorbed this information. Krystal finally broke the silence. "Seriously? I like Flannery's Fashion. It's a solid name. Now that I'm hearing it, give me a minute. I think that might have been what she called it." She jumped up and ran out of the room, clearly on a mission to find something specific.

A few minutes later, Krystal zoomed back in, triumphantly waving a dress over her head. "She did! Grannie B told you about how up-time clothing from the stores came with tags–labels. Mrs. Flannery made her own clothing and she bought labels with her name in them to show that she made them." She twisted the dress to let them read the label sewn into it. "The labels Mrs. Flannery used say 'Flannery Fashions'!"

Nils broke into a rare grin. "It is meant to be! We shall start this new 'label' so it can grow through the winter, while the armies are not campaigning and the wives can come to Grantville to shop. Maybe not so many wives but starting with a few who can spread the word will be good. Then they can buy something from Juniors for their daughters! The fathers will be pleased to spend less for their daughters than their wives. The daughters will be excited to shop without their mothers." He truly, deeply hoped what he said was true. He almost convinced himself.

November 1633

Nils updated Krystal and Sam on their great-grandparents health every time he visited them. Other than being half-deaf, Grandpa Eli seemed to be holding on just fine, but Grannie B's asthma was a different story. Without all the medicines she had relied on for years, she struggled to breathe more days than not now, and her asthma had always been worse in cold weather. That's why her Scottie dog scarf had been such a constant winter accessory for her. When Nils came home one Saturday afternoon and simply shook his head sadly, Krystal and Sam both thought the worst and started crying.

"No! I did not mean that. *Frau* Reed is still with us, but I think not for long. You should see her tomorrow and tell the rest of your family to visit her soon. This week. I have seen other old people who are like this and they never last more than a week or two, at the most." Nils remembered his own grandparents before they died.

Krystal sighed, deeply and dramatically. "I will tell Aunt Bethel and Uncle Raymond. Sam, you tell Donny's mom. Make sure both Donny and Ramona's mom hear since you know darn well Ramona won't think to take Donny out to say goodbye if he wants, but Delia Ruggles will make sure he says goodbye if she knows it's time. They can tell anyone else who lives in town. You should tell your dad, too, since he is their grandson."

"Nice try, cuz. That ain't happening. Telling my dad, at least. The others I'll take care of. If someone else wants to tell Donovan, they can."

Eli stood up in front of everyone at St. Mary's to give the eulogy for his wife. "All the clichés are true. She was my rock. I don't know what I will do without her. She was the strong one. Barbara and I have been married since 1934. That's three hundred years in the future now, but it was sixty-seven years of our lives. Barb was nineteen and I was twenty-two when we married. Since I was, and still am, a Methodist, we had a simple ceremony in her grandpa's back yard with the local justice of the peace officiating. My pastor and the priest from St. Vincent's blessed our marriage. This parish was named for St. Vincent de Paul before we came back to a time when he still lives, for those of you who didn't know. After we found that out, Barb kept hoping to meet a real-live-honest-to-goodness saint, preferably St. Vincent himself. It was a good dream, and one she wouldn't have had up-time. As much as we've lost, and it is a lot, including the medicines that kept so many of us, including my Barb alive, we have found much here.

"We have new businesses, new friends, new loves. Most of us have learned at least one new language. Some have learned many. Many of us West Virginia hillbillies are now rich! Anyone who still doubts the Ring of Fire was a miracle should think on that fact. If a passel of West Virginia hillbillies becoming rich and powerful (politically, economically, and socially) doesn't count as a gen-u-ine miracle, I surely don't know what does!" Eli's quick grin faded.

"I can barely remember a time before Barb was part of my life, but of course I can remember before the Ring of Fire. Barb and I were lucky to have many of our children, grandchildren, and even great-grandchildren come through with us, but not all of them did. To the day she died, Barb missed all those we left behind and prayed that they were well and safe. So do I. We pray for those who survived and came through with us, but we say extra prayers for those left behind, and for those who died here since we came through. There are too many to name them all, but she prayed for Irene Flannery in particular. For anyone who ever thinks that no one will remember or care when they die, knowing that someone other than a priest cared enough to pray for Irene Flannery should set your mind at ease." That got a small, nervous laugh.

"My Barb was a better person than I could ever be. She took care of us all. In the end, the Ring of Fire took her from me because it took her meds, but when we were younger, those meds didn't exist. She had a hard time outside for a lot of years. Walking to school was tough for her sometimes, and of course we didn't have buses back then. Most don't know it, but her asthma and allergies were part of the reason Barb dropped out of high school. She missed too much school because she was sick, and she got sick when she tried to walk to school. I hope that someone who is alive today will create asthma and allergy meds again to save lives like my Barb's. Those meds gave her a lot of good years." With tears threatening, Eli went back to his pew.

The next day, he bundled up and sat at her grave for an hour. A few minutes before the bus arrived, he walked over and placed a hand on the marker. As a teardrop fell off the end of his nose, he said his own private good-bye. "Barb, I've loved you since that first high school dance. In all those years, there haven't been many days, other than the war and when I went to college, we haven't been together. But, Barb, I can't come to your grave every day. I wish I could, my love, but I'm too old, and it's too far and too cold. It would just worry you up in heaven if I did. I'll come when I can, but don't take me not being here to mean I don't want to. I do. Oh, how I do! I miss you so much already. As you always said, my love, if wishes were fishes." His head bowed with tears shed and unshed, he turned and shuffled away from the love of his life and toward the bus-stop, grateful he still had family and new friends who would visit him and keep his empty room from becoming unbearably lonely.

Bethanne Kim

CHAPTER 26

December 1633

Nils' grin went from ear-to-ear. He didn't even try to stop himself. The new sign with the up-timer style "logo" for Flannery Fashions had just been hung. It included a long-stemmed lavender John Francis rose.

"The new logo does catch the eye, husband." Clara stood on the sidewalk admiring the sign. "When we have the new rose bushes lining the path to the door, it will be even better."

"Indeed. The glitter *Frau* Little gave us adds a little something special to the purple of the John Francis rose. I have to wonder why she was so insistent that we keep the glitter and never, ever, bring it back into her home." Nils put an arm around her as they walked up the path and inside together.

"Everyone knows up-timers can be *verrückt*. I know you asked the apprentices to clean up the glitter but please ask again. They did not get it all and now it is getting onto my clothing as well."

"Hmmm. Is that why your hair glinted in the moonlight yesterday? A bit of glitter in it? Hans told me they did a good job and cleaned everything. We will have a conversation about doing a job well tonight."

For the first official day of business, they had made appointments for customers to come and discuss what they wanted. Nils feared having the shop look unsuccessful if no one came, so a few of the appointments were friends of the Bowers' Broads. To help and not, as Grandpa Eli uncharitably said, to be nosy. Nils was extra proud because to have this new shop open on Hans' first day as a journeyman and employee of Flannery Fashions instead of an apprentice at Juniors.

* * *

"Director, I have received permission to take time off from the well-baby clinic over the Christmas holidays and I need to talk to you about my plans. There is a chance I won't be back at the start of the spring term." At the end of a long day, Krystal's expression was simply tired, giving nothing away.

Knowing Krystal had quit shortly after starting LPN training and taken a year-long break, Garnet's expression immediately, if subtly, gave away her concern. Krystal hastened to reassure her. "Nothing bad, I promise! I've helped several mid-wives for two years now. I'm going to help them with well-baby exams in some smaller towns that need them. They are farther out so the mobile clinic never made it either and they don't see a point in the mid-winter clinics in the bigger towns. I promised Grandpa Eli to come home for my birthday, so we won't go too far, but I know how easily travel is delayed now and don't want anyone worrying if I'm late."

The change in Garnet's expression was comical. Her relief, palpable. Her reply, unsurprising. "As long as you're going, there are a few things you can do for us…"

Krystal looked back over her notes. "To sum it all up, in addition to the well-baby clinic and helping the mid-wives, you want me to take information from the Sanitation Committee, someone from the CoC to look at how they are doing with hygiene and sanitation, do basic wellness checks to see if they need a larger medical team to go out, ask about herbal remedies, get seeds for herbal remedies if they have any to spare, look for any good candidates for medical training, and promote the medical program in general."

"Ahhh…"

Krystal flipped back a page. "Right, and make nice with any doctors or healers, try to temper everyone's expectations of up-timer 'miracles', and generally win over hearts and minds. If we visit any towns big enough to be part of the new public health project, which you will give me information on, try to find the best person and invite them to visit Jena and be part of it. Does that sum it up?" As she listed everything, the increase in her stress level was almost visible.

Garnet had the good grace to look sheepish. "Now that you read it all back to me, perhaps we can find another person or two who can go along with you, plus transport, and maybe drop a few things that are already part of the mid-winter clinics. If any other students want to go, let me know. Come back in a day or two and we'll finish coordinating everything. While you are here, though, I'll give you some good news, hot off the presses. You know we've been working on the new nursing program, hoping to have it up and running next month. It won't be until the fall, but that isn't the news. Well, it is, but not what you'll be excited about. Latin isn't required! It's still a good idea to learn, but at least you won't have to be fluent in a third language for the program."

"Can I tell the other students? This is the best early Christmas present for us all! Thank you. I don't know how you all did it but thank you so much! This is wonderful. I'm so relieved…"

"Krystal! Take a breath. Go ahead and tell the other students. Git, girl! And merry early Christmas to you all indeed!"

PART 4
1634

Bethanne Kim

CHAPTER 27

January 1634

The second (hopefully) annual mid-winter clinic was going well. "Hold out your hands, *Oma*." Krystal took a generous glob and smoothed it over the old woman's gnarled, dry hands. She winced at the slight pressure on her cracked skin but didn't try to pull back. When she finished, Krystal held onto the woman's hands as she explained. "This is something we called Vaseline up-time. The oil fields have started making it for us. One thing it's very good for is healing very dry, very cracked skin. It's supposed to feel greasy like that. Put your gloves on and keep them on for at least fifteen minutes. It will absorb into your skin soon, but the gloves will help."

Twenty minutes later, the *Oma* came back and patted Krystal's cheek. "You good girl. Hands much better. Some Vasa-leen go home?"

Krystal grinned. She knew a convert when she saw one, and this particular *Oma* had resisted up-timer medicine since their first visits in 1632. She only came because her granddaughter-in-law Renata insisted on bringing her children. "It just so happens that I have a small container for you to take home. But we don't have a whole lot yet, so just a small container for now."

Renata smothered a grin. "I didn't think you would ever get her to accept any up-timer cure. That Vasa-leen must be magic. And she does like Princess Kristina, so having it named after her family helps."

"We didn't think of that! The up-time brand name for petroleum jelly was Vaseline and none of us really knows why. Renaming it for the Vasa's is a great idea! Just for that, your *Oma*'s Vasa-leen is on the house! Free. 'On the house' means free."

"New subject. We heard that Johan Becker is doing well in Grantville. When he comes home in the spring, he is sure to pass the exams to be master, whenever he applies for it. Has he baked anything special for you?" Pink spots appeared on Krystal's cheeks. "Ah. So, you know his baking very well. He has fine strong arms, does he not?" Krystal blushed right up to her hairline, nodded, then rushed off to the sounds of soft, but friendly, laughter behind her.

February 1634

One Sunday in February, Elsa arrived at St. Mary's well before mass started, just as Grannie B said Mrs. Flannery always had. She wasn't there for long, barely long enough to add one purple rose to the altar flowers and to say a prayer for a bitter old woman who would be amazed if she knew how many would grow to think of her as a benefactor and philanthropist in the years to come. In the weeks to come, Elsa thought about that tradition, and she thought about the John Francis Flannery rose bushes outside St. Mary's. Mrs. Flannery had been keeping a secret, so she couldn't let anyone know that she was adding flowers from her garden to the altar flowers because they would ask why. Elsa wanted to keep the tradition, but also make it easier. Having roses bloom in February was not easy.

Irene chose February because of her anniversary but the month no longer held a meaning other than Mrs. Flannery had done it then. Starting that very spring and continuing every spring after, the first blooms from the John Francis Flannery rose bushes at St. Mary's were put into the altar flowers. Tending to those rose bushes came to be an honor among the women who volunteered at St. Mary's. Few knew about Irene's first baby, but the roses were named for her second one. It was a rare family who hadn't lost at least one child or didn't have someone close who had, so the stillbirth of John Francis was enough reason for them to honor the tradition.

May 1634

Nils was bored, and he didn't like it. Flannery's Fashions had a few clients, not a bad start at all for a new shop, but no real challenges for a master tailor. The Bowers' Broads had talked to him, over and over and over, about making down-time designs inspired by up-time designs. He had looked through the books and magazines in the library and ones people showed him, but he wasn't feeling inspired. Nothing spoke to him.

Frustrated, he left the shop and went on a walk, searching for inspiration. He soon found himself at Mrs. Flannery's house, where all that wonderful fabric had been stored. He knocked on the door to let *Frau* Gerandt know he was going into the garage to poke around in the boxes. Sam Reed still lived in the house, but his chemistry training for the military left him with little spare time. Elsa Gerandt was focused on growing more of the John Francis Flannery rose bushes, which meant she was at the house much of the time, so she was effectively the "lady" of the house.

In his search for buried treasure, one box yielded some interesting family photos, all in black and white and clearly old before the Ring of Fire. As he looked through, hoping for inspiration, he realized there was more under the photos. He found old travel brochures for California, Los Angeles, Hollywood, New York City, Broadway, Manhattan, Paris, London, and all manner of other glamorous-looking places. (Oddly, some seemed to be the same place with different names.) There were also a few old catalogs from "Sears", including one from 1923. The brochures didn't take long to leaf through, but the catalogs had a truly astounding amount in them.

He found more treasure in a shoebox: a small pile of brochures from museum showings of famous designers like Christian Dior and something called the "Theater de la Mode", which was apparently dolls showcasing the latest styles in 1945. Those were revolutionary! The shoes were positively unbelievable. How could someone make a shoe with a heel that high and thin? And how did women walk in them? Looking at them, the reason for using the Italian word "stiletto" was obvious. Of course, he had seen some in Grantville, but only when women dressed up for special events. These showed women wearing fabulous dresses and stiletto heels to go shopping and all kinds of everyday activities. One catalog showed women wearing "beach pajamas" with thick-soled "espadrilles." Any cobbler would be interested in selling these rope-soled espadrille shoes as a cheap indoor shoe, outdoor use being clearly limited to warm days with dry streets, but he had never heard of wearing pajamas except for sleeping.

He had been there for nearly two hours when Elsa came out to give him a glass of water and make sure he was okay. In the end, he took the whole box with him for further examination and decided to come back another day to investigate the rest of the boxes, even the ones marked "patterns." Up-time patterns were made of ridiculously flimsy paper (how did anyone use them multiple times?) and wasted sinful amounts of fabric, but perhaps he could find inspiration in them.

"*Frau* Gerandt, how are the roses coming? You have planted many more bushes outside this year. What are you doing with them next?"

"I wish I knew. We can only sell, and plant, so many in Grantville. We plan to sell blooms to the Higgins Hotel and for special events like weddings. Not many places have started growing ornamental flowers for those events, so there is little competition. But Sam seems to want this to be a big business and I don't know how we can make that happen. We need to build greenhouses to plant many rose bushes, find ways to sell them in other towns, and find ways to expand this business into other towns. For that matter, we need a *name* for whatever this is!"

"You really don't have a name yet? I'm surprised. Sam made sure we named the tailor shop immediately."

Elsa nodded. "He is too busy with the National Guard and school. I think this is maybe my business to run now, but it is hard to run a business when no one has told you what it is! The two things I know are that we need to spread these John Francis Flannery roses far and wide, and we need to use the money we make to help women who have dependent children but no husband. Are we to find them jobs? Train them? Take care of the children? Build them homes? There are so many questions I cannot answer."

"I think you should talk to *Herr* Reed and *Frau* Snodgrass at the Bowers. They knew *Frau* Flannery and were close to her age. Perhaps they would have a suggestion for what she might have wanted. Also, you could name it Flannery Flowers. Simple names are best."

Elsa lit up at that suggestion. "I love it! Flannery Flowers it will be. Now that we have a name, Sam can finish the paperwork to make this a 'charitable foundation', as he calls it. And perhaps *Herr* Reed and *Frau* Snodgrass will help me figure out what this foundation will actually *do*."

June 1634

Nils had so many ideas going through his head he couldn't focus. He wanted to make something fabulous that fused what he had seen in that marvelous box with what women wore down-time. If he could come up with something even half as popular as skorts, he could be famous. Needing a plan, he went back to the Bowers' Broads for advice.

"Ladies." He bowed in greeting. "I have a decision or two to make, and I would like your advice, once again. I have decided to make a special outfit for the Fourth of July. Something one of a kind and inspired by the Sears Roebuck catalog, but I need to decide what to make and who to make it for."

"We're in!" They basically all said it at the same time, then started talking over each other with ideas on what to make and who should wear it.

Nils took the easy path and started talking over them. "I want to make something that combines up-time and down-time, but in red, white, and blue colors for the holiday. That means full-length and modest, in a material I can buy here and now. It has to be for a grown, adult woman because it's for the Flannery Fashions line, not Juniors."

"Hmmm. So, something more along the lines of these new skorts, yes?" Nils nodded yes to Betty Ruth's question. "Linen palazzo pants. They have super wide legs. Not as full as a skirt and no underlayers, but they are very loose and flowing. Beach pajamas were a lot like palazzo pants."

"I saw these beach pajamas. They were in the catalog. I like them. I don't understand the point, but I like them. How are they different from palazzo pants?" No one could answer Nils' question, so they just looked back and forth at each other and shrugged. "Do you really think linen? It is such an inexpensive material it seems wrong to make an outer garment from it."

Once they got their snickers under control, Betty Ruth answered. "Two things. First, up-time good linen was expensive, so any up-timer is happy to wear it. Second, and most importantly, linen is very cool for summer wear. It also flows nicely for something like palazzo pants. Maybe you'll start a new trend for linen in the summer."

"I'll think about that. I'm not sure how down-time women will feel about using the same material for a dress that they use for their shifts. Moving on, ladies, do you have any suggestion who I might make them for?"

"Me!" Again, they all answered in unison.

Betty Ruth took the lead again. "Now that we've all volunteered, here's the real answer: someone who can get you some free PR. It doesn't do you much good if we're wearing your fabulous outfit up here in the county home. You need to find someone doing something that might end up in the paper, but don't aim too high. If Marla wore something during a concert, or Bitty had it on introducing a new ballet, everyone in the country would know, but something like that takes time to arrange. Plus, if Marla or Bitty wear a gown and anything goes wrong, everyone will know, so don't start with them, especially with such a short timeline. Someone opening a new business everyone is interested in and the newspaper might cover is a good choice for this year."

"How about that new bagel place? If you can convince them to introduce cheesecake, those two pieces of news just might make the front page, on a slow day. If they make cheesecake, it could even be above the fold, but below the fold is more likely. Front page, especially with a new style of clothing. The pastors might even decide to give their opinions on Sunday, if you time it right." Nils agreed on that point. Pastors were not prone to silence, not even when they were sick and the doctors ordered them to silence. It truly wasn't something they were good at.

"This is so cool. A *haute couture atelier* in Grantville!" Betty Ruth Snodgrass' sewing skills were never impressive, but her dedication to *Vogue* magazine had been.

Nils suddenly looked both suspicious and annoyed. "Why didn't you tell me you speak French and why are you doing it now? Are you trying to make me look foolish?"

Poor Betty Ruth was so flabbergasted she almost stuttered her answer. "Wha? But, but, everyone knew those words, *haute couture* for sure. *Vogue* magazine used them all the time. '*Haute couture*' was fancy, expensive clothing from famous designers, and the designers liked to show it off in their '*atelier*'. They did seem to mostly use those terms for things from Paris, now that you mention it. Especially *atelier*. But that's because Paris, France, was the center of the fashion world and had been since, well, a long time!"

Nils just about blew a gasket hearing that. Instead of being a man on a mission to build his own business, he became a man on a mission to make his newly formed country, which included the country of his birth, the center of the fashion world. He had a huge advantage because no one else had even imagined such a thing.

CHAPTER 28

The whole design and fitting process made Sam and Krystal's Aunt Bethel nervous. All the clothing she had ever owned was either store-bought or family made, not made by a professional tailor. The youngsters in the Flannery Fashion *werkstatt* were busy measuring parts of her she had never thought about measuring, like from her neck to her waist in the front *and* back, and from her waist to the floor, front *and* back. The experience was a lot to take in.

When the measuring was done, Nils walked in. "Now we decide on the design details and fabric." Two hours later, they had agreed on wide-legged red palazzo pants with a simple knee-length blue tunic edged in white. The pieces could be worn (and sold) separately. While simple and familiar to Bethel, the nearly knee-length untucked shirt would be both radically new to down-timers accustomed to women's fashions with tight bodyes or stays as the outer layer and ridiculously old-fashioned, to anyone who spent time looking at medieval tapestries. However, in warm summer weather, many women would welcome a lighter, looser outfit that could keep any skirts underneath admirably clean. There were times a woman just didn't want to keep her apron on.

July 1634

Bethel expected to feel self-conscious, but when the day rolled around, she was excited. The part-owner of a successful new business, she actually looked and felt the part in her new *couture* or, as Nils called it, "*die Artmode*" outfit. (The first step in his mission to make the United States of Europe (USE) the epicenter of fashion was defining the words in Ami-Deutsch instead of French; high fashion would be "*die Artmode*", which was made in a "*werkstatt*".) With a little help, he had found a cobbler to make espadrilles to go along with the outfit. As much as she liked the outfit overall, shoes with a woven straw sole seemed a bit iffy to Bethel. Definitely a bad choice on wet days. Since the forecast was for a sunny Fourth of July, she set aside her concerns and wore them to complete the *Zusammesetzung*, Nils' word for 'ensemble'.

All the glances and compliments on her outfit as she strolled from her home to the newly opened café were a pleasant surprise. It was so exciting to have a storefront and not just be a catering company! Bethel had never been unfashionable, but she had never received this many compliments for an outfit in her life and, being truthful, espadrilles were surprisingly comfortable on a warm day. When Betsy Springer of the *Grantville Times* arrived five minutes later, Bethel walked her through the café, making sure she had a fresh, hot bagel with cream cheese, while they discussed the Saalfeld expansion plans and how the café had come about.

"Nils, everything went perfectly! Exactly as you hoped. I talked about the business, and she kept asking me questions about my outfit. I finally told her she needs to interview you if she wants all the details. Whenever you see my niece, please tell her I hired Johan. She'll know the one I mean—Sibylle's brother. That should get her to stop in the bakery! Now, it's your turn. Who is this lovely young woman? Is this the *Frau* Zimmerman I have heard so much about?" Seeing Nils turn red wasn't unusual. Seeing him turn red because he was embarrassed? That was extraordinary.

222

"Um, yes, it is. *Frau* Clara Zimmerman, this is *Frau* Bethel Little. She gives us advice sometimes for the shop and she just opened the bagel and cream cheese store. You already know her nephew Sam and niece Krystal."

Elsa started to walk past as Bethel replied. "It is nice to meet you *Frau* Zimmerman. Have you met *Frau* Gerandt? I know your husband has met her. She lives in Sam's house and runs the Flannery Flowers operation."

Clara knew about the fabric stash and that Sam had decided that most of the fabric should go toward funding efforts to help single mothers and to spreading the purple roses. While the fabric stash had been locked securely away for safekeeping, she was pleased to meet the young woman in charge of the effort since her husband's business was indirectly related. "I am so pleased to meet you both. *Frau* Gerandt, how is it going for you?"

"I have made a good start with growing the flowers in Grantville, but I am not sure the best way to move forward with the whole project." Elsa sounded dejected, but looked frustrated. "I am meant to be helping women who have children without a husband, but I do not know how I should help them or what I should help them with."

"I don't know if you have heard of the Fugger, but they have a place called the 'Fuggerei' in Augsburg that may inspire you. The Fuggerei is a community within the city for people who have jobs but cannot afford a home. Jakob Fugger the Rich started it for his brothers Georg and Ulrich after they died. In addition to a small rent, the people who live there say three daily prayers for the Fugger family. It is quite famous, and one of the largest constructions near the city center."

"How do the people live? Do they have a room for each family, or a house, or barracks? How do they keep the women and children safe? Do they have gardens for their own food?" Elsa had a lot of questions.

"Americans would think them small, but they have generous rowhouses for each family. They have small gardens so they can grow food. The whole thing is surrounded by a wall with only two gates, which are closed at ten every night." Clara had never been inside the Fuggerei, but in the century plus since the Fugger first started construction on it, the people of Augsburg had a good idea what the inside was like. If nothing else, looking through the gates in the daytime was easy enough.

"I must go see this Fuggerei, although I still need a way for the residents to earn money. We cannot build a place that is too large. If we sell some of the fabric, we can buy land to build on to start, but not in Jena, Magdeburg, Augsburg, or anywhere in West Virginia. The land is just too expensive. Thank you for this wonderful idea." Elsa's quick hug startled Clara, but it was the start of a fast friendship. "Now I must find a way to visit this Fuggerei."

CHAPTER 29

August 1634

O nce Elsa told Sam about the Fuggerei, he was determined to go with her to see it, live and in person, before his classes started in earnest for the fall. As they walked up to the gate, he spoke. "*Frau* Gerandt, Flannery's Flowers is truly your project now. I will follow your lead."

"Ah, so formal today! Not Elsa, eh? Fair enough while we are here, but if I am not mistaken, our approach has been noticed. The gatekeeper sent a child running, as if to fetch someone or something. Going more slowly to allow time for whoever, or whatever, to arrive would be polite." Elsa had been a burgher's daughter before Tilly swept through and left her a widowed orphan with two small children. Sam was learning a lot about manners from her.

They paused to read the Fuggerei mission statement, carved in stone in the donors' plaques. "Out of piety and generous munificence grant, endow, and devote 106 dwellings with all provisions to their diligent but indigent fellow citizens." As they continued toward the gatekeeper, a rotund, pox-scarred burgher scurried around the corner, clearly having exerted himself far more than usual. "*Herr* von Uptime! I am *Herr* Ulrich.

You are most welcome here at the Fuggerei! We would have had a more appropriate greeting prepared if we had known you were coming!"

Sam looked distinctly uncomfortable at being called "von Up-Time". He wasn't a noble and he knew it. Unfortunately for him, like most down-timers, Elsa and the *Herr* Ulrich knew no such thing. She looked a bit smug at hearing him called "von Uptime." Elsa nudged him to reply. "Um, this is fine. My name is Sam Reed and I am helping *Frau* Gerandt. She is the head of Flannery's Flowers, which wants to do something like what you have done here but on a smaller scale. When she heard about the Fuggerei, we both wanted to see how you have done this to hopefully get some ideas. She can tell you more."

"An up-time woman killed when the Croats raided Grantville left *Herr* Reed von Up-Time funds for the purpose of helping single mothers. Your Fuggerei was mentioned as a model to look at and possibly copy, on a much smaller scale, so we came for a visit. Of course, we wouldn't do that in Augsburg or anywhere near here. You have amply, and generously, provided for the community here."

Lorentz Ulrich looked nervously between them, not quite sure he should really be addressing the down-time woman instead of the noble man. Even three years after the event, he hadn't interacted with up-timers enough to be entirely comfortable with their ways. "You honor us. You may already know the basics, but I will review in case you are not. Jakob Fugger the Rich founded the Fuggerei in 1516 to honor his deceased brothers, Georg and Ulrich. Residents are gainfully employed, respectable Augsburg citizens who do not earn enough to provide housing for their families as well as their other basic needs. They pay one Rheinish florin per year to live here, which is about one week's wages for most of our residents. They must also say one Our Father, one Ave Maria, and the Apostles' Creed every day for the Fugger family. Since the Fugger are Catholic, as are all our residents, they have seen to the residents' spiritual needs by building St. Markus Church. The walls have been there since the very beginning, as have the gardens and public spaces. The gates close at ten o'clock every night, so our residents are safe and secure inside. Our motto is 'assistance so others can help themselves.' What questions do you have for me?"

Elsa noticed how winded Lorentz became as they walked through the Fuggerei. "This is a lovely square, let's enjoy sitting here for a few minutes while we chat. Your residents must really enjoy these open spaces."

Sam had questions. "You mentioned everyone is Catholic and a citizen of Augsburg. Are those requirements?"

"Yes, those are requirements. We know, of course, that you up-timers don't like religious requirements, but this is a private charity, similar to something a church might start but ours is funded by the Fuggers and Saint Ulrich. It isn't government run, which is important because the government can't re-allocate the endowment for something else. Ideally, in our hopes and dreams, the Fuggerei will still be operating, and still charging one Rheinish florin per year and three prayers daily, hundreds of years from now."

"Wait, what? A saint funded this place? How is that possible?" Sam was Methodist so saints in general were a foreign concept to him, but he was pretty sure most saints were dead before they became saints. Being dead tended to complicate funding things.

"Technically, it isn't Saint Ulrich. He is on the account for the blessings he brings. You can see how the Fuggerei has flourished in the one hundred sixteen years of its existence! Our syphilis and smallpox ward has also helped many people." Lorentz's pride was palpable.

"I didn't know you had a hospital here. Can we see it?"

"Nothing so large, but we do have doctors, nurses, and aftercare for syphilis and smallpox. In addition, we have a surgery near here. Would you care to continue our tour now? You can see one of our residences. *Herr*

Fugger instructed me to show you one before bringing you to meet him. The Infirmary doesn't allow visitors to reduce spreading illness, but I can show you the building, if you wish."

By the end of their visit, Elsa and Sam were overwhelmed with information and contacts. The Fuggerei was the perfect model for them to base a Flannery Foundation on and the Fuggers had provided much excellent advice to get it on a sound financial footing. Instead of one large location, there would be smaller residences all over the USE and they would only house women with children, not entire families. In Elsa's dreams it eventually extended beyond the bounds of the USE, but that was a long way in the future. She had a lot of thinking and planning to get everything started.

* * *

"How did the trip go, Sam?" Krystal had rented out her room in their great-grandparents home and was staying with Sam for the last few days before moving to Jena for the fall term. The RN program was now officially a joint program with the University of Jena.

"Ask Elsa. This is her thing now. I'm officially in the National Guard and done fiddling about with flowers."

"The Fugger were generous with their time. They gave us much good advice, especially about how to set it up. I am just not sure how to do what they told us." Elsa alternated between looking and sounding excited and dejected. "I am just a Burgher's daughter! What do I know about setting up a foundation to last for centuries?"

"Whoa. That's some pressure there. Why not start by just setting up a regular foundation? Let the centuries take care of themselves, Elsa. Take a deep breath, hold it, then let it out. There you go. You look a little bit less tense. Now, let's figure out what you need to do next."

As Krystal and Elsa talked, Krystal had a lightbulb moment and asked Sam to call Ursula, Doctor Sims, and Nurse Sims and ask them all to come over. When they arrived, she started talking. "We have been trying to figure out how to expand the well-baby clinics without having to travel all over the countryside with everything we need, then find a place we can work, and either a place to spend the night or a way to get back home. We also need to find more people to work for us and, if possible, a way to grow more herbs in the communities we visit."

"Meanwhile, Elsa, here, has been trying to figure out a way to build small communities of women with clinics, herb and vegetable gardens, and possibly some kind of job training. Mrs. Flannery left a substantial fabric stash, which is funding the endeavor Elsa is working on. It needs a more over-arching name than Flannery Flowers, by the way, Elsa. That's good for the efforts to spread the roses, just not for the rest of it."

Krystal paused for a minute so everyone could think through the ramifications and permutations of what she had just said. "So, here's what I'm thinking. The Red Cross works with whatever the new Flannery Foundation is. They build clinics at each site. We provide a person who comes, maybe once a week, and they plant whatever herbs Ursula recommends. And, eventually, we start training some of the women who live there to be herbalists or at least to do some advanced first aid and help their community. What do you think?" She didn't notice it, but Krystal was so excited that she was bouncing up onto her toes as she spoke.

Alice and her husband glanced at each other. Krystal had come a long way from the deep depression of three years earlier. "It sounds like a lovely plan, sweetie, but a great deal of work. Too much for Doctor Sims and me. Not many people know it yet, but we are both going to retire next year. Ursula, dear, your opinion on this matters more than ours since with

Krystal in nursing school and Doctor Sims and me retired, you would be the one leading the effort." Seeing Ursula's stunned expression, Alice looked at her and cocked her head. "You really hadn't guessed? Even after we had you move to the brand-new, larger well-baby clinic in Jena instead of us?" Ursula just shook her head. "Ah, well, then you have some news to tell your husband. I hope you both think it's good news, unless you want to decline the offer."

Krystal grabbed Ursula into a big hug. "Don't you dare! You'll be fabulous at it! And before I forget, what do you think about my suggestions?"

"I. I. I. Um. I will take the job, yes. And the suggestions are. They are a lot right now. I think it will probably be good, but I need to think. It's a lot to take in all at once."

Alice stood up and held out her hand to her husband. "I think *Frau* Gerandt and Ursula have some talking to do, with more than a little input from Krystal. I'm sure you young women will come up with a fine plan for the Flannery Foundation and the well-baby clinic and Red Cross to work together without two old dinosaurs hanging around."

October 1634

Juniors was making some of the costumes for the upcoming ballet. The apprentices were all talking about the girls (pretty or not) in their extremely skimpy outfits, but the journeymen (for whom most of those girls were too young to be of interest) could talk about nothing except the extraordinary skirts that practically stood up by themselves but weighed almost nothing, considering the bulk.

Upon closer inspection of the tulle in the existing costumes, the first thing Nils noticed was that instead of being a woven or even knit fabric, tulle was a kind of superfine netting, possibly related to lacemaking.

Lacemaking was an exceptionally expensive handcraft. Replicating the tulle would be incredibly hard, but potentially quite lucrative. Seeing that all the ballet outfits seemed to include tulle, and that every picture he could find of a ballerina seemed to include tulle (except ones where they wore truly scandalous skin-tight outfits), Nils hoped that Bitty Matowski and her ballerinas were desperately wishing for a source of tulle. With a bit of luck, he could use the ballet company to help fund creating (re-creating) tulle, which he could then sell at a handsome profit.

With that goal in mind, Nils was hopeful and cautiously optimistic when *Frau* Bitty, as she asked to be called, took him up on his offer and visited Juniors the next time she was in town. "*Frau* Bitty, I am hoping you would like a source for tulle…" She was easily four times as excited as he expected. After a few minutes, he managed to explain that he didn't have tulle *yet* but was planning to recreate it, with the right backing.

Knowing someone wanted to manufacture tulle made Bitty's month. "I have to race back to the train station now, but if you can find a way to manufacture tulle, dancers will always want it! The Ballet will definitely be a strong customer, and you can tell that to potential investors. You can also tell them that we haven't given a sample of tulle to anyone else. It wasn't everywhere like cotton, but it wasn't particularly rare either, up-time, so someone else could have some, but I doubt anyone else is working on making it. They would've come to me or the ballet company if they were. You can tell them all of that. Oh, and don't forget the army! They'll buy tulle too. Don't look at me like I've lost my mind. It's great for mosquito nets, and eventually they'll send someone somewhere that they need them, and you can use it to keep bugs off of food. Dang it, I'm making myself late for the train. The medics, too. They can use big mosquito nets to cover whole beds in the field to keep flies and such off their patients."

As the door banged shut behind *Frau* Bitty, Nils collapsed into a chair, his thoughts awhirl. A market beyond tutus and fashion had never occurred to him. Armies spent *a lot* of money. This could be a real windfall!

November 1634

Elsa had lived through family members dying, plague epidemics, smallpox, being a camp follower, losing her husband, seeing cities destroyed, and being forced to flee her home. This just might be the most scared she had ever been. She stopped for a minute as she walked through the door, distracted by the sight of the man in front of her, who was most definitely not the elderly *Herr* Pridmore. "Sir," deep breath "I am *Frau* Elsa Gerandt, President of the Flannery Foundation. We would like to get a loan to buy land and construct several buildings. We have up-time fabric to use as the collateral."

As a brand-new loan officer, Valentin Friedrich's personal stress level was at DEFCON 1. His brain knew he was fully prepared to handle a loan without help, but knowing the bank's two most senior loan officers had recently not only quit but moved out of town left him a bundle of nerves doing his first entirely unreviewed up-time style loan. "*Frau* Gerandt, I can give you all the paperwork to complete but we will need a professional valuation for the fabric. The bank will store it until you repay the loan. Do you wish to fill out the paperwork here or take it with you?" He dabbed his forehead with a handkerchief as he awaited her reply. His leaned on habits and manners formed during his years working as a down-time banker to steady him. It didn't help that the client was so distractingly lovely and connected or rich enough to be running a foundation.

She paused to let her nerves calm down. "I will fill it out here so I can ask you questions, if I need to." *And so I can't lose any of the pages.* "May I have a glass of water, please?"

Sipping on her water, she took her time to ensure she made no mistakes on the paperwork. "What did you do before you came to work for the bank here?"

"I worked for a banker in Jena. With so many people coming back and forth with the medical schools working together, I moved here. I lost my parents and grandparents before the Ring of Fire. I still have a brother and two sisters, but they are married with children, and I don't see them much. We're close but they are so busy with their own lives that it's hard." He realized he was babbling but he couldn't stop himself. Once she finished and left, he didn't know when he would see her again. Grantville was a big place.

For her part, Elsa told him all about her children, the John Francis Flannery rose, and the oddities of living with an up-timer. As she handed him the last page, he stammered out something neither of them would ever remember, then gave a courtly bow and kissed her hand before she left in a bit of a daze, thinking about the charming banker and when she might see him again.

Bethanne Kim

PART 5
1635 AND 1636

CHAPTER 30

January 1635

"How did you manage it?" Bitty examined the first-ever piece of down-time made tulle.

Nils was proud of that tiny, two square inch piece of tulle. "I didn't. I found the right people to ask. First, I asked around to find lacemakers. Two Flemish lacemakers were headed home with their apprentice after doing some research here, but I convinced them to spend the winter by agreeing to let them have a room in Juniors while they worked on this. Central heating combined with not traveling in the winter made it an easy sell. Given how simple it is compared to most of what they do, they are pretty quick at it, but it's still complicated to make a machine to do it. All of which is my long-winded way of saying we still can't make much at a time."

"How much have they made so far?"

"A few yards, but having it hand-made that way is ridiculously expensive. Since they are living with us, they are spending more time making the more expensive laces for us. We are even working together to create a new lace pattern with stars and bars, to commemorate the American flag. Since they developed the pattern based on our request, we own the rights to the pattern jointly and should earn some nice income from having an exclusive new pattern, which they will sell to us at cost. It's quite exciting. But back to the tulle, now that they have worked out how to do it, they have handed over making the tulle to their apprentice, for the time being. The young lady had already wanted to stay in Grantville. Helping a master machinist create a machine to make tulle gives her a *reason* to stay. Assuming we can find a master machinist with the time and ability, gather the materials we need, and generally get the process worked out. It will be sooner than later, but that means maybe 1636-1637, not Christmas this year."

Nils chewed on his lip as he thought. "Can you keep a secret?" Now he really had Bitty's complete focus. "We are making another pattern together. This one, we'll give away for free. Copies of the pattern are being sent to lacemakers all over. The pattern will clearly say it is from '*die Artmode aus eine werkstatt*, Magdeburg' and the pattern may be freely used by all who wish."

"Don't keep me hanging! What is this new pattern?"

"Do You Hear the People Sing?"

"What? Of course. Marla's new song, translated from *Les Mis*. The broadsheet is everywhere. What does that have to do with lace?"

"The pattern. It is the musical notes for that phrase. That Swedish pig Oxensternia is no lord of mine, and Berlin is not my capital city. Now *Frau* Linder's song can literally be sewn into the fabric of the USE." He looked almost grim in his determination. "I *will* see Magdeburg as the fashion capital of Europe as surely as *Frau* Admiral Simpson will see it as the music capital."

Elsa,

I have talked to the teachers here. No one can do anything right now because they are overwhelmed with the new RN and DO programs, but in a few years, they will be happy to work on a program that can be taught through the Flannery Foundation to help train people in more substantial first aid for when it's longer than the "golden hour" to get to the hospital. Something less than a medic but more than plain old first aid.

They recommended starting by doing mid-wife training for women. I countered by asking to get at least some mid-wives trained so they can do C-sections, tubal ligations, and one or two other related surgeries for things like ectopic pregnancies, and so no one has to go through what Irene Flannery endured as a teenager. They aren't excited about it, but they haven't said no yet, so there's a chance. I know they really don't want anyone except doctors doing surgery, but they also understand that this could save a lot of lives, mothers and children. But for now, start looking for someone who can train mid-wives and women who would like to become mid-wives.

Also, congratulations on your betrothal to Valentin! I bet Sibylle is excited to be a bridesmaid. Will Johan bake your cake? I'll be very disappointed if you don't have a bouquet full of Flannery roses. Let me know when it is so I can get back for the whole thing. Just don't plan it for right when I graduate.

— Krystal

February 1635

"Krystal, we wanted to talk to you first about your plans after graduation because it seems like you are already set so it should go quickly. Are we right that you plan on continuing to work in maternal and pediatric care?" Garnet's task for the week was to interview all the nursing students who were about to graduate to place them following graduation. Having known Krystal the longest, she was the easiest to place.

"Absolutely. I know how much you need help here and at Leahy, but I am going to work with the Flannery Foundation full time. Thanks to Grandpa Eli making a deal for me to be part-owner of Miasma Masks, and the increasing income from Irene's Intimates, I don't have to worry about my salary. The initial plan is for me to help them set up a model clinic in the first community. I will continue to travel around doing a version of the Red Cross well-baby clinics and helping communities add to their herbal remedies. We are hoping that the medical school will work with me to develop a curriculum to train first responders at the Foundation homes and living in the more rural areas."

"We already talked about that, Krystal. You know how short we are on staff and how much we already need to do. Are you going to be able to spend any time helping us here or are you leaving the area entirely?"

"I know there will probably be roadblocks for what the Foundation is trying to do and that the hospitals and medical school are short-staffed, but I also know how much you want to help people who can't get to the hospital either at all or quickly enough for a serious injury. Even splinting and setting broken bones would be a huge help. To answer your question, no, I don't expect to spend any time working here or in Grantville, but I *do* expect to gather a lot of information on what people really need help with, what they can already do, and who might be a good candidate for either training or teaching. I'm hoping to find some herbalists who can help me build part of the curriculum around down-time remedies. Did you know that when they have tiny babies, usually preemies but not always, they keep them warm by putting hot bricks wrapped in cloth in their bedding with them? It isn't always enough, but it saves a lot of babies."

Garnet let out a breath. "You are a woman on a mission, and it's a mission I approve of. I'm sure the rest of the staff will as well. We will help when we can, just keep our limitations in mind. No matter how much we want to help, we are only human. Do you have any other plans we should know about?"

"There is one thing. When we cleaned out Irene Flannery's house back in thirty-two, I found a box of clippings, booklets, and other parenting and baby related information buried under a biohazard of insulation and critter droppings in a closet. Mice had gotten in and chewed on some of it and I never got back to read what all was there. I was still pretty depressed over the whole lost-everyone-and-everything aspect of life at the time. Since everything in the room was from before 1958, I'm hoping to find some useful ideas for gadgets, techniques, and whatever to help parents. When I go back after graduation, I'm going to grab that and start looking through for ideas to help babies and moms. I think Sam still has all the actual nursery items boxed up somewhere, so I may look at those, too, whenever I'm in Grantville. I know Grannie B and Grandpa Eli stored some baby gear in their attic because I see a highchair whenever I go up there. I'm hoping Grandpa Eli is having a good day when I visit and can help me find things or explain what any odd gadgets are."

Garnet whistled. "That sounds like quite a project. I hope you find some great things in all of that. How is your grandpa doing, by the way? I know losing your grandma was hard on him."

"Honestly, not well. His memory is failing. I'm going to go visit in a few weeks, right after exams. The Bowers' staff doesn't think he has very long. As much as we'll all miss him, he'll be happier once he's with Grannie B again. Of course, there's always the chance he'll be seeing Mrs. Flannery, but that's a risk I'm sure he's willing to take to see his 'Barb' again." They were both silent for a minute, lost in their own thoughts.

Krystal cleared her throat. "Ah, there is one other thing. It's a bit unusual and not really a hospital or medical school thing, but I think you should know. The book *The Lady with the Lamp* is quite popular. I've heard the talk about the Fourth of July Arts Festival in Magdeburg this summer. With the new RN program graduating its first class in June and, knowing that what down-timers think of nurses is pretty much what the book shows in the beginning, I had this idea, and I talked to a few people and, well, it's being made into a play. It will debut at the Festival. They show Miss Nightingale as an English lady who learns about being a proper nurse in Germany, then goes to war and saves many of the soldiers with the help of nuns and hard-working peasant women. The CoC is happy with how it's coming along. It really fits in with their mania for hygiene and sanitation. By the end, nurses are respected by the medics and doctors, and respectable women are signing up to be nurses. The very last scene will be a group of new nurses in their uniforms reciting the Nightingale Pledge."

"Do you think we could review the final manuscript before they perform it? I wouldn't want it to give people the wrong expectations."

"Of course. They mentioned somehow listing the names of the 'brave' nursing students when they perform the show. Another thing to think about: the uniform Miss Nightingale used for her nurses was practical and would work now just as well as it did in her time. It might be a good model for new nursing uniforms."

"All good thoughts, Krystal, and I'll bring them up at our next department meeting. We do need to finalize the uniforms. Please thank *Frau* Gerandt for donating the Flannery roses and all those herbs she found in Grantville gardens to the hospital gardens. For now, I heard the door open a few minutes ago and someone settling into a chair, and I believe we're done?" Krystal nodded. "Please ask them to wait for just a minute while I make some notes about our conversation. And please, tell your grandfather we are all praying for him and wish him the best."

March 1635

"I wish we could ask her about the up-time." Krystal's nursing classmates were walking down the hall toward their classroom.

"She talks about it more now than she did at first. Back in '31, when we were in refugee housing, someone asked Krystal about the before and she walked away and didn't talk to the woman for days. Krystal only talks about it if it explains something, not just to remember, especially right now with her grandfather having just died." Nicol Steinmetz had known who Krystal was since she helped her fill out paperwork at the Refugee Center, an interaction Krystal had long since forgotten.

"Like when she talks about *M*A*S*H*? She must love that show. I really do not want to hear about Klinger and his fake 'mental illness' wearing dresses again! It is wrong. Although I wouldn't mind seeing pictures of the dresses, and I would love to meet a real-life Radar O'Reilly. Compared to my old clothing, I love our warm, sturdy uniforms, but that doesn't mean I don't appreciate a pretty dress!" Anna said.

"If she has some tapes of *M*A*S*H,* maybe we could all meet at her house to watch them! Oh, fudge, that won't work. She was just visiting Grantville that day. Which is why she doesn't like to talk about 'before'."

"Fudge, Margarete?"

"I can't remember where I heard it. I think on a TV show, but maybe in a book. Apparently, fudge is a sugary treat, but sometimes people used the word when they were annoyed or upset, and I like the sound of it. Even the strictest priest can't accuse me of taking the Lord's name in vain with that one! Sometimes, I dream about trying fudge." Margarete Dietrich's childhood home had a generous library by seventeenth century standards, and she enjoyed reading and watching TV, on the rare times she had the chance.

"Huh. Interesting. 'Fudge!' I like the word too. Anyhow, maybe we could find some *M*A*S*H* tapes. If we ask around, someone might know where to find a copy or two and we could organize a watch-party together, as a surprise for her. We could invite some of the student doctors too! I don't know about you, but my dowry might stretch to a doctor now, if I'm lucky."

They hadn't noticed the up-time instructor walking behind them. "Fudge? Is one of our nursing students fudging their data? I certainly hope not!"

Anna, Nicol, and Margarete looked at each other. "What does dessert have to do with data?"

"If you 'fudge' your data, that means you made it up or changed it to make it reflect, well, whatever it is you want it to reflect. Nothing to do with the kind of fudge you eat, which I haven't seen since before the Ring of Fire, now that I think about it. If you like, I'll reserve a room for the party. I'll also take care of finding some episodes of *M*A*S*H* and see if the Deans will let us all have a watch party together, RN and DO students. Deal?" The medical school staff had been trying to find ways to get them all together socially and this seemed ideal.

As they turned to walk into their classroom, Anna, Nicol, and Margarete were suddenly self-conscious as they realized Krystal had been close behind them, hidden by others in the busy hallway and could have heard their conversation.

"I lost my parents. When we came here, they were left up-time." Krystal spoke more softly than she usually did.

Anna spoke quickly. "We didn't mean anything bad. It's just that your old world sounds fascinating! We've heard stories but there is so much that is different and we all have questions no one but an up-timer can answer." It was time for class to start, but their instructor felt this conversation was too important to interrupt. She simply motioned the other students to sit quietly and listen.

Krystal spoke again when Anna finished, ignoring her comment. "I lost my parents. They were left up-time. So were all of my grandparents, my best friend, my new boyfriend, my house, and almost all my things. I never wanted to live in West Virginia, much less Grantville, but I got stuck there with nothing but my car, some laundry, a few music CDs, and the odds and ends in my car. Talking about The Before just makes me remember what I lost. I was just in town for the afternoon, working and visiting. I didn't even live in Grantville, before."

"We're really sorry, Krystal, but now I'm confused. You have a house in Grantville and we have all heard you talk about your Grannie B and Grandpa Eli dying, but you just said all your grandparents were left up-time and you didn't live here?"

"They are my great-grandparents and it's their house. Was their house. My cousin Sam and I both got stranded here when the Ring of Fire happened. Since neither of us had parents to live with, they let us live in their house. When Sam inherited a house and moved out, I stayed. When Grandpa Eli died, I inherited their house. We've all had the classes Caroline Platzer designed, especially the Five Stages of Grief. I went through them all. Sometimes it feels like I've gone through them all too many times to remember, but you're right that I don't like remembering and talking about times from before. I've accepted our new lives and I'm happy now, but that doesn't make remembering Before anything but sad for me.

"I spent a long time depressed and in denial when we moved here and I don't want to go back to that, however briefly. I hope you understand why I don't like to talk about it, just as I understand why you are curious. I mean, do you think people who went through Tilly's sack want to think or talk about it? What I went through wasn't that bad, but I can't even do something as simple as go back and look at the woods near my home, because my home is still up-time. I've really focused on my life here and now, as a nurse in 1635, and how I can help others here."

"Excuse me, ladies, but we do need to start class. Krystal, I don't want an answer right now, but please consider taking a class to discuss what it was like up-time and answer any questions your classmates have. It is a great way to see the world differently from how we were born, and that is one of the things we want our RNs and doctors to do: see things the way their patients might to help figure out the source of problems. Now, let's review for the upcoming test."

CHAPTER 31

May 1635

"Husband, you need to make a decision. Last year you created a Fourth of July outfit for *Frau* Little. If this is to be an annual event, as you said you wished it to be, you are almost out of time to create something worthy of Flannery Fashions." Clara was young but she was no quiet mouse, content to let her husband make all the decisions and watch opportunities slip out of his grasp. She had seen women ruined by foolish husbands.

"But who should I dress? I must be inspired for this. What yells freedom? I have been searching and no one comes to mind." For a moment, Nils looked as down-in-the-dumps as he felt.

"Brillo. Few things speak more strongly of freedom, right here and now, than Brillo the Ram. I hear they are even doing a ballet about him. Make Flo, the woman who cares for Brillo, an outfit to wear to the ballet." Seeing Nils' jaw drop at her perfect suggestion, Clara felt more than a little bit smug. "I went out to see the famous Brillo yesterday and spoke to Flo. If you make her an outfit, I believe she would agree to wear it to the ballet in July. After that, perhaps even *Frau* Admiral Simpson would decide to have you dress her."

* * *

"*Frau* Coffman, I do not know if you remember, but last summer, I made a Fourth of July dress for *Frau* Bethel Little. My hope is to do a special Fourth of July dress every year and this year, I would like to make one for you. All I ask in exchange, is to be able to promote my work and have the newspapers know that you are wearing a Flannery Fashions original." Most people liked getting new clothing, especially something custom made to suit them, but one never knew with up-timers, so Nils held his breath just a bit until she answered.

"My own *haute couture* dress? And all I need to do is let you tell people you made it and take pictures? Sign me up!" Flo didn't let out a whoop of excitement or wave her hat in the air, but somehow left the impression that she had.

"Not *haute couture*." Nils' response was stiff, but not angry. "In this timeline, the USE, not France, will be the country everyone looks to for fashion, and the terms will be in Amideutsch, not French. What was *haute couture* in your old timeline will be '*die Artmode*'. Now, I have some ideas and books for inspiration, but tell me what you like to wear."

Twenty minutes later, Nils and Flo had agreed on dark blue pants in light-weight summer wool with a fitted and belted white cotton blouse (not tucked in) and a red swing-style jacket made of the new American-pattern lace.

"Nils, that takes me back to when I was a schoolgirl. All I need is some ballet flats and I'll feel like Audrey Hepburn her own self!" Flo was grinning like a schoolgirl.

"But I thought only ballet dancers with years of training wore the famous ballet shoes, and I have heard that they hurt very much. Was this Audrey a famous ballerina?"

"Good gracious, no! She was a movie star. If you watch the movie *Roman Holiday*, I'm pretty sure she wears them in that. I think ballet flats were inspired by ballet slippers, but they have an actual sole instead of a suede bottom. Not much more, though. Soft leather surrounds your foot and covers your toes, but they are fairly skimpy as shoes go. Now that I think about it, they look a lot like the shoes the Burghers wear in town, but without any kind of decorations on them. I think they even run a string or ribbon through a casing along the top edge of the shoe, but I don't know why. They were decorative, or something. Ballet flats definitely weren't designed for working on a farm!"

"Hmmm. Perhaps the cobbler can make you a pair of these ballet flats to finish your *Zusammesetzung*–ensemble."

"Fabulous! You know, I'm going to the Arts Festival in Magdeburg. Maybe some of the court ladies will see what I'm wearing and decide to have you dress them. One can hope!" Hearing that, Nils did indeed hope, and pray, very hard every day for just such a small miracle to happen for him.

June 1635

"I have been dreaming of this day since I was a little boy. After this I finally start on my training to become a doctor!"

"Your rank is showing again, Marcus. We are about to graduate, and I *still* can't believe I'm in college. As a little girl, my biggest dream was marrying a kind man who wasn't old enough to be my grandfather. When I was really feeling 'big in my pants', I dreamed of a man not old enough to be my father."

Krystal winced. Even after four years, some of the down-time marriage customs still made her uncomfortable. "The phrase is 'too big for your britches', Nicol, and this is definitely not how I ever imagined my college graduation. The robes and a bunch of people wasting our time with fancy speeches are about the only things I recognize. Well, and the diploma. But the robes! I wish they had managed to get us graduated last month. These suckers are too thick and too hot for June!"

"Krystal." She looked over at Marcus. "There is a paper that says 'Princess Kristina' on some boxes over there. Do you think she's attending?"

Krystal paled a bit under the layer of sweat but breathed a sigh of relief when she heard the first strains of Pomp and Circumstance. "They wouldn't start without the Princess, if she was coming, and I don't see her. So, I don't know what that is, but it doesn't mean the Princess is coming and giving a speech."

An interminable time later, the speeches were done, awards given, and diplomas handed out. A groan was quickly stifled when the Dean stood up again instead of the Chaplain. To almost everyone's distress, he picked up a letter and started reading.

Dear New Nurses,

I have heard about your fondness for the word fudge and your interest in trying some. At my request, the royal dessert maker found fudge recipes. It really is quite delicious and can be made in a surprising variety of flavors. As a personal congratulations from me, you are each receiving one half pound of fudge in different colors and flavors.
— Princess Kristina.

Her note received thunderous applause and fudge from Princess Kristina for graduating RNs became a tradition. (Graduating doctors were rumored to be envious.) The only items left before the final benediction and dismissal were for each for each newly minted RN to receive her cap and pin, and to recite the Nightingale Pledge, as preserved in the newly-repopularized Scholastic children's book. New nurses even received a copy when they started their training. It was the easiest way to get the expectations across.

I solemnly pledge myself before God and in the presence of this assembly, to pass my life in purity and to practice my profession faithfully. I will abstain from whatever is deleterious and mischievous, and will not take or knowingly administer any harmful drug. I will do all in my power to maintain and elevate the standard of my profession, and will hold in confidence all personal matters committed to my keeping and all family affairs coming to my knowledge in the practice of my calling. With loyalty will I endeavor to aid the physician in his work, and devote myself to the welfare of those committed to my care.

Bethanne Kim

CHAPTER 32

June 1635

"They have pockets. Nils, I love you. These pants have real pockets. I can fit my whole entire hand inside." Nils could not understand her extreme excitement over simply having pockets big enough to fit her whole hand inside, but the other up-time woman with her seemed impressed by this as well. "When do you expect to have the blouse?"

"Next week, when we have made all the marked changes for the pants and jacket, you can try them on with the blouse and, just possibly, with the shoes." Nils tried to look severe but failed.

"You didn't! You found someone to make ballet flats? They will make this outfit perfect!"

"A cobbler named Hans Bauer has been helping to make shoes for the ballet company. He was most pleased to have a simple up-time style shoe he can make and sell for a nice profit, considering how little work the shoes are, and how close they are to the men's shoes he is familiar with. If you stop by his shop, he'll make a pair to fit you. On the Fourth of July, he will have an entire window display of these shoes in red, ivory, and blue, plus the regular shades of brown and tan. He's calling one shade Brillo

Brown and has high hopes that will be his best seller. He says they are a muddy brown."

Flo guffawed long and hard at that. "I don't care what you had in mind; I have to wear the Brillo Brown Ballet Flats!"

July 1635, Magdeburg

Flo plopped bonelessly into a chair. "I still can't believe I met a real-life future Empress! She was even more excited than I was about the sky-diving demonstration. She was less excited about the Fourth of July Arts Week, but she sees these things a lot more often than skydiving. Today was a long day and the week has barely started. Why are you here, Krystal? You haven't moved to Magdeburg, have you?"

"No, not at all. Although I did buy a house here last year. I'm pretty sure my instructions were for something sufficient for my personal needs in a good neighborhood. I had the money from my car, some money in OPM, and tenants had to cover the rest of any mortgage and bills. No one has asked me for an additional penny, but I just went by it and *wow*! I did not expect anything that fancy, or large. I can't imagine walking up to the front door and being welcomed in as a guest, much less owning the place! And yet, apparently, I do. Own the place, that is. But I don't quite live anywhere just now. I graduated from the RN program in Jena and I'm going to visit Grantville before I start work for the Flannery Foundation in September. We have our first location about a six hour walk from Jena and I'll be based there at first.

"As for this week, I came here to see the world premiere of a play based on the old book *The Lady with the Lamp* about Florence Nightingale. They want to have a real live nurse, preferably up-time, to introduce to the audience at the end of the play and I got the job."

"I heard something about that. It sounds influential, in a good way." Flo slipped out of her shoes.

"Where on earth did you find those shoes?" Krystal was notoriously disinterested in fashion, but several years of living and working with tailors had worn her down and she noticed things now.

"Master Jorgensen from Flannery Fashions made my outfit and found a cobbler to make the shoes. They have them in red, white, and blue, but these are Brillo Brown Ballet Flats. Princess Kristina wants a few pairs and I think she said she would like a jacket similar to mine but in Swedish blue and yellow. Marla Linder liked my outfit, too. First Brillo, now this. I'm turning into a regular trend-setter, I am."

Bethanne Kim

CHAPTER 33

September 1635

G ebhard wasn't sure what to expect. Being called to the master's house in the evening was rarely good news. He wracked his head as hard as he could, but he couldn't think of anything he had done wrong recently. The other possibility, being elevated to master, didn't even occur to him because it was pointless. He hadn't saved enough money to even consider buying his own shop. When he entered and saw Master Warner Rudolen and Master Bruno Schroeder both in the living room with Master Jorgensen, he felt light-headed from shock, and slightly ill with fear that he was being forced out of Flannery Fashions.

"Gebhard, as you are probably guessing, we asked you here this evening to talk to you about becoming a master tailor yourself. Master Rudolen and Master Schroeder have both examined your work and agree that the coat you completed for *Frau* Dreeson qualifies. We know that you have not saved enough to open your own shop, so this probably comes as a surprise to you. Please, sit down while we talk. New times call for new approaches. You have already been running Juniors. As I said, Master Rudolen and Master Schroeder agreed that you qualify as a Master." Nils paused and took a good look at Gebhard. "Are you unwell?"

"I. I. I. Well, this is unexpected. I don't have any money to buy a shop. I enjoy working for you. I don't really want to leave, but I... If it's time and I must go, then I have to go." Gebhard looked stunned and ready to panic.

Nils grinned and waved him to sit back down. "No need to panic, Master Rabe! We are all in agreement that you may, if you choose, take over as the Master Tailor for Juniors LLC, and oversee the Grantville branch of Flannery Fashions. It isn't the usual way of doing things, but this is a new world. You will earn a small salary and for every year that you remain the master, you will earn five percent of my share of Juniors, which has been made into a separate company from Flannery Fashions for just this purpose. I will receive profits as long as I am part owner, which will repay me for my ownership stake. In twenty years, you will own half and I will no longer own any. If you choose, you may buy my shares more quickly, but we will have to negotiate that separately. As you own more shares of the company, you will, of course, earn more as a result."

Gebhard was overwhelmed. When almost everyone in his village was killed by a random gang of bandits, he had survived only by luck. He happened to be in the woods searching for mushrooms and other edibles. With nothing to his name and little chance to continue his training when he arrived in Grantville, becoming a journeyman again had been an unexpected joy in his life. Even before his village was attacked, he had little hope of earning enough to becoming a master. All he could do was nod his thanks.

"You may wonder at the timing. I am moving to Magdeburg with Clara and Eleonore to open a new branch of Flannery Fashions. Now that he is a journeyman, Hans will be going to study further with Master Rudolen. Soon, Eleonore will become a journeyman and study with Master Schroeder. You will need to recruit more journeymen and apprentices to replace the ones I take. I promise not to take them all!"

Regaining his voice, Gebhard answered, "Thank you so much! I never expected this. You will not regret trusting me with Juniors. I…thank you. Just, thank you."

Clara bustled in with a tray. "This is a special day, deserving of a special treat! One of my friends helped me get the famous bagels and cream cheese from American Bagels & Cream Cheese. Master Rudolen and Master Schroeder, you probably haven't tried cream cheese yet, but once you do you will understand why there is sometimes a waiting list for it. Master Rabe, my sincere congratulations on your achievement!"

February 1636, Magdeburg

Nils was determined to top his Fourth of July successes from the previous two years. This year, he would finally have enough of the accursed, blessed tulle to make a stunning gown, but he needed someone worthy to wear such a treasure, young enough to show it off, old enough to appreciate it, and a public figure the news would cover to help make Flannery Fashions famous. In this universe, the USE, not the French, would be creating the high fashion. People would speak of *die Artmode* instead of *haute couture* and *das werkstatt* instead of an *atelier* when they wanted the highest quality, latest fashions.

Marla. If he could convince Marla Linder to wear one of his dresses for the Fourth of July concert, Flannery Fashions could become *the couture atelier*. No, not *couture*. *Die Artmode werkstatt*.

April 1636, Magdeburg

"She agreed! Marla Linder will wear a Flannery Fashions dress for her Fourth of July concert this year! To celebrate, you all have the afternoon off. You will go somewhere else while I design her gown. Be gone with you!" As Nils finished speaking, the apprentices and journeymen practically evaporated into thin air, delighted at the prospect of roaming free on a beautiful spring day.

Clara beamed at the news. Marla Linder wearing one of her husband's gowns would be a triumph for them.

After a celebratory small beer with Clara, Nils sighed deeply and started talking. "I met with *Frau* Linder this afternoon. I already knew from other tailors that she doesn't wear down-time clothing for her concerts and now I understand better why. Between the weight, the layers, and the stiff constructions, she can't move well enough in them. She was clear when we talked that if she can't move in what I make, she will wear a gown she already owns. Her favorite is dark blue velvet with a high neckline she called 'empire'. I can't explain that. But her not wearing our gown would be a catastrophe!" Nils was stressed. He was counting on publicity from the great Marla wearing his gown to propel his tulle-making enterprise to profitability.

"We know that ballerinas are able to leap about in skirts made of a similar material, so what concerns you?" Clara had a knack of getting to the heart of his worries and allaying them.

"The pedals. I have seen the new-style piano she plays, and it has pedals. True, only three, nothing like an organ, but she must be able to reach the pedals without her gown getting in the way. The flute isn't a problem because her arms aren't constrained at all, and of course we already took her singing into account. But those pedals!"

"You are worrying too much. She is not playing an organ. There are only three pedals, and they are close together. For an organist, yes, this might be a problem. But *Frau* Linder is a singer, flautist, and pianist."

Nils sat considering Clara's comment for so long she thought he had fallen asleep with his eyes open. Suddenly, he slapped the arm of his chair and said, "You're right! She will be fine. I just replayed the last time I saw her perform in my head and you are right! Now I have a good idea of what

I want to make. It will use all the tulle we have, but she will be resplendent. This gown will be the talk of the continent and I must go back to Grantville to oversee making it. We need the electric lights. Thank you!" He jumped up, planted a kiss on top of Clara's head, and started heading for the *werkstatt* to begin working on the gown.

"Do you wish me to leave as well, husband?"

Nils paused, then turned and headed back to her. "No! In fact, I will wait to start work. At the moment, I think what I truly need is a few hours of not thinking about work. Now that we have the house entirely to ourselves, do you have any ideas?" Nils' grin matched that of his lovely bride.

CHAPTER 34

July 1, 1636, Magdeburg

Nils was beyond nervous. "Hold the dress up higher! I know, Krystal gave us two 'dry cleaner bags' to use under the regular dress bag to make sure it stays clean and dry, but you must be careful! You saw how easily those thin bags rip." Three apprentices had traveled with Marla's gown, overseen by Master Rabe, from the shop in Grantville to the new train station in Magdeburg. Electric lights made working with such fine material easier, but they were all still nervous. Any damage was likely to be irreparable and they weren't at the new shop yet. Flannery's Fashions was the most exclusive new tailor's shop for women in Magdeburg, and this dress for Marla's Fourth of July concert would cement that in place, hopefully making them famous.

A few hours later, the small bell over the shop door tinkled as Marla Linder entered the shop. "Hello? Master Jorgensen?"

"*Frau* Linder! How wonderful to see you! Please, come in here and make yourself comfortable. Master Jorgensen is waiting for you in our *werkstatt*." Gebhard guided her into the room in question and toward a seat in the center of the room. "Would you care for a refreshment? A drink or snack, perhaps?" When she declined, he bowed slightly and left.

Master Jorgensen stood next to a genuine up-time mannequin (a painfully expensive purchase from the back room of the thrift store) with a sheet covering the gown on it. A simple pair of blue suede ballet flats sat on a small table next to it. "An artist such as yourself with the voice of an angel deserves a dress that looks as light and ethereal as the heavens themselves. I found such an up-time material, but no one here knew how to make it." With a flourish, Nils gestured for two apprentices to gently remove the covering. "Until now!"

Marla gasped in surprise. "It's tulle! How did you manage it? How much is in that dress? Does Bitty Matowski know? It's gorgeous!"

Her response was everything Nils could have hoped for. "Yes, it is tulle. I spoke to *Frau* Matowski, and she very much wanted more tulle for her dancers, just as I wanted tulle to make gowns and more. She gave me a sample for lace-makers to examine and learn from. People are trying to make a machine but, for now, it is all handmade. As to how much, this is all the tulle made from the time God created the earth until the last batch was shipped to us last week. The dress is cotton tulle. The jacket is a single yard of silk tulle, all that we could afford to have made. But once people see and hear about this gown, we will have so many orders we will be able to pay to develop the machines to make it."

Marla walked over to stroke her new gown. "I will feel like a fairytale princess in this gown, and I love the blue suede shoes. My feet will be far happier at the end of the night than wearing high heels! Being practical for a moment, though, I don't have a strapless bra that fits. None of my old ones fit since... None of them fit now. Also, can the cobbler add ties onto my new Blue Suede Shoes to make sure they don't slip off?" For some reason Nils couldn't understand, Marla had clearly capitalized the words Blue Suede Shoes and started humming a tune.

Nils picked up a small box from the table and handed it to her. "We will take them to the cobbler and ask this very afternoon. As for your other concern, this is the newest design from Irene's Intimates. Since we had your measurements, they made this to go with your gown." Seeing Marla's troubled expression as she pulled the stiff strapless stays out of the box, he continued. "Since you are singing, your breathing can't be constrained in any way, we understand that. Most bodices have very rigid 'boning', to use the up-time term. These do not. Go ahead and flex it. Don't bend it too sharply or you will damage it, but your body can't do that anyway. These bodices, stays I believe *Fräulein* Reed called them, use reeds to keep the shape while allowing you total freedom of movement, most particularly including breathing. Just for you, one of the up-time ladies sacrificed a wide elastic belt, so the sides are up-time elastic. You won't find another set of stays this well suited to your performing needs, possibly ever." Everyone involved was extremely proud of Marla's new strapless stays in the up-time style.

Marla looked relieved. "Thank you so much for your attention to detail on this. Most non-singers don't realize how important that is. Where can I try my new outfit on?"

"Right here. I will wait outside. We at Flannery's Fashion specifically chose to include women as apprentices and journeymen so they can help our customers during fittings and other times you might feel uncomfortable with a man nearby. This room was designed as a place for our most exclusive clients to not only be fitted and view new items, but also to prepare for truly special events, such as your concert. My daughter Eleonore has newly risen to the rank of journeyman and will ring a bell when you are ready for me to return."

As Nils walked back in a few minutes later, Marla was beaming. "It's perfect! I love the way the blue at the bottom fades to ivory for the bodice and the gentle upward curve of the hem in the front will make walking up steps *so* much easier! Down-time women may prefer stark white, but, as pale as I am, I know it makes me look pasty. With the red jacket, this screams Fourth of July! And I'll be able to wear them separately for other events, when the good old red, white, and blue aren't appropriate." She twirled in place and took a few deep breaths before giving Nils a hug. "And you are right about the stays. They are comfortable and I will be able to sing in them. They are actually better than my old underwire strapless bra! I definitely didn't expect that. It's from Irene's Intimates? I'll make sure to buy more from them and recommend them to my friends. One more question. I seem to remember that Mrs. Flannery's first name was Irene. Do you own Irene's Intimates, too?"

"Ah, no. *Frau* Flannery left all her things to young Sam Reed, and he is our semi-silent partner in this business. His cousin, Krystal, started Irene's Intimates a few years ago when her bras started wearing out. I'm not sure why she chose the name. I think she just liked it. But since she was around while we were starting Flannery Fashions, and she is related to our largest investor, we work quite closely."

Marla removed her jacket and examined it more carefully. "The jacket cuffs. Is that embroidery what I think it is?"

Eleonore grinned. Nils looked a bit embarrassed as he answered. "When young *Herr* Reed found out we were making you a red jacket, he insisted it 'must have' gold cuffs and gave us the fabric for it. The embroidery was Eleonore's idea, and she did the work on her own, without telling me."

"But is it what I think it is?"

This time, Eleonore answered. "If you think one cuff has the notes for 'do you hear' and the other one has 'the people sing', then yes, it is exactly what you think it is."

"Franz, you have to see this." He had been patiently waiting outside but came in at Marla's call to see her new gown. She held out her wrists. "They embroidered the notes into the cuffs. Isn't that a lovely touch? So personal. Would you like a set of cuffs for your own concert suit?" At his nod, Nils made a note to have a set in a far more sedate color combination rushed to be ready for Franz to wear at the concert. Gold cuffs draw attention to a person's hands, which Franz Sylwester wouldn't want.

As she was about to walk out the door, Marla turned. "It was you, wasn't it? The lace pattern 'Do You Hear the People Sing'? It was you. Maybe I will have a gown made from that someday." With his next client waiting for him, Nils simply smiled and bowed, neither admitting nor denying his involvement.

Fourth of July, 1636, Magdeburg

"We wanted you to have a handbag to go with the gown, but finding one was hard. Tulle is too delicate to make into a bag, and every other fabric we found is too heavy to go with the tulle. This was the only material we found that was as light and airy as tulle." With that, Gebhard handed her a small, translucent bag, and Marla burst into belly laughs, eyes tearing up from laughing so hard.

"Where" gasp "did you" gasp "find" gasp "*bubble wrap*??" Marla was desperately trying to stop laughing, but the hilarious combination of a hand-sewn gown made of such precious fabric with a purse made of something she still really thought of as garbage, or maybe entertainment for a kid, was too much. "It's been more than five years. Seriously, guys, where did you get it? Don't get me wrong, this is great, perfect in its own way, but that doesn't mean every single up-timer won't find a bubble-wrap purse hilarious."

Slightly hurt, Gebhard responded stiffly. "*Fräulein* Krystal gave it to us. This was, in fact, her idea. She said they found the 'bubble wrap' in Grandpa Eli's things after he died and were saving it for something special. Then she handed it to Master Jorgensen."

"Master Rabe, Master Jorgensen, this really is perfect in its own way. I will treasure my bubble-wrap purse. Who knows? Maybe it will become a signature item that I carry for my biggest performances—for as long as it lasts! But now, I really have to go." Gebhard motioned her toward the window. "Whatever you want, I don't have any more time, I have to leave right now. I promise to come back tomorrow so you can show me." Marla started heading toward the front door.

"*Frau* Linder, I really must insist you come this way. I promise it will not make you late." Eleonore moved unobtrusively to block her way and steer her back toward the window, which made her uncharacteristically angry. As a professional, she worked hard to never be late for a performance. "Please, but a moment. This is part of the service for our most exclusive clients." Gebhard and Eleonore pulled open first the wooden shutters and then the windows while Nils guided Marla to step up onto the windowsill, then out onto the boards over the sidewalk and directly into the curtained carriage waiting for her. The room had truly been designed to make everything as easy and painless as possible for the most exclusive clientele, even down to getting into their carriage without dirtying their hem or shoes, or needing chopins (if she came from somewhere they were common), even on the dreariest days.

Looking back at the shop, Marla giggled. "I feel like the paparazzi are after me! Oh, never mind, I know you don't understand paparazzi, but this is a lot of fuss for a West Virginia girl!"

"This is not all of the 'fuss', as you put it. When you arrive, several people will meet you when you alight from the carriage to ensure no one sees your gown until you walk on stage. The reveal will be magnificent!" As Marla left in the curtained carriage, Nils was practically crowing with anticipation of his masterpiece being seen, and at successfully keeping it a secret from everyone else.

* * *

A few weeks later, Nils sat at the kitchen table in the back of Flannery Fashions with clippings spread out on the table. "It worked. It really worked! Paris, Vienna, Venice, Florence, Rome, Amsterdam—at least one newspaper in all the biggest cities had a photo or drawing with a description of her gown, along with my name. They all said it was the '*die Artmode aus werkstatt* Flannery Fashions, Magdeburg.' We are famous! And our nation, not France, is the fashion center of Europe!" In an utterly uncharacteristic display of exuberance, he jumped up, grabbed Clara by the waist, and started twirling her around the room while she grinned at him, before turning green, pushing off, and running away.

She returned a few minutes later. "So, husband, are you hoping for another boy, or another girl?"

CAST OF CHARACTERS

Adam Fuchs, senior apprentice at Flannery Fashion.

Ada Schrickel, employee of Miasma Masks. Cuts masks.

Agatha Schulte, lives with Sam and Krystal. Close friend of Krystal.

Alice Sims, nurse at the Red Cross well-baby clinic.

Anna Banz, refugee who rents from Wooly Snyder. She is married to Mathias Heydman and up-timers sometimes call her Frau Heydman.

Anna Kruger, nursing student in Krystal Reed's class at the University of Jena. 1635 graduate.

Anna Maria Schneider, lives with Sam and Krystal.

Bethel Little, Sam and Krystal's aunt. Co-owner of a new bagel shop.

Bethel Little, Sam and Krystal's cousin, daughter of Bethel and Raymond Little.

Betsy Springer, reporter for the Grantville Times and Grantville Inquisitor.

Betty Ruth Snodgrass, member of the Bowers' Broads advising Nils and Sam.

Beulah Ann MacDonald, Director of Nursing.

"Bitty" Matowski, ballet teacher.

Bruno Schroeder, master tailor.

Caroline Platzer, mental health counselor.

Clara Zimmerman, widow who marries Nils Jorgenson. Fifty-one percent owner of Miasma Masks.

Curt Bauer, master mason and husband of Ursula Durer.

Dieter Ulrich, Augsburg Burgher.

Dietrich Schulte, lives with Sam and Krystal.

Donovan Higgins, Sam's half-brother.

Donovan Reed, Sam's estranged father.

Eleonore Jorgensen, daughter of Nils, twin sister of Hans. Apprentice at Flannery Fashion. Graduates Grantville HS in 1632.

Elsa Gerandt, widow and mother of Katherine and Ernst. A burgher's daughter, she becomes the head of Flannery Flowers.

Ermegart Zimmerman, herbalist and teacher.

Flo Coffman, farmer and owner of Brillo.

Franz Sylwester, musician married to Marla Linder.

Garnet Szymanski, nurse and Director of the LPN program.

Gebhard Rabe, senior journeyman at Flannery Fashion

Gisela Schulte, lives with Sam and Krystal. Excellent baker.

Grandpa Eli/Eli Reed, great-grandfather to cousins Krystal and Sam Reed. Married to Barbara Reed.

Grannie B/Barbara Reed, lifelong frenemy with Irene Flannery. Great-grandmother to cousins Krystal and Sam Reed. Married to Eli Reed.

Gretchen Dieter, she and her family lived with Krystal and Sam for a few months after the New Year's Eve fire.

Hannelore Evertz, wife of the curate of St. Mary's Catholic church in Grantville.

Hans Jorgensen, son of Nils, twin sister of Eleonore. Apprentice at Flannery Fashion. Graduates Grantville HS in 1632.

Hans Schruer, Grantville police officer.

Henry Dreeson, mayor of Grantville.

Irene Flannery, cantankerous old widow and steadfast parishioner of St. Vincent's/St. Mary's. Long-time seamstress. Her maiden name was MacClanahan.

Johan Becker, journeyman baker who moves to Grantville with his sister, Sibylle.

John Thompson Sims, doctor at the Red Cross well-baby clinic.

Jürgen Neubert, police force auxiliary and later member of the police force.

Justin Marbury, Englishman and LPN student.

Krystal Reed, employed to help with the well-baby clinics starting in 1631. Nursing student. RN in 1635. Forty-nine percent owner of Miasma Masks.

Lorentz Ulrich, Herr Fugger's representative at the Fuggerei who talks to Sam Reed and Elsa Gerandt and gives them a tour.

Marcus Rasch, nursing student in Krystal Reed's class at the University of Jena. 1635 graduate.

Marla Linder, singer and musician.

Margarete Dietrich, nursing student in Krystal Reed's class at the University of Jena. 1635 graduate.

Margaretha Kniess, refugee and Irene Flannery's next door neighbor.

Marquise Clevenger, rented the Reed home Sam and Krystal live in. Left up-time, getting married shortly after the Ring of Fire happened, becoming Mrs. King.

Marlon Pridmore, Grantville bank loan officer.

Mathias Banz, refugee who rents from Wooly Snyder.

Mike Stearns, Grantville politician.

Mikki Barnes, nursing student.

Nicol Steinmetz, nursing student in Krystal Reed's class at the University of Jena. 1635 graduate.

Jorgen "Nils" Jorgensen, master tailor. Fifty-one percent owner of Flannery Fashions. Father of Hans and Eleonore. Married to Clara Zimmerman.

Raymond Little, pharmacist and Krystal and Ursula's boss. Sam and Krystal's uncle.

Sam Reed, forty-nine percent owner of Flannery Fashions. Graduates high school in 1632 and joins the National Guard.

Sarah Jager, employee of Miasma Masks. Sews masks.

Sibylle Becker, rural young woman who has gradually lost most of her vision. Works for the well-baby clinic. Named for the wife of the childless founder of the Fuggerei.

Ursula Durer, herbalist. Works for the pharmacy starting in 1631 and the well-baby clinic starting in 1632, and wife of Curt Bauer.

Valentin Friedrich, Bank of Grantville loan officer.

Warner Rudolen, master tailor.

Wooly Snyder, owner and builder of poorly constructed housing for refugees.

Made in the USA
Las Vegas, NV
08 September 2021

29884153R00154